P9-DNU-062

THE SLAYING OF THE DRAGON

THE SLAYING OF THE DRAGON

MODERN TALES OF THE PLAYFUL IMAGINATION

EDITED AND WITH AN INTRODUCTION BY

FRANZ ROTTENSTEINER

Harcourt Brace Jovanovich, Publishers
San Diego New York London

Library of Congress Cataloging in Publication Data
Main entry under title:
The Slaying of the dragon.
Contents: The slaying of the dragon / Dino Buzzati — Axolotl / Julio Cortázar — The lottery in Babylon / Jorge Luis Borges — [etc.]
1. Fantastic fiction. I. Rottensteiner, Franz.
PN6120.95 F25S58 1984 808.83'876 83–26542
ISBN 0–15–182975–6

Designed by Amy Hill
Printed in the United States of America
First edition
A B C D E

CONTENTS

INTRODUCTION

FAREWELL TO DRAGONS: A LITERATURE OF DOUBT

"Why are Americans afraid of dragons?" asked the eminent science-fiction writer Ursula K. Le Guin in a speech she made in 1973. Today, more than a decade later, that fear has certainly been overcome. Fantasy books regularly grace the best-seller lists, and, inspired by the great success of J. R. R. Tolkien's *Lord of the Rings* trilogy, many writers have jumped on the bandwagon.

This kind of fantastic literature, sometimes called "high" fantasy, is mostly about vast imaginary lands wholly unlike this world, rich in people and real and invented beings, and usually contains a liberal injection of sorcery and magic. Noble heroes may undertake quests that can last them through a trilogy, although some have been known to act nobly and heroically for three times that number of volumes. These fantasy worlds are invariably simple in intellectual background, without much science or technology.

There are artisans and craftsmen, and plenty of monks, priests, soldiers, and peasants. No industrial wastes, trade unions, or big corporations threaten; only guilds and merchants, kings and nobility. True, many dangers loom, even supernatural ones, sometimes powerful enough to threaten the whole world (though in the end overcome without undue effort)—but there is no stress, and none of the other pressures of modern civilization. What results is a sort of nostalgic historical novel with supernatural elements. The authors need not acquaint themselves with history or familiarize themselves with the political and social conditions of the past, for they can invent everything to their heart's content.

These stories are actually fairy tales, though, to be sure, considerably longer than most fairy tales. But why always a supernatural element? Maybe because it is just part of the formula, or because the authors want to invest their stories with the "deep meaning" of the myths and legends of the past. Perhaps, however, there is a more psychological and more significant reason: perhaps only through wizardry can man become fully reconciled with his world, can his purpose and that of the world he lives in become one, in a way impossible in the real world. Modern fantasy in this sense is, I am inclined to think, the equivalent of the utopias of the eighteenth and nineteenth centuries. But while those utopias contain plans—however unrealistic—for changing and perfecting the world, these latter-day utopias are escapes into a world that is everything ours is not. Such fantasy creates no intellectual blueprints for a better world, offers no course of action, no hope for the future, and provides little insight into the modern world or the human mind. It turns to imaginary worlds that are essentially idealized pasts, and instead of intellectual stimulation it presents a variety of physical details and sensual impressions, human (and nonhuman) acts divorced from reality. Since genuine philosophy is lacking, the void is filled with myths and legends, or constructs analogous to them, usually bowdlerized.

The existence of a thriving field of commercial fiction looking to the past for its inspiration is more an expression of yearning for bygone days than a sign of respect for the past or an indication that those old beliefs are still alive. In fact, the contrary may be true: precisely because the old myths no longer have any real power over the minds of men, because they have lost their sacred qualities, they can be used with impunity as literary building blocks. They can be varied infinitely. Everything is of equal value because nothing is of value any more, and there is nobody to protest against the new use of myths. This type of fantasy is a reaction against the modern world, a by-product of industrialization and the emergence of mass culture. It is for this reason, I think, that "high" fantasy first developed in England, where the pressures of the machine age were felt as early as the nineteenth century (historians of fantasy usually trace the genre to William Morris, the nostalgic utopian), and took on a firmer shape through the work of English and Irish writers united in their dislike of the modern world (C. S. Lewis, Eric Rucker Eddison, Lord Dunsany, and Tolkien); significantly, it became a full-fledged genre in the United States, England's successor as the world's most industrialized country.

But of course there have always been fantastic tales less

easy to classify than those of the "high" variety. While nobody in the more distant past thought of imagining every detail of other worlds, of concocting rivals to the "real" world, man continually felt a desire to go beyond the everyday, to imagine the impossible. Miracles and dreams have always provided a strong impulse in literature: to escape from the fetters of time and space and causality, but not so much that the link to our world is totally lost. The fantasy thus created oscillates between different states rather than firmly adhering to any one state, weaves a fabric of speculations about possibilities that transcend the everyday world, lights on ingenious and playful inventions which are no mere escapes from an age that may be experienced as too complex, confused, and chaotic. It challenges the certainties of life.

Fantasy need not mean flight into a never-never land, a yearning for a time and codes of behavior that are irrevocably past. It can be a protest against a too complacent world, a challenge to fixed norms, an expression of the rebellious romantic spirit against classical standards and order, a call to dare to think differently, to question what is usually taken for granted. It can stress the irrational side of man, the unknown and perhaps unknowable aspects of the world. It is, ultimately, literature of doubt, not of affirmation. That so many writers of stature, including those noted for their painstaking realism, have at some point in their careers turned to writing fantasy suggests that fantasy satisfies a deep human need and fulfills a genuine function in life and literature.

Fantasy as I am speaking of it now does not re-create fairy tales or pile gruesome horrors upon one another, but, instead, raises rather unsettling questions about the nature of reality, life, and the human psyche. This is not to say that there may not be a touch of terror; indeed, a metaphysical horror may be more deeply disturbing than simple gruesomeness. Carlos Fuentes's "Aura," with its Poe-like atmosphere and situation, is surely as horrible as anything to be found in Stephen King, but it is presented with much greater subtlety and psychological penetration. Likewise, the killing machine in Stanislaw Lem's "The Mask" is definitely horrific. But the primary aim of these authors is not to terrify the reader, and in the case of Dino Buzzati and J. G. Ballard what terrifies is not a monstrous being but the monstrousness of the acts human beings are capable of. Like Kafka, these authors show that the only fantastic world is everyday reality.

Other writers change ontological properties of the world. Ilse Aichinger, for instance, reverses the natural flow of time; her "Story in a Mirror" is a journey back in time through the personal history of the heroine, ending inevitably in the womb. This idea has attracted many other writers of fantasy, from Velimir Khlebnikov at the beginning of this century to Jorge Luis Borges, to say nothing of popular science-fiction writers like Roger Zelazny, Philip K. Dick, and Ballard. But Aichinger's story is easily the most deeply felt and brilliantly imagined among them, and has brought her justified acclaim.

Borges's famous "The Lottery in Babylon," with its dazzling joining of chance and necessity, is one of those stories that defy classification and become instant classics, so powerful is the imagination at work—or at play. The story can be read as philosophy, for in Borges's hands fantasy becomes a branch of philosophy—or, rather, philosophy, as Borges has claimed, becomes a branch of fantastic literature. Who could deny that this is much more exciting and entertaining than yet another excursion into dragon territory?

Most of the stories in this anthology take an ironical stance and do not yearn for a dead past. Mircea Eliade's "With the Gypsy Girls" is a powerful evocation of the mystery of temporal existence that for the author decidedly includes the mythical and the numinous, but knights, the paraphernalia of sorcery, and simple virtues are lacking. If there is a quest, as in Donald Barthelme's hilarious "The Emerald," it is a takeoff of other quest stories (and many other things besides). When the alphabet of popular fantasy fiction is used, as in Joyce Carol Oates's "Further Confessions," it is subtly to corrode narrative clichés as well as reality, and the author has her tongue well in cheek. Italo Calvino, too, is a master at shaping elegantly ironic, strange, and curious tales that defy the banality of reality.

These stories set out to undermine fixed notions of reality; the real may appear unreal, truth may become a dream, and dreams may divulge strange truths. The rug is pulled from under the reader, not by some mad ax murderer, but by an unexpected challenge to the fundamental certainties of the world. A man may become a salamander, as in Julio Cortázar's "Axolotl," and a beautiful woman may turn out to be a robot, as in Lem's "The Mask." The latter story is clearly science fiction with a difference. Its heroine and narrator is a Frankenstein-like creature, a robot in human shape, sent out by a king in an unspecified fantasy land to kill an enemy. Or is she? "The Mask" derives its poignancy and humanity from the fact that the heroine herself does not know what she is, or how she will act. Perhaps she is a programed killing machine, but at the same time she is "our sister," she feels and suffers like a human being, is beset by the same doubts and anxieties. What is consciousness? Lem asks. And what makes a human being?

Fantasy, although deviating from what is considered possible in the "real" world, is nevertheless not arbitrary, and certainly not irrelevant. By moving between the real world and the other reality that is glimpsed, by questioning what exists, by casting tenaciously held beliefs into doubt, it probes and illuminates the real world, often more sharply than realistic writing can. By distorting reality, it may arrive at a clearer view of the world and its inhabitants, and make the reader see what could not be seen otherwise; it does this moreover in dreams and visions that are marvelously entertaining and of considerable value as fiction. It is ambiguity and skepticism that make for good fiction, not the unreflected expression of understandable but vain human longings.

DINO BUZZATI

THE SLAYING OF THE DRAGON

In May 1902 a peasant in the service of Count Gerol, one Giosue Longo, who often went hunting in the mountains, reported that he had seen a large animal, resembling a dragon, in Valle Secca. Palissano, the last village in the valley, had long cherished a legend that one such monster was still living in certain arid passes in the region. But no one had ever taken it seriously. Yet on this occasion Longo's obvious sanity, the exactitude of his account, the absolutely accurate and unwavering repetition of details of the event convinced people that there might be something in it and Count Martino Gerol decided to go and find out. Naturally he was not thinking in terms of a dragon; but it was possible that some huge rare serpent was still living in those uninhabited valleys.

He was to be accompanied on the expedition by the governor of the province, Quinto Andronico, and his beautiful and intrepid wife, the naturalist Professor Inghirami and by his colleague Fusti, who was an expert in taxidermy. Quinto Andronico was a weak, sceptical man and had known for some time that his wife felt drawn to Count Gerol, but this did not worry him. In fact he agreed willingly when Maria suggested that they should accompany the Count on his hunt. He was not the least bit jealous, nor even envious, although Gerol was greatly superior to him in wealth, youth, good looks, strength and courage.

Two carriages left the town shortly after midnight with an escort of eight mounted hunters and arrived at Palissano at about six the following morning. Gerol, Maria and the two naturalists slept; only Andronico remained awake and he stopped the carriage in front of the house of an old friend of his, the doctor Taddei. After a few moments the doctor, woken by a coachman and still half asleep, with a nightcap on his head, appeared at a first-floor window. Andronico greeted him jovially from below and explained the object of the expedition, expecting his listener to burst out laughing at the mention of dragons. To his surprise Taddei shook his head disapprovingly.

"I don't think I'd go, if I were you," he said firmly.

"Why not? Don't you think there's anything to it? You think it's all a lot of nonsense?"

"I don't know about that," replied the doctor. "No, personally I think there is a dragon, though I've never seen it. But I wouldn't get involved in this business. I don't like the sound of it."

"Don't like the sound of it? Do you mean you really believe in the dragon?"

"My dear sir, I'm an old man," said the doctor, "and

I've seen many things. It may be a lot of nonsense, but it may also be true; if I were you, I wouldn't get involved. And I warn you: the way is hard to find, the rocks are very disaster, and there isn't a drop of water. Give up the whole thing—why not go down to the Crocetta [he pointed to-unsafe, you only need a gust of wind to precipitate sheer wards a rounded grassy hill rising behind the village], you'll find plenty of hares there." He was silent for a moment, then added: "I assure you, I wouldn't go. I once heard it said—but it's useless, you'll only laugh . . ."

"Why should I laugh?" protested Andronico. "Please go on."

"Well, some people say that this dragon gives out smoke, and that it's poisonous and a small quantity can kill you."

Forgetting his promise, Andronico laughed loudly. "I always knew that you were reactionary," he snorted, "reactionary and eccentric. But this is too much. You're medieval, my dear Taddei. I'll see you this evening, and I'll be sporting the dragon's head."

He waved good-bye, climbed back into the carriage and ordered the coach to move on. Giosue Longo, who was one of the hunters and knew the way, went at the head of the convoy.

"What was that old man shaking his head at?" enquired Maria, who had woken up in the interim.

"Nothing," replied Andronico. "It was only old Taddei, who's an amateur vet; we were talking about foot and mouth disease."

"And the dragon?" enquired Count Gerol, who was sitting opposite him. "Did you ask him about the dragon?"

"No, I didn't, to be quite honest," replied the governor. "I didn't want to be laughed at. I told him we'd come up here to do a bit of hunting, that's all I said."

The passengers felt their weariness vanish as the sun rose; the horses moved faster and the coachmen began to hum.

"Taddei used to be our family doctor. Once"—it was the governor speaking—"he had a fashionable practice. Then suddenly he retired and went into the country, perhaps because of some disappointment in love. Then he must have been involved in some other trouble and came to this one-eyed place. Lord knows where he could go from here; he'll be a sort of dragon himself soon."

"What nonsense!" said Maria, rather annoyed. "Always talking about the dragon—you've talked of nothing else since we left and it's really becoming rather boring."

"It was your idea to come," replied her husband, mildly amused. "Anyway, how could you know what we were talking about if you were asleep the whole way? Or were you just pretending?"

Maria did not reply but looked worriedly out of the window; at the mountains, which were becoming higher, steeper and more arid. At the far end of the valley there appeared a chaotic succession of peaks, mostly conical in shape and bare of woods or meadows, yellowish in color and incredibly bleak. The scorching sunlight clothed them in a hard, strong light of their own.

It was about nine o'clock when the carriages came to a standstill because the road came to an end. As they climbed down, the hunting party realized that they were now right in the heart of those sinister mountains. On close inspection the rock of which they were made looked rotten and friable as though they were one vast landslide from top to bottom.

"Look, this is where the path starts," said Longo, pointing to a trail of footsteps leading upwards towards the mouth of a small valley. It was about three-quarters of an hour's journey from there to the Burel, where the dragon had been seen.

"Have you seen about the water?" Andronico asked the hunters.

"There are four flasks, and two of wine, your Excellency," one of them answered. "That should be enough . . ."

Odd. But now that they were so far from the town, locked in the mountains, the idea of the dragon began to seem less absurd. The travelers looked around them but saw no signs of anything reassuring. Yellowish peaks where no human being had ever trod, endless little valleys winding off into the distance: complete desolation.

They walked without speaking: first went the hunters with the guns, culverins and other hunting equipment, then Maria and lastly the two naturalists. Fortunately the path was still in the shade; the sun would have been merciless amid all that yellow earth.

The valley leading to the Burel was narrow and winding too; there was no stream in its bed and no grass or plants growing on its sides, only stones and debris; no birdsong or babble of water, only the occasional hiss of gravel.

At a certain point a young man appeared below them, walking faster than the hunting party and with a dead goat slung over his shoulders. "He's going to the dragon," said Longo, as if it were the most natural thing in the world.

The inhabitants of Palissano, he then explained, were highly superstitious and sent a goat to the Burel every morning to placate the monster. The young men of the region took turns taking the offering. If the dragon was heard to roar, this portended untold disaster; all kinds of misfortunes might follow.

"And the dragon eats the goat every day?" enquired Count Gerol, jokingly.

"There's nothing left of it the next day, that's for certain."

"Not even the bones?"

"No, not even the bones. It takes the goat into the cave to eat it."

"But couldn't it be someone from the village who eats the goat?" asked the governor. "Everyone knows the way. Has no one really ever seen the dragon actually take the goat?"

"I don't know, your Excellency," replied the hunter.

Meanwhile the young man with the goat had caught up with them.

"Hey there, young man!" called the Count Gerol in his usual stentorian tones, "how much do you want for that goat?"

"I can't sell it, sir," he replied.

"Not even for ten crowns?"

"Well, I could go and get another one, I suppose . . ." he weakened. "For ten crowns . . ."

"What do you want the goat for?" Andronico enquired. "Not to eat, I trust?"

"You'll see in due course," replied Gerol evasively.

One of the hunters put the goat over his shoulders, the young man from Palissano set off back to the village (obviously to get another animal for the dragon) and the whole group moved off again.

After another hour's journey they finally arrived. The valley suddenly opened out into a vast rugged amphitheatre, the Burel, surrounded by crumbling walls of orange-colored earth and rock. Right in the center, on top of a cone-shaped heap of debris, was a black opening: the dragon's cave.

"That's it," said Longo. They stopped quite near it, on a gravelly terrace which offered an excellent observation point, about thirty feet above the level of the cave and almost directly in front of it. The terrace had the added advantage of not being accessible from below because it stood at the top of an almost vertical wall. Maria could watch from there in absolute safety.

They were all quiet, listening hard, but they could hear nothing except the endless silence of the mountains, broken by the occasional swish of gravel. Here and there lumps of earth would give way suddenly, streams of pebbles would pour down the mountainside and die down again gradually. The whole countryside seemed to be in a state of constant dilapidation: these were mountains abandoned by their creator, being allowed to fall quietly to pieces.

"What if the dragon doesn't come out today?" enquired Quinto Andronico.

"I've got the goat," answered Gerol. "You seem to forget that."

Then they understood: the animal would act as a bait to entice the dragon out of its lair.

They began their preparations: two hunters struggled up to a height of about twenty yards above the entrance to the cave, to be able to hurl down stones if necessary. Another placed the goat on the gravelly expanse outside its cave.

Others were posted at either side, well-protected by large stones, with the culverins and guns. Andronico stayed where he was, intending to remain a spectator.

Maria was silent; her former boldness had vanished altogether. Although she wouldn't admit it, she would have given anything to be able to go back. She looked round at the walls of rock, at the scars of the old landslides and the debris of the recent ones, at the pillars of red earth which looked to her as though they might collapse any minute. Her husband, Count Gerol, the two naturalists and the hunters seemed negligible protection in the face of such solitude.

When the dead goat had been placed in front of the cave, they began to wait. It was shortly after ten o'clock and the sun now filtered into every crevice of the Burel, filling it with its immense heat. Waves of heat were reflected back from one side to the other. The hunters organized a rough canopy with the carriage covers for the governor and his wife, to shield them from the sun; Maria drank avidly.

"Watch out!" shouted Count Gerol suddenly from his point of vantage on a rock down on the scree, where he stood with a rifle in his hand and an iron club hanging from his hip.

A shudder went through the company, and they held their breath as a live creature emerged from the mouth of the cave. "The dragon! The dragon!" shouted several of the hunters, though whether in joy or terror it was not clear.

The creature moved into the light with the hesitant sway of a snake. So here it was, this legendary monster whose voice made a whole village quake.

"Oh, how horrible!" exclaimed Maria with evident relief, having expected something far worse.

"Come on, courage!" shouted one of the hunters jokingly. Everyone recovered their self-assurance.

"It looks like a small Ceratosaurus!" said Professor Inghirami, now sufficiently confident to turn to the problems of science.

The monster wasn't really very terrible, in fact, little more than six feet long, with a head like a crocodile's only shorter, a long lizard-like neck, a rather swollen thorax, a short tail and floppy sort of crest along its back. But its awkward movements, its clayey parchment color (with the occasional green streak here and there) and the general apparent flabbiness of its body were even more reassuring than its small dimensions. The general impression was one of extreme age. If it was a dragon, it was a decrepit dragon, possibly moribund.

"Take that!" scoffed one of the hunters who had climbed above the mouth of the cave. And he threw a stone down towards the animal.

It hit the dragon exactly on the skull. There was a hollow "toc," like the sound of something hitting a gourd. Maria felt a movement of revulsion.

The blow had been hard but not sufficient. The reptile was still for a few moments, as though stunned, and then began to shake its head and neck from side to side as if in pain. It opened and closed its jaws to reveal a set of sharp teeth, but it made no sound. Then it moved across the gravel towards the goat.

"Made you giddy, did they, eh?" cackled Count Gerol,

suddenly abandoning his arrogant pose. He seemed eager and excited in anticipation of the massacre.

A shot from the culverin, from a distance of about thirty yards, missed its mark. The explosion tore the stagnant air; the rock faces howled with the echo, setting in motion innumerable diminutive landslides.

There was a second shot almost immediately. The bullet hit the animal on one of its back paws, producing a stream of blood.

"Look at it leaping around!" exclaimed Maria; she too was now enthralled by this show of cruelty. In the agony of its wound the animal had started to jump around in anguished circles. It drew its shattered leg after it, leaving a trail of black liquid on the gravel.

At last the reptile managed to reach the goat and to seize it with its teeth. It was about to turn round when Gerol, to advertise his own daring, went right up to it and shot it in the head from about six feet away.

A sort of whistling sound came from its jaws; and it was as though it were trying to control itself, to repress its anger, not to make as much noise as it could, as though some incentive unknown to mere men were causing it to keep its temper. The bullet from the rifle had hit it in the eye. After firing the shot Count Gerol drew back promptly and waited for it to collapse. But it didn't collapse, the spark of life within it seemed as persistent as a fire fed by pitch. The ball of lead lodged firmly in its eye, the monster calmly proceeded to devour the goat and its neck swelled like rubber as the gigantic mouthfuls went down. Then it went back to the foot of the rocks and began to climb up the rock face beside the cave. It climbed with difficulty, as the earth kept giving way beneath its feet, but it was obviously seeking a way of escape. Above it was an arch of clear, pale sky; the sun dried up the trails of blood almost immediately.

"It's like a cockroach in a basin," muttered Andronico to himself.

"What did you say?" enquired his wife.

"Nothing, nothing," he replied.

"I wonder why it doesn't go into its cave," remarked Professor Inghirami, calmly noting all the scientific aspects of the scene.

"It's probably afraid of being trapped," suggested Fusti.

"But it must be completely stunned. And I very much doubt whether a Ceratosaurus is capable of such reasoning. A Ceratosaurus . . ."

"It's not a Ceratosaurus," objected Fusti. "I've restored several for museums, but they don't look like that. Where are the spines on its tail?"

"It keeps them hidden," replied Inghirami. "Look at that swollen abdomen. It tucks its tail underneath and that's why they can't be seen."

As they were talking one of the hunters, the one who had fired the shot with the culverin, came running hurriedly towards the terrace where Andronico was, with the evident intention of leaving.

"Where are you going?" shouted Gerol. "Stay in your position until we've finished."

"I'm going," the hunter answered firmly. "I don't like it. This isn't what I call hunting."

"What do you mean? That you're afraid? Is that it?"

"No sir, I'm not afraid."

"You're afraid, I tell you, or you'd stay in your place."

"No I'm not. But you, sir, should be ashamed of yourself."

"Ashamed of myself?" cursed Martino Gerol. "You young swine. You're from Palissano, I suppose, and a coward. Get away before I teach you a lesson."

"And where are *you* off to now, Beppi?" he shouted again, seeing another hunter moving off.

"I'm going too, sir. I don't want to be involved in this horrible business."

"Cowards!" shrieked Gerol. "Cowards, you'd pay for this if I could get at you!"

"It isn't fear, sir," repeated the second hunter. "It's not fear. But this will end badly, you'll see."

"I'll show you how it'll end right now!" and seizing a stone from the ground, the count hurled it at the hunter with all his force. But it missed.

There was a few moments' pause while the dragon scrambled about on the rock without managing to climb any higher. Earth and stones gave way and forced him back to his starting point. Apart from the sound of falling stones, there was silence.

Then Andronico spoke. "How much longer is this going to go on?" he shouted to Gerol. "It's fearfully hot. Finish off the animal once and for all, can't you? Why torture it like that, even if it is a dragon?"

"It's not my fault," answered Gerol, annoyed, "can't you see that it's refusing to die? It's got a bullet in its skull and it's more lively than ever."

He stopped speaking as the young man they had seen earlier came over the brow of the rock with another goat over his shoulders. Amazed at the sight of the men, their weapons, at the traces of blood and above all the dragon (which he had never seen out of its cave) struggling on the rocks, he had stood still in his tracks and was staring at the whole strange scene.

"Oy! Young man!" shouted Gerol. "How much do you want for that goat?"

"Nothing, I can't sell it!" he replied. "I wouldn't give it to you for its weight in gold. But what have you done to the dragon?" he added, narrowing his eyes to look at the blood-stained monster.

"We're here to settle the matter once and for all. You should be pleased. No more goats from tomorrow."

"Why not?"

"Because the dragon will be dead," replied the count smiling.

"But you can't, you can't do that," exclaimed the young man in terror.

"Don't you start too," shouted Gerol. "Give me that goat at once."

"I said no," the young man answered firmly, drawing back.

"Good God!" The count rushed at him, punched him full in the face, seized the goat from his back and threw him to the ground.

"You'll regret this one day, I tell you, you see if you don't," swore the young man quietly as he picked himself up, not daring to react more positively.

But Count Gerol had turned his back on him.

Now the whole valley basin was ablaze with the sun's heat and the glare from the yellow scree, the rocks, the stones and the scree again was such that they could hardly keep their eyes open; there was nothing, absolutely nothing, remotely restful to the eye.

Maria became more and more thirsty and drink gave no relief. "Good Lord, what heat," she moaned. Even the sight of Count Gerol had begun to pall.

In the meantime dozens of men had appeared, apparently springing from the earth itself. They had presumably come up from Palissano at the news that strangers were up at the Burel and they stood motionless on the brows of the various peaks of yellow earth, watching silently.

"Fine audience you've got now," remarked Andronico in an attempt at a joke, directed at Gerol, who was involved in some maneuvers concerning the goat with two hunters.

The young man looked up and saw the strangers staring at him. He assumed an expression of disdain and continued with what he was doing.

The dragon, exhausted, had slithered down the rock face on to the gravel; it was lying there, motionless except for its swollen stomach, which was still throbbing.

"Ready!" shouted one of the hunters, lifting the goat from the ground with Gerol's help. They had opened its stomach and put in an explosive charge with a fuse attached.

The Count then advanced fearlessly across the scree until he was about thirty feet from the dragon, put the goat carefully on the ground and walked away, unwinding the fuse.

They had to wait for half an hour before the creature moved. The strangers standing on the crests of the hills stood like statues: silent even among themselves, their faces expressed cold disapproval. Indifferent to the sun which was now immensely strong, they stared fixedly at the reptile, as though willing it not to move.

But at last the dragon, with another bullet in its back, turned suddenly, saw the goat and dragged itself slowly towards it. It was about to stretch out its head and seize its prey when the count lit the fuse. The spark ran rapidly along it, reached the goat and the charge exploded.

The report was not loud, much less so in fact than the culverin shots: sharp yet muffled, like a plank breaking. Yet the dragon's body was hurled violently backwards, its belly had obviously been ripped open. Once again the head began to move slowly from side to side as though it were saying no, that it wasn't fair, that they had been too cruel and that there was now no more it could do.

The Count laughed gleefully, but this time he laughed alone.

"Oh how awful! That's enough!" gasped Maria, covering her face with her hands.

"Yes," said her husband slowly, "I agree, this may end badly."

The monster was lying in a pool of black blood, apparently exhausted. And now from each of its two flanks there rose a column of dark smoke, one on the left and one on the right, two slow-moving plumes rising, it seemed, with difficulty.

"Do you see that?" said Inghirami to his colleague.

"I do," affirmed the other.

"Two blow-holes just like those of the Ceratosaurus, the so-called opercula hammeriana."

"No," said Fusti, "it's not a Ceratosaurus."

At this juncture Gerol emerged from behind the boulder where he'd been hiding and came forward to deliver the final blow. He was right in the middle of the stretch of gravel with his iron club in his hand, when the assembled company gave a shriek.

For a moment Gerol thought it was a shout of triumph for the slaying of the dragon. Then he became aware of movement behind him. He turned round sharply and saw —ridiculous—two pathetic little creatures tumbling out of the cave and coming towards him at some speed. Two small half-formed reptiles no more than two feet long, diminutive versions of the dying dragon. Two small dragons, its children, probably driven out of the cave by hunger.

It was a matter of minutes. The Count gave a wonderfully skillful performance. "Take that! and that!" he shouted gleefully, swinging the iron club. And two blows were enough. Aimed strongly and decisively, the club struck the two little monsters one after the other and smashed in their heads like glass bowls. They collapsed and lay dead looking, from a distance, like half-deflated bagpipes.

But now the strangers, without a word, turned and fled up the stony gulleys as though from some unexpected danger. Without making a sound, without dislodging a pebble or turning for a moment to look at the dragon's cave, they disappeared as mysteriously as they had come.

Now the dragon was moving again—it seemed as though it were never going to make the final effort to die. Dragging itself like a snail and still giving out two puffs of smoke, it went towards the two little dead creatures. When it had reached them it collapsed on to the stones, stretched out its head with infinite difficulty and began to lick them gently, perhaps hoping to resuscitate them.

Finally the dragon seemed to collect all its remaining strength: it raised its neck towards the sky to emit, first very softly but then with a rising crescendo, an unspeakable, incredible howl, a sound neither animal nor human but one so full of loathing that even Count Gerol stood still, paralyzed with horror.

Now they saw why it had not wanted to go back into its den (where it could have found shelter) and why it hadn't roared or howled but merely hissed. The dragon was thinking of its children, to save them it had given up its own hope of escape; for if it had hidden in its cave the men would have followed it and discovered its young; and had it made any noise, the little creatures would have come out to see what was happening. Only now, once it had seen them die, did the monster give this terrible shriek.

It was asking for help, and for vengeance for its children. But from whom? From the mountains, parched and uninhabited? From the birdless, cloudless sky, from those men who were torturing it? The shriek pierced the walls of rock and the dome of the sky, it filled the whole world. Unreasonably enough it seemed completely impossible that there should be no reply.

"Who can it be calling?" said Andronico, trying in vain to adopt a light-hearted tone. "Who is it calling? There's no one coming, as far as I can see."

"Oh if only it would die!" said the woman.

But the dragon would not make up its mind to die even though Count Gerol, suddenly maddened by the desire to conclude the business once and for all, shot at it with his rifle. Two shots. In vain. The dragon continued to lick its dead children; ever more slowly, yet surely, a whitish liquid was welling up in its unhurt eye.

"The saurian!" exclaimed Professor Inghirami. "Look, it's crying!"

The governor said: "It's late. That's enough, Martino, it's time to go."

Seven times the monster raised its voice, and the rocks and sky resounded. The seventh time it seemed as though the sound were never going to end, but then it suddenly ceased, dropped like a plumb-line, vanished into silence.

In the deathly quiet that followed there was a sound of coughing. Covered with dust, his face drawn with effort, weariness and emotion, Count Gerol, throwing his rifle down among the stones, came across the debris coughing, with one hand pressed to his chest.

"What is it?" asked Andronico, no longer joking but with a strange presentiment of disaster. "What's happened?"

"Nothing," said Gerol, trying to sound unconcerned. "I just swallowed a bit of that smoke."

"What smoke?"

Gerol didn't reply but indicated the dragon with his hand. The monster was lying still, its head stretched out on the stones; except for the two slight plumes of smoke, it looked very dead indeed.

"I think it's all over," said Andronico.

It did indeed seem so. The last breath of obstinate life was coming from the dragon's mouth.

No one had answered his call, no one in the whole world had responded. The mountains were quite still, even the diminutive landslides seemed to have been reabsorbed, the sky was clear without the slightest cloud and the sun was setting. No one, either from this world or the next, had come to avenge the massacre. Man had blotted out this last remaining stain from the world, man so powerful and cunning that wherever he goes he establishes wise laws for maintaining order, irreproachable man who works so hard for the cause of progress and cannot bring himself to allow the survival of dragons, even in the heart of the mountains; man had been the executioner, and recrimination would have been pointless.

What man had done was right, absolutely in accordance with the law. Yet it seemed impossible that no one should have answered the last appeal. Andronico, his wife and the hunters all wanted to escape from the place without more ado; even the two naturalists were willing to give up the usual embalming procedure in order to get away more quickly.

The men from the village had disappeared as though they had felt forebodings of disaster. The shadows climbed the walls of loose rock. The two plumes of smoke continued to rise from the dragon's shriveled carcass, curling slightly in the still air. All seemed over now, an unhappy incident to be forgotten as soon as possible. But Count Gerol went on coughing. Exhausted, he was seated on a boulder and his friends around him did not dare speak to him. Even the fearless Maria averted her gaze. The only sound was his sharp coughing. All attempts at controlling it were unsuccessful: there was a sort of fire burning ever deeper within him.

"I knew it," whispered Andronico to his wife, who was trembling a little. "I knew it would end badly."

Translated from the Italian
by Judith Landry

JULIO CORTÁZAR

AXOLOTL

There was a time when I thought a great deal about the axolotls. I went to see them in the aquarium at the Jardin des Plantes and stayed for hours watching them, observing their immobility, their faint movements. Now I am an axolotl.

I got to them by chance one spring morning when Paris was spreading its peacock tail after a wintry Lent. I was heading down the boulevard Port-Royal, then I took Saint-Marcel and L'Hôpital and saw green among all that grey and remembered the lions. I was friend of the lions and panthers, but had never gone into the dark, humid building that was the aquarium. I left my bike against the gratings and went to look at the tulips. The lions were sad and ugly and my panther was asleep. I decided on the aquarium, looked obliquely at banal fish until, unexpectedly, I hit it off with the axolotls. I stayed watching them for an hour and left, unable to think of anything else.

In the library at Sainte-Geneviève, I consulted a dictionary and learned that axolotls are the larval stage (provided with gills) of a species of salamander of the genus Ambystoma. That they were Mexican I knew already by looking at them and their little pink Aztec faces and the placard at the top of the tank. I read that specimens of them had been found in Africa capable of living on dry land during the periods of drought, and continuing their life under water when the rainy season came. I found their Spanish name, *ajolote,* and the mention that they were edible, and that their oil was used (no longer used, it said) like cod-liver oil.

I didn't care to look up any of the specialized works, but the next day I went back to the Jardin des Plantes. I began to go every morning, morning and afternoon some days. The aquarium guard smiled perplexedly taking my ticket. I would lean up against the iron bar in front of the tanks and set to watching them. There's nothing strange in this, because after the first minute I knew that we were linked, that something infinitely lost and distant kept pulling us together. It had been enough to detain me that first morning in front of the sheet of glass where some bubbles rose through the water. The axolotls huddled on the wretched narrow (only I can know how narrow and wretched) floor of moss and stone in the tank. There were nine specimens, and the majority pressed their heads against the glass, looking with their eyes of gold at whoever came near them. Disconcerted, almost ashamed, I felt it a lewdness to be peering at these silent and immobile figures heaped at the bottom of the tank. Mentally I isolated one, situated on the right and somewhat apart from the others, to study it better. I saw a rosy little body, translucent (I thought of those Chinese figurines of milky glass), looking like a small lizard about six inches long, ending in a fish's tail of extraordinary delicacy, the most sensitive part of our body. Along the back ran a transparent fin which joined with the tail, but what obsessed me was the feet, of the slenderest nicety, ending in tiny fingers with minutely human nails. And then I discovered its eyes, its face. Inexpressive features, with no other trait save the eyes, two orifices, like brooches, wholly of transparent gold, lacking any life but looking, letting themselves be penetrated by my look, which seemed to travel past the golden level and lose itself in a diaphanous interior mystery. A very slender black halo ringed the eye and etched it onto the pink flesh, onto the rosy stone of the head, vaguely triangular, but with curved and irregular sides which gave it a total likeness to a statuette corroded by time. The mouth was masked by the triangular plane of the face, its considerable size would be guessed only in profile; in front a delicate crevice barely slit the lifeless stone. On both sides of the head where the ears should have been, there grew three tiny sprigs red as coral, a vegetal outgrowth, the gills, I suppose. And they were the only thing quick about it; every ten or fifteen seconds the sprigs pricked up stiffly and again subsided. Once in a while a foot would barely move, I saw the diminutive toes poise mildly on the moss. It's that we don't enjoy moving a lot, and the tank is so cramped—we barely move in any direction and we're hitting one of the others with our tail or our head—difficulties arise, fights, tiredness. The time feels like it's less if we stay quietly.

It was their quietness that made me lean toward them fascinated the first time I saw the axolotls. Obscurely I seemed to understand their secret will, to abolish space and time with an indifferent immobilty. I knew better later; the gill contraction, the tentative reckoning of the delicate feet on the stone, the abrupt swimming (some of them swim with a simple undulation of the body) proved to me that they were capable of escaping that mineral lethargy in which they spent whole hours. Above all else, their eyes obsessed me. In the standing tanks on either side of them, different fishes showed me the simple stupidity of their handsome eyes so similar to our own. The eyes of the axolotls spoke to me of the presence of a different life, of another way of seeing. Gluing my face to the glass (the guard would cough fussily once in a while), I tried to see better those diminutive golden points, that entrance to the infinitely slow and remote world of these rosy creatures. It was useless to tap with one finger on the glass directly in front of their faces; they never gave the least reaction. The golden eyes continued burning with their soft, terrible light; they continued looking at me from an unfathomable depth which made me dizzy.

And nevertheless they were close. I knew it before this, before being an axolotl. I learned it the day I came near them for the first time. The anthropomorphic features of a monkey reveal the reverse of what most people believe, the distance that is traveled from them to us. The absolute lack of similarity between axolotls and human beings proved to me that my recognition was valid, that I was not propping myself up with easy analogies. Only the little hands . . . But an eft, the common newt, has such hands also, and we are not at all alike. I think it was the axolotls' heads, that triangular pink shape with the tiny eyes of gold. That looked and knew. That laid the claim. They were not *animals*.

It would seem easy, almost obvious, to fall into mythology. I began seeing in the axolotls a metamorphosis which did not succeed in revoking a mysterious humanity. I imagined them aware, slaves of their bodies, condemned infinitely to the silence of the abyss, to a hopeless meditation. Their blind gaze, the diminutive gold disc without expression and nonetheless terribly shining, went through me like a message: "Save us, save us." I caught myself mumbling words of advice, conveying childish hopes. They continued to look at me, immobile; from time to time the rosy branches of the gills stiffened. In that instant I felt a muted pain; perhaps they were seeing me, attracting my strength to penetrate into the impenetrable thing of their lives. They were not human beings, but I had found in no animal such a profound relation with myself. The axolotls were like witnesses of something, and at times like horrible judges. I felt ignoble in front of them; there was such a terrifying purity in those transparent eyes. They were larvas, but larva means disguise and also phantom. Behind those Aztec faces, without expression but of an implacable cruelty, what semblance was awaiting its hour?

I was afraid of them. I think that had it not been for feeling the proximity of other visitors and the guard, I would not have been bold enough to remain alone with them. "You eat them alive with your eyes, hey," the guard said, laughing; he likely thought I was a little cracked. What he didn't notice was that it was they devouring me slowly with their eyes, in a cannibalism of gold. At any distance from the aquarium, I had only to think of them, it was as though I were being affected from a distance. It got to the point that I was going every day, and at night I thought of them immobile in the darkness, slowly putting a hand out which immediately encountered another. Perhaps their eyes could see in the dead of night, and for them the day continued indefinitely. The eyes of axolotls have no lids.

I know now that there was nothing strange, that that had to occur. Leaning over in front of the tank each morning, the recognition was greater. They were suffering, every fiber of my body reached toward that stifled pain, that stiff torment at the bottom of the tank. They were lying in wait for something, a remote dominion destroyed, an age of liberty when the world had been that of the axolotls. Not possible that such a terrible expression which was attaining the overthrow of that forced blankness on their stone faces should carry any message other than one of pain, proof of that eternal sentence, of that liquid hell they were undergoing. Hopelessly, I wanted to prove to myself that my own sensibility was projecting a nonexistent consciousness upon the axolotls. They and I knew. So there was nothing strange in what happened. My face was pressed against the glass of the aquarium, my eyes were attempting once more to penetrate the mystery of those eyes of gold without iris, without pupil. I saw from very close up the face of an axolotl immobile next to the glass. No transition and surprise, I saw my face against the glass, I saw it on the outside of the tank, I saw it on the other side of the glass. Then my face drew back and I understood.

Only one thing was strange: to go on thinking as usual,

to know. To realize that was, for the first moment, like the horror of a man buried alive awaking to his fate. Outside, my face came close to the glass again, I saw my mouth, the lips compressed with the effort of understanding the axolotls. I was an axolotl and now I knew instantly that no understanding was possible. He was outside the aquarium, his thinking was a thinking outside the tank. Recognizing him, being him himself, I was an axolotl and in my world. The horror began—I learned in the same moment—of believing myself prisoner in the body of an axolotl, metamorphosed into him with my human mind intact, buried alive in an axolotl, condemned to move lucidly among unconscious creatures. But that stopped when a foot just grazed my face, when I moved just a little to one side and saw an axolotl next to me who was looking at me, and understood that he knew also, no communication possible, but very clearly. Or I was also in him, or all of us were thinking humanlike, incapable of expression, limited to the golden splendor of our eyes looking at the face of the man pressed against the aquarium.

He returned many times, but he comes less often now. Weeks pass without his showing up. I saw him yesterday; he looked at me for a long time and left briskly. It seemed to me that he was not so much interested in us any more, that he was coming out of habit. Since the only thing I do is think, I could think about him a lot. It occurs to me that at the beginning we continued to communicate, that he felt more than ever one with the mystery which was claiming him. But the bridges were broken between him and me, because what was his obsession is now an axolotl, alien to his human life. I think that at the beginning I was capable of returning to him in a certain way—ah, only in a certain way—and of keeping awake his desire to know us better. I am an axolotl for good now, and if I think like a man it's only because every axolotl thinks like a man inside his rosy stone semblance. I believe that all this succeeded in communicating something to him in those first days, when I was still he. And in this final solitude to which he no longer comes, I console myself by thinking that perhaps he is going to write a story about us, that, believing he's making up a story, he's going to write all this about axolotls.

Translated from the Spanish
by Paul Blackburn

JORGE LUIS BORGES

THE LOTTERY IN BABYLON

Like all men in Babylon, I have been proconsul; like all, a slave. I have also known omnipotence, opprobrium, imprisonment. Look: the index finger on my right hand is missing. Look: through the rip in my cape you can see a vermilion tattoo on my stomach. It is the second symbol, Beth. This letter, on nights when the moon is full, gives me power over men whose mark is Gimmel, but it subordinates me to the men of Aleph, who on moonless nights owe obedience to those marked with Gimmel. In the half light of dawn, in a cellar, I have cut the jugular vein of sacred bulls before a black stone. During a lunar year I have been declared invisible. I shouted and they did not answer me; I stole bread and they did not behead me. I have known what the Greeks do not know, incertitude. In a bronze chamber, before the silent handkerchief of the strangler, hope has been faithful to me, as has panic in the river of pleasure.

Heraclides Ponticus tells with amazement that Pythagoras remembered having been Pyrrhus and before that Euphorbus and before that some other mortal. In order to remember similar vicissitudes I do not need to have recourse to death or even to deception.

I owe this almost atrocious variety to an institution which other republics do not know or which operates in them in an imperfect and secret manner: the lottery. I have not looked into its history; I know that the wise men cannot agree. I know of its powerful purposes what a man who is not versed in astrology can know about the moon. I come from a dizzy land where the lottery is the basis of reality. Until today I have thought as little about it as I have about the conduct of indecipherable divinities or about my heart. Now, far from Babylon and its beloved customs, I think with a certain amount of amazement about the lottery and about the blasphemous conjectures which veiled men murmur in the twilight.

My father used to say that formerly—a matter of centuries, of years?—the lottery in Babylon was a game of plebeian character. He recounted (I don't know whether rightly) that barbers sold, in exchange for copper coins, squares of bone or of parchment adorned with symbols. In broad daylight a drawing took place. Those who won received silver coins without any other test of luck. The system was elementary, as you can see.

Naturally these "lotteries" failed. Their moral virtue was nil. They were not directed at all of man's faculties, but only at hope. In the face of public indifference, the merchants who founded these venal lotteries began to lose money. Someone tried a reform: The interpolation of a few unfavorable tickets in the list of favorable numbers. By means of this reform, the buyers of numbered squares ran the double risk of winning a sum and of paying a fine that could be considerable. This slight danger (for every thirty favorable numbers there was one unlucky one) awoke, as is natural, the interest of the public. The Babylonians threw themselves into the game. Those who did not acquire chances were considered pusillanimous, cowardly. In time, that justified disdain was doubled. Those who did not play were scorned, but also the losers who paid the fine were scorned. The Company (as it came to be known then) had to take care of the winners, who could not cash in their prizes if almost the total amount of the fines was unpaid. It started a lawsuit against the losers. The judge condemned them to pay the original fine and costs or spend several days in jail. All chose jail in order to defraud the Company. The bravado of a few is the source of the omnipotence of the Company and of its metaphysical and ecclesiastical power.

A little while afterward the lottery lists omitted the amounts of fines and limited themselves to publishing the days of imprisonment that each unfavorable number indicated. That laconic spirit, almost unnoticed at the time, was of capital importance. *It was the first appearance in the lottery of nonmonetary elements.* The success was tremendous. Urged by the clientele, the Company was obliged to increase the unfavorable numbers.

Everyone knows that the people of Babylon are fond of logic and even of symmetry. It was illogical for the lucky numbers to be computed in round coins and the unlucky ones in days and nights of imprisonment. Some moralists reasoned that the possession of money does not always determine happiness and that other forms of happiness are perhaps more direct.

Another concern swept the quarters of the poorer classes. The members of the college of priests multiplied their stakes and enjoyed all the vicissitudes of terror and hope; the poor (with reasonable or unavoidable envy) knew that they were excluded from that notoriously delicious rhythm. The just desire that all, rich and poor, should participate equally in the lottery, inspired an indignant agitation, the memory of which the years have not erased. Some obstinate people did not understand (or pretended not to understand) that it was a question of a new order, of a necessary historical stage. A slave stole a crimson ticket, which in the drawing credited him with the burning of his tongue. The legal code fixed that same penalty for the one who stole a ticket. Some Babylonians argued that he deserved the burning irons in his status of a thief; others, generously, that the executioner should apply it to him because chance had determined it that way. There were disturbances, there were lamentable drawings of blood, but the masses of Babylon finally imposed their will against the opposition of the rich. The people achieved amply its general purposes. In the first place, it caused the Company to accept total power. (That unification was necessary, given the vastness and complexity of the new operations.) In the second place, it made the lottery secret, free and general. The mercenary sale of chances was abolished. Once initiated in the mysteries of Baal, every free man automatically participated in the sacred drawings, which took place in the labyrinths of the god every sixty nights and which determined his destiny until the next drawing. The consequences were incalculable. A fortunate play could bring about his promotion to the council of wise men or the imprisonment of an enemy (public or private) or finding, in the peaceful darkness of his room, the woman who begins to excite him and whom he never expected to see again. A bad play: mutilation, different kinds of infamy, death. At times one single fact—the vulgar murder of C, the mysterious apotheosis of B—was the happy solution of thirty or forty drawings. To combine the plays was difficult, but one must remember that the individuals of the Company were (and are) omnipotent and astute. In many cases the knowledge that certain happinesses were the simple product of chance would have diminished their virtue. To avoid that obstacle, the agents of the Company made use of the power of suggestion and magic. Their steps, their maneuverings, were secret. To find out about the intimate hopes and terrors of each individual, they had astrologists and spies. There were certain stone lions, there was a sacred latrine called Qaphqa, there were fissures in a dusty aqueduct which, according to general opinion, *led to the Company*; malignant or benevolent persons deposited information in these places. An alphabetical file collected these items of varying truthfulness.

Incredibly, there were complaints. The Company, with its usual discretion, did not answer directly. It preferred to scrawl in the rubbish of a mask factory a brief statement which now figures in the sacred scriptures. This doctrinal item observed that the lottery is an interpolation of chance in the order of the world and that to accept errors is not to contradict chance: it is to corroborate it. It likewise observed that those lions and that sacred receptacle, although not disavowed by the Company (which did not abandon the right to consult them), functioned without official guarantee.

This declaration pacified the public's restlessness. It also produced other effects, perhaps unforeseen by its writer. It deeply modified the spirit and the operations of the Company. I don't have much time left; they tell us that the ship is about to weigh anchor. But I shall try to explain it.

However unlikely it might seem, no one had tried out before then a general theory of chance. Babylonians are not very speculative. They revere the judgments of fate, they deliver to them their lives, their hopes, their panic, but it does not occur to them to investigate fate's labyrinthine laws nor the gyratory spheres which reveal it. Nevertheless, the *unofficial* declaration that I have mentioned inspired many discussions of judicial-mathematical character. From some one of them the following conjecture was born: If the lottery is an intensification of chance, a periodical infusion of chaos in the cosmos, would it not be right for chance to intervene in all stages of the drawing and not in one alone? Is it not ridiculous for chance to dictate someone's death and have the circumstances of that death—secrecy, publicity, the fixed time of an hour or a century—not subject to chance? These just scruples finally caused a considerable reform, whose complexities (aggravated by centuries' practice) only a few specialists understand, but which I shall try to summarize, at least in a symbolic way.

Let us imagine a first drawing, which decrees the death of a man. For its fulfillment one proceeds to another drawing, which proposes (let us say) nine possible executors. Of these executors, four can initiate a third drawing which will tell the name of the executioner, two can replace the adverse order with a fortunate one (finding a treasure, let us say), another will intensify the death penalty (that is, will make it infamous or enrich it with tortures), others can refuse to fulfill it. This is the symbolic scheme. In reality *the number of drawings is infinite.* No decision is final, all branch into others. Ignorant people suppose that infinite drawings require an infinite time; actually it is sufficient for time to be infinitely subdivisible, as the famous parable of the contest with the tortoise teaches. This infinity harmonizes admirably with the sinuous numbers of Chance and with the Celestial Archetype of the Lottery, which the Platonists adore. Some warped echo of our rites seems to have resounded on the Tiber: Ellus Lampridius, in the *Life of Antoninus Heliogabalus*, tells that this emperor wrote on shells the lots that were destined for his guests, so that one received ten pounds of gold and another ten flies, ten dormice, ten bears. It is permissible to recall that Heliogabalus was brought up in Asia Minor, among the priests of the eponymous god.

There are also impersonal drawings, with an indefinite purpose. One decrees that a sapphire of Taprobana be thrown into the waters of the Euphrates; another, that a bird be released from the roof of a tower; another, that each century there be withdrawn (or added) a grain of sand from the innumerable ones on the beach. The consequences are, at times, terrible.

Under the beneficent influence of the Company, our customs are saturated with chance. The buyer of a dozen amphoras of Damascene wine will not be surprised if one of them contains a talisman or a snake. The scribe who writes a contract almost never fails to introduce some erroneous information. I myself, in this hasty declaration, have falsified some splendor, some atrocity. Perhaps, also, some mysterious monotony . . . Our historians, who are the most penetrating on the globe, have invented a method to correct chance. It is well known that the operations of this method are (in general) reliable, although, naturally, they are not divulged without some portion of deceit. Furthermore, there is nothing so contaminated with fiction as the history of the Company. A paleographic document, exhumed in a temple, can be the result of yesterday's lottery or of an age-old lottery. No book is published without some discrepancy in each one of the copies. Scribes take a secret oath to omit, to interpolate, to change. The indirect lie is also cultivated.

The Company, with divine modesty, avoids all publicity. Its agents, as is natural, are secret. The orders which it issues continually (perhaps incessantly) do not differ from those lavished by impostors. Moreover, who can brag about being a mere impostor? The drunkard who improvises an absurd order, the dreamer who awakens suddenly and strangles the woman who sleeps at his side, do they not execute, perhaps, a secret decision of the Company? That silent functioning, comparable to God's, gives rise to all sorts of conjectures. One abominably insinuates that the Company has not existed for centuries and that the sacred disorder of our lives is purely hereditary, traditional. Another judges it eternal and teaches that it will last until the last night, when the last god annihilates the world. Another declares that the Company is omnipotent, but that it only has influence in tiny things: in a bird's call, in the shadings of rust and of dust, in the half dreams of dawn. Another, in the words of masked heresiarchs, *that it has never existed and will not exist.* Another, no less vile, reasons that it is indifferent to affirm or deny the reality of the shadowy corporation, because Babylon is nothing else than an infinite game of chance.

Translated from the Spanish
by John M. Fein

MIRCEA ELIADE

WITH THE GYPSY GIRLS

Inside the streetcar the heat was scorching, stifling. Walking quickly down the aisle, he said to himself, "You're in luck, Gavrilescu!" He had spotted an empty seat beside an open window at the other end of the car. He sat down, took out his handkerchief, and for a long time mopped his brow and his cheeks. Then he stuffed the handkerchief under his collar all the way around his neck and began fanning himself with his straw hat. An old man sitting across from him had been staring at him the whole time, as if trying to recall where he had seen him before. He was holding a metal box carefully on his knees.

"This heat is awful!" he said all of a sudden. "It hasn't been this hot since 1905!"

Gavrilescu nodded and continued to fan himself with his hat. "It certainly is hot," he said. "But when a man is cultured, he can stand anything more easily. Colonel Lawrence, for instance. Do you know anything about Colonel Lawrence?"

"No."

"Too bad—I don't know much about him either. If those young men had got on this streetcar, I would have asked them. I always like to strike up a conversation with cultured people. Those young men, sir, must have been students. Outstanding students. We were all waiting together at the car stop, and I listened to what they were saying. They were talking about a certain Colonel Lawrence and his adventures in Arabia. And what memories they had! They were reciting by heart whole pages from the colonel's book.* There was one sentence I particularly liked, a very beautiful sentence, about the intense heat he encountered—the colonel, that is—somewhere in Arabia, which smote him on the top of the head, smote him like a saber. Too bad I can't remember it word for word. That terrible heat of Arabia smote him like a saber. It smote him on the top of the head like a saber, and struck him dumb."

The conductor, who had been listening with a smile, handed him his ticket. Gavrilescu put his hat on his head and began searching through his pockets.

"Excuse me," he murmured finally, when he was unable to find his wallet. "I never know where I put it."

"That's all right," said the conductor, with unexpected good humor. "We've got time—we haven't got to the gypsy girls' yet."

And turning to the old man, he winked at him. The

* Mircea Eliade himself as a young man translated T. E. Lawrence's *Revolt in the Desert* into Romanian, under the title *Revolta în Deşert* (Bucharest 1934).—TRANS.

old man blushed and nervously held on to the metal box more tightly, with both hands. Gavrilescu handed the conductor a bill, and he began counting out the change, still smiling.

"It's a scandal!" muttered the old man after a few moments. "It's a crime!"

"Everybody's talking about them," said Gavrilescu, starting to fan himself again with his hat. "It certainly is a fine-looking house, and what a garden! What a garden!" he repeated, nodding his head in admiration. "Look, you can almost see it from here," he added, leaning forward a little in order to see better.

A number of men moved their heads closer to the windows, as if by chance.

"It's a scandal!" the old man repeated, looking severely straight in front of him. "It ought to be forbidden."

"They have some ancient walnut trees," continued Gavrilescu. "That's why it's so shady and cool there. I've heard that walnut trees begin to throw a thick shade only after thirty or forty years. Do you suppose that's true?"

But the old man pretended not to hear. Gavrilescu turned to one of his neighbors, who had been gazing out of the window lost in thought.

"They have some ancient walnut trees which must be at least fifty years old," he began. "That's why there's so much shade. And in the heat like this, that's a real pleasure. Those lucky people!"

"Lucky girls," said his neighbor, without raising his eyes. "They're gypsy girls."

"That's what I've heard too," continued Gavrilescu. "I ride on this streetcar three times a week. And I give you my word of honor, never once has it happened that I didn't hear people talking about them, about the gypsy girls. Does anyone know who they are? I wonder where they came from?"

"They came here a long time ago," said his neighbor.

"They've been here twenty-one years," someone interrupted him. "When I first came to Bucureşti, the gypsy girls were already here. But the garden was much larger. The lyceum hadn't been built yet."

"As I was telling you," Gavrilescu began again, "I ride this streetcar regularly three times a week. Unfortunately for me, I'm a piano teacher. I say unfortunately for me," he added, with an attempt at a smile, "because that's not what I was made for. I have the soul of an artist."

"Why then I know you," said the old man suddenly, turning his head. "You're *Domnul* Gavrilescu, the piano teacher. I have a little granddaughter, and you've been giving her lessons for five or six years now. I've been wondering the whole time why your face was so familiar."

"Yes, that's me," Gavrilescu resumed. "I give piano lessons and I travel a lot by streetcar. In the spring, when it's not too hot and there's a breeze blowing, it's a real pleasure. You sit at a window like this, and as the streetcar goes along you see lots of gardens in bloom. As I was telling you, I travel on this line three times a week. And I always hear people talking about the gypsy girls. Many times I've asked myself, 'Gavrilescu,' I say to myself, 'assuming they're gypsies, I wonder where they get so much money?' A house like that, a real palace, with gardens and ancient walnut trees—that takes millions."

"It's a scandal!" the old man exclaimed again, turning his head away in disgust.

"And I've also asked myself another question," continued Gavrilescu. "In terms of what I earn, a hundred lei a lesson, it would take ten thousand lessons to make a million. But you see, things aren't as simple as that. Let's say I had twenty lessons a week, it would still take me five hundred weeks—in other words almost ten years—and I would have to have twenty pupils with twenty pianos. And then there's the problem of summer vacations, when I'm left with only two or three pupils. And Christmas and Easter vacations too. All those lost lessons are lost for the million too—so that I shouldn't speak of five hundred weeks with twenty lessons, and twenty pupils with twenty pianos, but of much more than that, much more!"

"That's right," said one of his neighbors. "These days people don't learn to play the piano any more."

"Oh!" exclaimed Gavrilescu suddenly, tapping his forehead with his hat. "I thought I'd forgotten something, but I couldn't think what it was. My portfolio! I forgot the portfolio with my music. I stopped to chat with Mrs. Voitinovici, Otilia's aunt, and I forget the portfolio. Of all the luck!" he added, pulling the handkerchief out from under his collar and stuffing it in his pocket. "In all this heat, back you go, Gavrilescu, all the way back on the streetcar to Strada Preoteselor."*

He looked about him desperately, as if he expected someone to stop him. Then he stood up suddenly.

"It's been a pleasure meeting you," he said, lifting his hat and bowing slightly from the waist.

Then he quickly stepped out onto the platform just as

* Street of the Priests' Wives.—TRANS.

the car was stopping. Alighting on the street, he was again enveloped in the intense heat and the smell of melted asphalt. With some difficulty he crossed the street to wait for the streetcar going in the opposite direction. "Gavrilescu," he murmured, "watch out! for it looks . . . it really looks as if you're starting to grow old. You're getting decrepit, you're losing your memory. Again I say, watch out! because there's no excuse for it. At forty-nine a man is in the prime of life."

But he felt worn out and weary, and he sank down on the bench, right out in the sun. He pulled out his handkerchief and began to mop his face. "Somehow this reminds me of something," he said to himself to give himself courage. "A little effort, Gavrilescu, a little effort of the memory. Somewhere, on a bench, without a cent in my pocket. It wasn't as hot as this, but it was summer just the same." He looked around him at the deserted street, at the houses with the shutters drawn and the blinds lowered as if they had been abandoned. "Everybody is going to the shore," he said to himself, "and tomorrow or the day after Otilia is going too." And then it came to him: it was in Charlottenburg; he was sitting, just as he was now, on a bench in the sun, only then he was hungry and hadn't a cent in his pocket. "When you're young and an artist, you can bear anything more easily," he said to himself. He stood up and took a few steps out into the street to see if the streetcar was in sight. As he walked, it seemed as if the heat was losing some of its intensity. He returned, and leaning against the wall of a house, took off his hat and began fanning himself.

A hundred meters or so up the street was what looked like an oasis of shade. From inside a garden the branches of a tall linden tree with their dense foliage hung down over the sidewalk. Gavrilescu looked at them, fascinated but hesitating. He turned his head once more to see if the streetcar was coming, then set off determinedly, taking long steps and keeping close to the walls. When he got there, the shade did not seem so thick. But the coolness of the garden could still be felt, and Gavrilescu began to breathe deeply, throwing his head back a little. "What must it have been like a month ago, with the lindens all in flower!" he said to himself dreamily. He went up to the iron grillwork gate and gazed in at the garden. The gravel had recently been wet down, and one could see beds of flowers, while farther back was a pool with statues of dwarves around the edge. At that moment he heard the streetcar pass by him with a dry screech, and he turned his head. "Too late!" he exclaimed with a smile. "*Zu spät!*" he added, and raising his arm, he waved farewell several times with his hat, as at the North Station in the good old days, when Elsa was leaving to spend a month with her family in a village near Munich.

Then, sensibly and without haste, he continued on his way. On reaching the next stop he took off his coat and prepared to wait, when all at once he caught the rather bitter odor of walnut leaves crushed between the fingers. He turned his head and looked around him. He was alone. As far as eye could see, the sidewalk was empty. He didn't dare look up at the sky, but he felt above his head that same dazzling, incandescent, white light, and he felt the scorching heat of the street strike him on the mouth and cheeks. Then he set off again resignedly, his coat under his arm and his hat pulled down firmly on his forehead. Seeing from a distance the heavy shade of the walnut trees, he felt his heart beat faster, and he quickened his pace a little. He had almost reached there when he heard the metallic screech of the streetcar behind him. He stopped and waved his hat after it for a long time. "Too late!" he exclaimed. "Too late!"

In the shade of the walnut tree he was bathed in an unexpected, unnatural coolness, and Gavrilescu stood there a moment, bewildered but smiling. It was as if he suddenly found himself in a forest up in the mountains. In astonishment he began to look almost with awe at the tall trees and the stone wall covered with ivy, and gradually an infinite sadness stole over him. For so many years he had been going past this garden on the streetcar, without even once having the curiosity to get off and take a closer look at it. He walked along slowly, his head thrown back a little, his gaze fixed on the tall tops of the trees. And all at once he found himself just outside the gate, and there, as if she had been hiding a long time watching him, a young girl stepped out in front of him, beautiful and very swarthy, with a golden necklace and big golden earrings. Taking him by the arm, she asked him in a soft voice:

"Are you looking for the gypsy girls?"

She smiled at him with her whole mouth and with her eyes; and seeing him hesitate, she pulled him gently by the arm into the yard. Gavrilescu followed her, fascinated; but after a few steps he stopped, as if he wanted to say something.

"Won't you come to the gypsy girls'?" the girl asked him again, in a still softer voice.

She looked him in the eye fleetingly but deeply, then

took his hand and quickly led him to a little old house, which you would scarcely have guessed was there, hidden among lilac and dwarf elder bushes. She opened the door and gently pushed him inside. Gavrilescu found himself in a curious semidarkness, as if the windows had blue and green panes. Far away he heard the streetcar approaching, and the metallic screech struck him as so unbearable that he put his hand to his forehead. When the racket died away, he discovered near him, seated at a short-legged table, with a cup of coffee in front of her, an old woman who was looking at him curiously, as if waiting for him to wake up.

"What is your heart's desire for today?" she asked him. "A gypsy girl, a Greek girl, a German girl?"

"No," Gavrilescu interrupted her, raising his arm, "not a German girl."

"Well then, a gypsy girl, a Greek girl, a Jewish girl?" the old woman went on. "Three hundred lei," she added.

Gavrilescu smiled, but it was a grave smile.

"Three piano lessons!" he exclaimed, beginning to search his pockets. "And that's not counting the round trip on the streetcar."

The old woman took a sip of coffee and seemed lost in thought.

"You're a musician?" she asked him suddenly. "Then I'm sure you'll be satisfied."

"I am an artist," said Gavrilescu, taking a number of wet handkerchiefs out of one trousers pocket, one after the other, and transferring them methodically, one by one, to the other. "Unfortunately for me, I became a piano teacher, but my ideal has always been art for its own sake. I live for the soul. I'm sorry," he added, a bit embarrassed, setting his hat on the little table and putting in it the things he was taking out of his pockets. "I never can find my wallet when I need it."

"There's no hurry," said the old woman. "We've got lots of time. It's not even three o'clock yet."

"I'm sorry to contradict you," Gavrilescu interrupted her, "but I think you're mistaken. It must be almost four. It was three when I finished the lesson with Otilia."

"Then the clock must have stopped again," murmured the old woman, and once again was lost in thought.

"There, at last!" exclaimed Gavrilescu, showing her the wallet triumphantly. "It was right where it was supposed to be."

He counted out the bills and handed them to her.

"Take him to the cottage," said the old woman, raising her eyes.

Gavrilescu felt someone take his hand. Startled, he turned his head and saw beside him once again the girl who had lured him into entering the gate. He followed her timidly, holding under his arm the hat loaded with the things from his pockets.

"Now remember them well," the girl told him, "and don't get them mixed up: a gypsy girl, a Greek girl, a Jewish girl."

They crossed the garden, passing in front of the tall building with the red-tiled roof which Gavrilescu had seen from the street.

She stopped and looked deep into his eyes for a moment, then burst out in a brief, soft laugh. Gavrilescu had just started to put all the things from his hat back in his pockets.

"Oh!" he said. "I am an artist. If I had any choice in the matter, I would stay here, in these groves," and he waved his hat toward the trees. "I love nature. And in all this heat, to be able to breathe pure air, to enjoy a coolness like that in the mountains. But where are we going?" he asked, seeing that the girl was approaching a wooden fence and opening the gate.

"To the cottage. That's what the old woman said."

She took his arm again and led him along after her. They entered a neglected garden, with roses and lilies lost among the weeds and sweetbrier bushes. The heat was beginning to make itself felt again, and Gavrilescu hesitated, disappointed.

"I was deceiving myself," he said. "I came here for coolness, for nature."

"Wait till you go in the cottage," the girl interrupted him, pointing to a little old house, rather ramshackle-looking, which could be seen at the end of the garden.

Gavrilescu put his hat on and followed her morosely. But when he reached the vestibule, he felt his heart beating faster and faster, and he stopped.

"I'm all excited," he said, "and I don't know why."

"Don't drink too much coffee," the girl said softly, as she opened the door and pushed him inside.

It was a room whose limits he could not see, for the curtains were drawn, and in the semidarkness the screens looked like the walls. He started to walk forward into the room, treading on carpets each one thicker and softer than the last, as if he were stepping on mattresses, and at every step his heart beat faster, until finally he was afraid to go any farther, and he stopped. At that moment he suddenly felt happy, as if he had become young again, and the whole world was his, and Hildegard too was his.

"Hildegard!" he exclaimed, addressing the girl. "I

haven't thought of her for twenty years. She was my great love. She was the woman of my life!"

But on turning his head, he found that the girl had left. Then his nostrils caught a subtle, exotic scent, and suddenly he heard hands clapping, while the room began to get light in a mysterious way, as if the curtains were being drawn back slowly, very slowly, one by one, allowing the light of the summer afternoon to come in a little at a time. But Gavrilescu scarcely had time to notice that not one of the curtains had been touched, when he caught sight of three young girls standing a few meters in front of him, clapping their hands softly and laughing.

"We're the ones you chose," said one of them. "A gypsy girl, a Greek girl, a Jewish girl."

"Now let's see if you can guess which is which," said the second.

"Let's see if you know which is the gypsy girl," added the third.

Gavrilescu had dropped his straw hat and was looking at them with a vacant stare, transfixed, as if he didn't see them, as if he were looking at something else, beyond them, beyond the screens.

"I'm thirsty!" he whispered all at once, putting his hand to his throat.

"The old woman sent you some coffee," said one of the girls.

She disappeared behind a screen and returned with a round wooden tray on which were a cup of coffee and a coffeepot. Gavrilescu took the cup and drank it all down, then handed it back to her with a smile.

"I'm terribly thirsty," he murmured.

"This will be very hot, for it's right out of the pot," said the girl, refilling his cup. "Drink it slowly."

Gavrilescu tried to sip it, but the coffee was so hot that he burned his lips, and he put the cup back on the tray, disappointed.

"I'm thirsty!" he said again. "If I could just have a little drink of water!"

The other two girls disappeared behind the screen and returned at once with two full trays.

"The old woman sent you some jam," said one of them.

"Rose jam and sherbet," added the other.

But Gavrilescu saw only the jug full of water, and although he had noticed the heavy, frosted, green-glass tumbler beside it, he seized the jug with both hands and put it to his lips. He took his time, drinking in noisy gulps, with his head thrown back. Then he heaved a sigh, set the jug back on the tray, and took one of the handkerchiefs out of his pocket.

"Ladies!" he exclaimed, starting to mop his brow. "I really was awfully thirsty. I've heard about a man, Colonel Lawrence . . ."

The girls exchanged knowing glances, then all burst out laughing. This time they laughed unrestrainedly, harder and harder as time went on. At first Gavrilescu gazed at them in astonishment, then a broad smile crept over his face, and finally he too began to laugh. He mopped his face for a long time with the handkerchief.

"If I too may ask a question," he said at last, "I'd be curious to know what got into you."

"We were laughing because you called us ladies," said one of them. "Did you forget you're with the gypsy girls?"

"That's not so!" another interrupted. "Don't pay any attention to her, she's just trying to fool you. We were laughing because you got mixed up and drank from the jug instead of the glass. If you had drunk from the glass . . ."

"Don't listen to her!" the third interrupted. "She's just trying to fool you. I'll tell you the real truth: we were laughing because you were afraid."

"That's not so! That's not so!" the other two burst out. "She wanted to test you, to see if you were afraid."

"He was afraid! He was afraid!" repeated the third girl.

Gavrilescu took a step forward and raised his arm solemnly.

"Ladies!" he cried, offended. "I see you don't know who you have before you. I'm not just anybody. I'm Gavrilescu, the artist. And before becoming, unfortunately for me, a miserable piano teacher, I experienced a poet's dream. Ladies," he exclaimed with emotion, after a pause, "when I was twenty I knew, I fell in love with, I adored Hildegard!"

One of the girls brought up an armchair for him, and Gavrilescu sat down with a deep sigh.

"Ah!" he began after a long silence. "Why have you reminded me of the tragedy of my life? Because, you understand, Hildegard never became my wife. Something happened, something terrible happened."

The girl handed him the cup of coffee, and Gavrilescu began to sip it, pensively.

"Something terrible happened," he resumed, after some time. "But what? What could have happened? It's strange that I can't remember. Of course, I hadn't thought of Hildegard for many, many years. I had grown accustomed to the situation. I told myself: 'Gavrilescu, the past is past.

That's the way it is with artists—they never have any luck.' And then suddenly, just now, when I came in here to you, I remembered that I too have known a noble passion, I remembered that I have loved Hildegard!"

The girls exchanged glances and began to clap their hands.

"So I was right after all," said the third girl. "He was afraid."

"Yes," the others agreed. "You were right: he was afraid."

Gavrilescu raised his eyes and looked at them sadly for a long time.

"I don't understand what you mean."

"You are afraid," one of the girls proclaimed tauntingly, taking a step toward him. "You've been afraid from the moment you first came in."

"That's why you were so thirsty," said the second.

"And ever since then you keep changing the subject," added the other. "You chose us, but you're afraid to guess which is which."

"I still don't understand," said Gavrilescu defensively.

"You should have guessed right at the start," continued the third girl. "You should have guessed which is the gypsy girl, which is the Greek girl, and which the Jewish girl."

"Try it now, since you say you're not afraid," the first one said again. "Which is the gypsy girl?"

"Which is the gypsy girl? Which is the gypsy girl?" The voices of the others came to Gavrilescu like an echo.

He smiled and looked at them again searchingly.

"How do you like that!" he began, suddenly feeling in high spirits. "Now that you've finally grasped the fact that

I'm an artist, you think I live up in the clouds and don't know what a gypsy girl looks like."

"Don't change the subject again," one of the girl interrupted him. "Guess!"

"I mean," Gavrilescu continued stubbornly, "you think I don't have sufficient imagination to pick out the gypsy girl, especially when she's young, beautiful, and naked."

For of course he had guessed which was which as soon as he set eyes on them. The one who had taken a step toward him, completely naked, very swarthy, with black hair and eyes, was without doubt the gypsy girl. The second girl was naked too, but covered with a pale-green veil; her body was preternaturally white, so that it gleamed like mother-of-pearl; on her feet she wore gilded slippers. She could only be the Greek girl. The third was without doubt the Jewish girl: she had on a long skirt of cherry-colored velvet, which hugged her body at the waist, leaving her breasts and shoulders bare; her abundant hair, red with fiery glints, was skillfully braided and piled on the top of her head.

"Guess! Which is the gypsy girl? Which is the gypsy girl?" cried all three.

Gavrilescu suddenly got up from the chair, and pointing to the naked, swarthy girl in front of him, he pronounced solemnly: "Since I am an artist, I consent to be put to the test, even such a childish test as this, and I respond: You are the gypsy girl!"

The next instant he felt himself taken by the hands, and the girls began turning him round and round, shouting and whistling; their voices seemed to come to him from very far away.

"You didn't guess it! You didn't guess it!" he heard as if in a dream.

He tried to stop, to escape from those hands which were turning him around at such a furious pace, as if in a witches' dance, but it was beyond his power to tear himself loose. His nostrils were filled with the emanation of their young bodies and that exotic, remote perfume, and he heard inside himself, but also outside of himself, on the carpet, the sound of the girls' feet dancing. He felt at the same time how the dance was carrying him gently between chairs and screens toward the other end of the room. After a time he ceased to resist—and was no longer aware of anything.

When he awoke, he found the swarthy, naked girl kneeling on the carpet in front of the sofa, and he sat up.

"Did I sleep very long?" he asked her.

"You weren't really asleep," the girl reassured him. "You just dozed a little."

"But what on earth have you done to me?" he asked, putting his hand to his forehead. "I feel as if I'd been drugged."

He looked around him in amazement. It no longer looked like the same room, and yet, scattered among the armchairs, sofas, and mirrors were the screens which had made such an impression on him from the moment he entered. He couldn't see any rhyme or reason to the way they were arranged. Some were very tall, almost touching the ceiling, and might have been mistaken for walls, except that here and there they projected at acute angles out into the middle of the room. Others, lighted up in some mysterious way, looked like windows, half covered with curtains, opening on interior corridors. And other screens, many-colored and curiously painted, or covered with shawls and embroideries, which fell in folds to the carpets and merged with them, were placed in such a way, you would have said, as to form alcoves of various shapes and sizes. But he had only to fix his gaze for a moment or two on one such alcove in order to realize that it was all an illusion, that what he was really seeing was two or three separate screens whose reflections in a large mirror with a greenish-gold shimmer caused them to appear to be joined together. At the very moment that he became aware of the illusion, Gavrilescu felt the room start turning around him, and he put his hand to his forehead again.

"What on earth have you done to me?" he repeated.

"You didn't guess who I am," the girl said softly, with a sad smile. "And yet I winked at you as a sign that *I'm* not the gypsy girl. I'm the Greek girl."

"Greece!" exclaimed Gavrilescu, getting to his feet suddenly. "Eternal Greece!"

His weariness seemed to have vanished as if by magic. He could hear his heart beating faster, and a bliss never before experienced suffused his entire body with a warm throb.

"When I was in love with Hildegard," he continued enthusiastically, "that's all we dreamed of—taking a trip to Greece together."

"You were a fool," the girl interrupted him. "You shouldn't have been dreaming, you should have loved her."

"I was twenty and she wasn't quite eighteen. She was beautiful. We were both beautiful," he added.

At that moment he became aware that he was dressed in a strange costume: he had on wide pantaloons, like Indian shalwars, and a short tunic of golden-yellow silk. He looked at himself in the mirror with astonishment, and had some difficulty even recognizing himself.

"We dreamed of going to Greece," he continutd after a few moments, in a calmer voice. "No, it was much more than a dream, for we had plans to make it come true: we had decided to leave for Greece right after the wedding. And then something happened. But what on earth could have happened?" he asked himself after a pause, putting both hands to his temple. "Everything was just the same, a day as hot as this, a terrible summer day. I saw a bench and started toward it, and then I felt the intense heat smite me on the top of the head, smite me like a saber on the top of the head. No, that's what happened to Colonel Lawrence; I heard about it today from some students while I was waiting for the streetcar. Oh, if I only had a piano!" he exclaimed in despair.

The girl sprang to her feet, and taking his hand, said softly, "Come with me!"

Shc led him quickly between the screens and mirrors, going faster and faster, and before long Gavrilescu found himself running. He wanted to stop a moment to catch his breath, but the girl wouldn't let him.

"It's late!" she murmured as she ran; and again her voice seemed to him like the sound of a whistle reaching him from far away.

But this time he didn't get dizzy, although as they ran he had to avoid innumerable soft sofas and cushions, chests and boxes covered with rugs, and mirrors large and small, some of them cut in strange shapes, which unexpectedly appeared in front of them, as though they had just been put there. All of a sudden they emerged from a sort of corridor formed by two rows of screens and entered a large, sunny room. There, leaning against a piano, the other two girls were waiting for them.

"Why are you so late?" the red-haired one asked them. "The coffee's gotten cold."

Gavrilescu caught his breath, and taking a step toward her, raised both arms as if to defend himself.

"Oh, no," he said, "I won't drink any more. I've drunk enough coffee. Though I have the soul of an artist, ladies, I lead a regular life. I don't like to waste my time in cafés."

But as if she hadn't heard him, the girl turned to the Greek girl.

"Why are you so late?" she asked again.

"He thought of Hildegard."

"You shouldn't have let him," said the third girl.

"Pardon, allow me," Gavrilescu broke in, approaching the piano. "This is a strictly personal matter. No one else has any right to interfere. It was the tragedy of my life."

"Now he'll be late again," said the red-haired girl. "He's confused all over again."

"Allow me," Gavrilescu burst out. "I'm not at all confused. It was the tragedy of my life. I thought of her when I first entered here. Listen!" he exclaimed, approaching the piano again. "I'll play you something and then you'll understand."

"You shouldn't have let him," he heard the two girls whisper. "Now he'll never guess us."

Gavrilescu sat there a few moments concentrating, then

hunched his shoulders over the keyboard as if he were about to attack *con brio*.

"Now I remember!" he exclaimed all at once. "I know what happened!"

He got up from the piano bench in excitement and began pacing the floor, his gaze fixed on the carpet.

"Now I know," he repeated several times, in a low voice. "It was just like now, it was in the summer. Hildegard had left with her family for Königsberg. It was terribly hot. I was living in Charlottenburg, and had gone out for a walk under the trees. They were tall, ancient trees, with heavy shade. Everything was deserted. It was too hot. No one dared leave the house. And there under the trees I came upon a young girl sobbing bitterly, sobbing with her face buried in her hands. And there was one surprising thing: she had taken off her shoes and was resting her feet on a small suitcase lying on the pavement in front of her. 'Gavrilescu,' I said to myself, 'there's an unhappy creature.' How could I guess that . . ."

Suddenly he stopped and turned abruptly to the girls.

"Ladies!" he exclaimed with emotion. "I was young, I was handsome, and I had the soul of an artist. An abandoned girl simply rent my heart. I stopped to talk with her and tried to console her. And that's how the tragedy of my life began."

"And now what are we to do?" asked the red-haired girl, addressing the others.

"Let's wait and see what the old chatterbox says," said the Greek girl.

"If we wait any longer, he'll never guess us," said the third girl.

"Yes, the tragedy of my life," continued Gavrilescu. "Her name was Elsa . . . But I became resigned to it. I said to myself, 'Gavrilescu, thus it was written. An evil hour!' That's the way artists are, they never have any luck."

"See!" said the red-haired girl. "He's getting all confused again, and he'll never be able to straighten himself out."

"Ah, fate!" exclaimed Gavrilescu, raising both arms in the air and turning toward the Greek girl.

The girl looked at him with a smile, her hands joined behind her back.

"Eternal Greece!" he continued. "I never did get to see you."

"Stop that! Stop that!" cried the other two girls, coming closer to him. "Remember how you chose us!"

"A gypsy girl, a Greek girl, a Jewish girl," said the Greek girl, looking him deeply and significantly in the eye. "That's the way you wanted it, that's the way you chose us."

"Guess us," cried the red-haired girl, "and you'll see how nice everything will be."

"Which is the gypsy girl? Which is the gypsy girl?" asked all three at once, surrounding him.

Gavrilescu retreated quickly and leaned against the piano.

"Well," he began after a pause, "that may be the way *you* think things are here. Artist or ordinary mortal, you've got a good thing going: I have to guess the gypsy girl. But why, I ask you? Who gave the order?"

"That's our game here at the gypsy girls'," said the Greek girl. "Try and guess. You won't find it so bad."

"But I'm not in the mood to play games," Gavrilescu continued with fervor. "I have remembered the tragedy of my life. And now, you see, I understand very well how it all happened: if on that evening, in Charlottenburg, I had not gone to a beer hall with Elsa . . . Or even if I had gone, but if I had had any money with me, and had been able to pay the check, my life would have been different. But as it happened I had no money, and it was Elsa who paid. And the next day I went all over everywhere looking for a few marks to pay my debt. But I couldn't get any anywhere. All my friends and acquaintances had gone on vacation. It was summer and it was terribly hot."

"He's afraid again," murmured the red-haired girl, with downcast eyes.

"Listen, I haven't told you the whole story," cried Gavrilescu with emotion. "For three days I couldn't find any money, and every evening I would go to see her, Elsa, at her lodgings, to apologize because I hadn't got the money. And afterward we would both go to the beer hall. If only I had been firm and hadn't agreed to go to the beer hall with her! But I couldn't help it, I was hungry. I was young, I was handsome, Hildegard had gone to the shore, and I was hungry. I tell you frankly, there were days when I went to bed with an empty stomach. That's an artist's life for you!"

"And now what are we to do?" the girls asked him. "For time is passing, time is passing."

"Now?" exclaimed Gavrilescu, raising his arms again. "Now it's good and hot, and I like you because you are young and beautiful, and are standing here before me ready to serve me sweets and coffee. But I'm not thirsty any more. Right now I feel fine, I feel just great. And I say to myself: 'Gavrilescu, these girls expect something of you. Why not oblige them? If they want you to guess them, then guess them. But watch out! Watch out, Gavrilescu, for if you guess wrong again, they'll take you on their wild dance and you won't wake up until dawn.' "

Smiling, he walked around the piano in such a way as to keep it as a shield between himself and the girls.

"So, then, you want me to tell you which one is the gypsy girl. All right then, I'll tell you."

The girls lined up excitedly, without a word, looking him in the eye.

"I'll tell you," he said again, after a pause.

Then he abruptly, melodramatically, raised his arm and pointed at the girl in the pale-green veil, and waited. The girls froze in place, as if they couldn't bring themselves to believe it.

"What's the matter with him?" the red-haired one finally asked. "Why can't he guess us?"

"Something's happened to him," said the Greek girl. "He remembered something, and he's lost his way, he's lost in the past."

The girl he had taken for the gypsy girl came forward a few steps, picked up the coffee tray, and passing in front of the piano, murmured with a sad smile: "I'm the Jewish girl."

Then she disappeared behind a screen without another word.

"Oh!" exclaimed Gavrilescu, striking his forehead. "I should have understood. There was something in her eyes that came from very far away. And she had a veil, which didn't really hide anything, but it was still a veil. It was just like the Old Testament."

Suddenly the red-haired girl burst out laughing.

"The gentleman didn't guess us!" she cried. "He didn't guess which is the gypsy girl."

She ran her hand through her hair. Then, as she shook herself several times, her braids fell, red and fiery, on her shoulders. She began to dance, turning slowly round and round in a circle, clapping her hands and singing.

"Tell him, Greek girl, what it would have been like!" she cried, shaking her braids.

"If you had guessed her, everything would have been wonderful," said the Greek girl softly. "We would have sung for you and danced for you and we would have taken you through all the rooms. It would have been wonderful."

"It would have been wonderful," repeated Gavrilescu with a sad smile.

"Tell him, Greek girl!" cried the gypsy girl, stopping in front of them, but continuing to clap her hands rhythmically and stamping her bare foot harder and harder on the carpet.

The Greek girl moved close to him and began talking. She spoke quickly, in a whisper, occasionally nodding her head or brushing her fingers over her lips. But Gavrilescu couldn't make out what she was saying. He listened to her with a smile, with a faraway look in his eyes, and from time to time he murmured, "It would have been wonderful."

He heard the foot of the gypsy girl stamping on the carpet harder and harder, with a muffled, subterranean sound, until that wild, unfamiliar rhythm became more than he could stand. Then, with a great effort, he dashed to the piano and began to play.

"Now you tell him too, gypsy girl!" cried the Greek girl.

He heard her approach him, as if she were dancing on a huge bronze drum; and a moment later he felt her ardent breath on the back of his neck. Gavrilescu bent still lower over the piano and struck the keyboard with all his force, almost with fury, as if he wanted to send the keys flying, to tear them out, and so make a way for himself with his fingernails right into the belly of the piano, and then farther still, deeper still.

He was no longer thinking of anything, absorbed as he was in the new, strange melodies, which he seemed to be hearing for the first time; and yet they came to his mind one after the other, as though he were remembering them after a very long time. Finally he stopped, and only then did he realize that he was alone in the room and that it had become almost completely dark.

"Where are you?" he cried in alarm, getting up from the bench.

He hesitated a few moments, then walked over to the screen behind which the Jewish girl had disappeared.

"Where are you hiding?" he called again.

Slowly, walking on tiptoe, as if he wanted to take them by surprise, he slipped behind the screen. Here you would have said a new room began, which seemed to be continued in a winding corridor. It was a curiously constructed room, with a low and irregular ceiling and somewhat serpentine walls that disappeared and reappeared in the darkness. Gavrilescu took a few tentative steps, then stopped to listen. At that very moment he thought he heard rustling sounds and rapid steps on the carpet passing very close to him.

"Where are you?" he called.

He listened to the echo of his voice while trying to penetrate the darkness with his gaze. He thought he caught sight of the three of them hiding in a corner of the corridor, and he headed in that direction, groping with his arms extended in front of him. But he soon realized that he had started off in the wrong direction, for he discovered that after a few meters the corridor turned left and continued a long way in that direction, so he stopped again.

"It's no use hiding, I'll find you just the same!" he called. "Better show yourselves of your own accord!"

He strained to hear, gazing down the corridor. Not a sound could be heard. But then he began to feel the heat again, and he decided to go back and play the piano while waiting for them. The direction from which he had come was fixed in his mind, and he knew he had gone only twenty or thirty steps. He extended his arms and proceeded slowly and cautiously. But after a few steps his hands touched a screen, and he drew back frightened. He was certain the screen had not been there a few moments before.

"What's gotten into you?" he cried. "Let me pass!"

Again he thought he heard stifled laughter and rustling sounds. He plucked up his courage.

"Perhaps you think I'm afraid," he began after a short pause, doing his best to appear in good humor. "Allow me, allow me!" he added quickly, as if he expected to be interrupted. "If I agreed to play hide-and-seek with you, I did so because I was sorry for you. That's the honest truth, I was sorry for you. Right from the start I saw you, innocent girls shut up here in a cottage at the gypsy girls', and I said to myself: 'Gavrilescu, these girls want to play tricks on you. Pretend to be taken in. Let them think you can't guess which is the gypsy girl. It's all part of the game!' It's all part of the game!" he shouted as loud as he could. "But now we've been playing long enough; come on out into the light!"

He stopped to listen, smiling, his right hand resting on the screen. At that moment he heard the sound of quick steps in the darkness, very close to him. He turned suddenly and extended his arms in front of him.

"Let's see which one of you it is," he said. "Let's see whom I've caught. Did I catch the gypsy girl?"

But after waving his arms around for some time, hardly realizing what he was doing, he stopped again to listen, and this time not the slightest sound reached him from any direction.

"It doesn't matter," he said, as if he knew that the girls were there somewhere nearby, hiding in the darkness. "We can wait. I see you still don't know whom you have to deal with. Later on you'll be sorry. I could have taught you to play the piano. Your musical culture would have been enriched. I would have explained Schumann's *Lieder* to you. What beauty!" he exclaimed with fervor. "What divine music!"

Now he could feel the heat again, and it seemed hotter than ever. He began to mop his face with the sleeve of his tunic. Then, discouraged, he started off to the left, feeling his way along the screen the whole time. From time to time he stopped to listen, then continued again at a faster pace.

"Why did I ever allow myself to be pitted against a bunch of girls?" he burst out all at once, suddenly overcome with anger. "Pardon me! I said girls out of courtesy. But you're something else. You know very well what you are. You're gypsies. Completely lacking in culture. Illiterate. Does any one of you know where Arabia is? Has any one of you ever heard of Colonel Lawrence?"

The screen seemed to be endless, and the farther he went, the more unbearable the heat became. He took off his tunic, and after furiously mopping his face and neck, he put it over his bare shoulder like a towel, then began groping with both arms extended once more, trying to find the screen again. But this time he encountered a smooth, cool wall, and he clung to it with outstretched arms. He remained thus a long time, clinging to the wall and breathing deeply. Then he began to move slowly, keeping close to the wall and inching his way along it. After a time he discovered that he had lost his tunic, and as he was still perspiring constantly he stopped, took off his shalwars, and began mopping his face and his whole body. Just then he thought he felt something touch his shoulder, and with a shriek he jumped aside, frightened.

"Let me pass!" he cried. "I told you to let me pass!"

Again someone or something, a creature or an object whose nature he could not determine, touched him on the face and shoulders; at that he began whirling his shalwars blindly over his head in an effort to defend himself. He felt hotter and hotter, he could feel the drops of sweat trickling down his cheeks, and he was gasping for breath. Suddenly, as he swung them around too vigorously, the shalwars flew out of his hand and disappeared somewhere far off in the darkness. For a moment Gavrilescu stood there with his arm extended above his head, clenching his fist spasmodically, as if hoping to discover, from one moment to the next, that he had been mistaken, that the shalwars were still in his possession.

All at once it came to him that he was naked, and he made himself as small as possible, dropping to a crouching position, supporting himself with his hands on the carpet, his head lowered, as if he were ready to take to flight. He began to move forward, groping all around him on the carpet with his hands, still hoping he might find the shalwars again. From time to time he encountered things that it was difficult for him to identify. Some at first resembled small chests, but when he felt of them more carefully they turned out to be giant pumpkins draped with kerchiefs. Others, which at first seemed like cushions or bolsters for a sofa, became, upon closer examination, balls, old umbrellas stuffed with bran, laundry baskets full of newspapers—but he didn't really have time to decide what they might be, for he was continually coming across new objects ahead of him, and would start feeling of them. Sometimes big pieces of furniture suddenly loomed up before him, and Gavrilescu cautiously went around them, for he couldn't discern their shapes and was fearful of knocking them over.

He had no idea how long he had been moving like this, on his knees or dragging himself along on his belly in the darkness. He had given up all hope of ever finding the shalwars. What bothered him more and more was the heat. It was like moving around in the attic of a house with a tin roof on a very hot afternoon. He felt the scorching air in his nostrils, and the things he touched seemed to be getting hotter and hotter. His whole body was dripping wet, and he had to stop from time to time to rest. When he did he would stretch out as far as he could, extending his legs and arms like a cross, pressing his face to the carpet, breathing deeply but jerkily and with difficulty.

Once he thought he had dozed off and was awakened by an unexpected breeze, as if a window had been opened somewhere, letting in the cool of night. But he understood immediately that it was something else, something different from anything he was familiar with, and for a moment he remained petrified, feeling how the sweat on his back grew cold. He couldn't remember what happened after that. He let out a yell and was startled by it himself. When he next became aware of his actions, he found himself running around madly in the dark, colliding with screens, overturning mirrors and all sorts of small objects scattered over the carpet in a curious fashion, stumbling and falling repeatedly, but getting up immediately and taking to flight once more. He caught himself jumping over small chests and avoiding the mirrors and screens; and then he realized that he had reached a region of semidarkness, where he could begin to make out the shapes of things. At the end of the corridor there seemed to be a window, unusually high in the wall, through which was coming the light of a summer twilight. When he entered the corridor the heat became unbearable. He had to stop to catch his breath, and with the back of his hand he wiped the sweat from his forehead and cheeks. He heard his heart beating as if it would burst.

Before reaching the window he stopped again, frightened. He could hear voices, laughter, and the sound of chairs being dragged across the floor, as if a whole group had got up from the table and were coming toward him. At that moment he saw that he was naked, thinner than he had ever been. His bones were plainly visible under his skin, and yet his belly was swollen and hanging down. He had never seen himself like this before. He had no time to turn back. He reached out, grabbed a curtain, and started pulling on it. The curtain seemed about to give. Bracing his feet against the wall, he leaned back with all his weight. But then something unexpected happened. He began to feel the curtain pulling him to itself with ever-increasing force, so that a few moments later he found himself pressed to the wall; and although he tried to free himself, letting go of the curtain, he was unsuccessful, and before long he felt himself all wrapped up, squeezed from all sides, as if he had been tied up and stuffed into a bag. Once again it was dark and very hot, and Gavrilescu realized that he couldn't hold out very long, that he would smother. He tried to scream, but his throat was dry and wooden, and the sounds that came out seemed to be muffled in thick felt.

He heard a voice that he thought he recognized.

"Go on, sir, tell me more."

"What more can I tell you?" he said in a low voice. "I've told you everything. There's nothing more to tell. Elsa and I came to Bucureşti. We were both penniless. I started giving piano lessons."

He raised his head from the pillow a little and saw the old woman. She was sitting at the little table with the coffeepot in her hands and was about to fill the cups again.

"No, thank you, I won't drink any more," he said, raising his arm. "I've drunk enough coffee. I'm afraid I won't sleep tonight."

The old woman filled her cup, then set the pot on a corner of the table.

"Tell me more," she insisted. "What else did you do? What else happened?"

Gavrilescu remained lost in thought for some time, fanning himself with his hat.

"Then we began to play hide-and-seek," he said all at once, in a changed and rather stern voice. "Of course, they didn't know whom they were dealing with. I'm a serious-minded person, I'm an artist and a piano teacher. I came here out of sheer curiosity. I'm always interested in new, unfamiliar things. I said to myself, 'Gavrilescu, here's an opportunity to broaden your experience.' I didn't know that it would involve silly, childish games. Just imagine suddenly I saw that I was naked, and I heard voices; I was sure that the very next moment . . . You know what I mean."

The old woman nodded her head and took a leisurely sip of coffee.

"What a time we had looking for your hat," she said. "The girls turned the cottage upside down before they could find it."

"Yes, I admit it was partly my fault," Gavrilescu continued. "I didn't know that if I didn't guess them by daylight, I would have to hunt for them, catch them, and guess them in the dark. No one told me anything. And, let me repeat, when I saw that I was naked, and when I felt the curtain wrap itself around me like a shroud—I give you my word of honor, it was like a shroud."

"What a time we had getting you dressed again!" said the old woman. "You just didn't want to let us dress you."

"I tell you, that curtain was like a shroud, it squeezed me from all sides, it enveloped me and squeezed me until

I could no longer breathe. And was it hot!" he exclaimed, fanning himself still harder with his hat. "It's a wonder I didn't smother!"

"Yes, it was very hot," said the old woman.

At that moment the metallic screech of the streetcar could be heard in the distance. Gavrilescu put his hand to his forehead.

"Oh!" he exclaimed, getting up from the sofa with difficulty. "How time flies. We've been chatting, and what with one thing and another, I forgot I have to go to Strada Preoteselor. Just imagine, I forgot the portfolio with my music: I was saying to myself after lunch today, 'Gavrilescu, watch out. I'm afraid . . . I'm afraid you . . .' Well, I was telling myself something of the sort, but I don't quite remember what."

He started toward the door, but after a few steps he turned around, bowed slightly from the shoulders, and waved his hat.

"A pleasure to have met you," he said.

Outside in the yard he had an unpleasant surprise. Although the sun had set, it was hotter than it had been in the middle of the afternoon. Gavrilescu took off his jacket and put it over his shoulder. He crossed the yard and went out the gate, fanning himself with his hat all the while. Once he was outside the tree-shaded wall he was again overwhelmed by the burning heat of the pavement and the odor of dust and melted asphalt. He walked dejectedly, with drooping shoulders, staring straight ahead of him. There was no one waiting at the streetcar stop. When he heard the car approaching, he raised his arm and signal it to stop.

The car was almost empty, and all the windows were

open. He sat down across from a young man in shirt sleeves, and as he saw the conductor approaching, he began looking for his wallet. He found it more quickly than he expected.

"It's unheard of!" he exclaimed. "I give you my word of honor that it's worse than in Arabia. If you've ever heard of Colonel Lawrence . . ."

The young man smiled absent-mindedly, then turned his face toward the window.

"Can you tell me what time it is?" Gavrilescu asked the conductor.

"Five minutes after eight."

"What rotten luck! They'll be eating dinner when I get there. They'll think I came this late on purpose, so they would be eating dinner. You understand, I wouldn't want them to think that I . . . You understand what I mean. And then, if I tell them where I've been, Mrs. Voitinovici is very curious and will keep me there till midnight to tell her all about it."

The conductor had been watching him with a smile; now he winked at the young man.

"Tell her you've been to the gypsy girls', and you'll see, she won't ask you anything more."

"Oh, no, out of the question. I know her well. She's a very curious woman. Better I don't say anything."

At the next stop a number of young couples got on, and Gavrilescu moved closer to them so that he could listen to their conversation better. When he saw a chance to join in, he raised his arm a little.

"If you'll allow me, I must contradict you. I, unfortunately for me, am a piano teacher, but that's not what I was made for . . ."

"Strada Preoteselor," he heard the conductor announce, and getting up suddenly, he waved and walked quickly down the aisle.

He set off slowly, fanning himself with his hat. In front of No. 18 he stopped, straightened his necktie, ran his hand over his hair, and went in. He climbed the stairs to the first floor slowly, then rang the bell hard. A few moments later he was joined by the young man from the streetcar.

"What a coincidence!" exclaimed Gavrilescu, when he saw the young man stop beside him.

The door opened suddenly, and on the threshold appeared a woman, still young, but with a pale and withered face. She was wearing a kitchen apron and in her left hand she had a pot of mustard. Seeing Gavrilescu, she frowned.

"What can I do for you?" she asked.

"I forgot my portfolio," Gavrilescu began nervously. "I got to talking and I forgot it. I had business in town and couldn't come any earlier."

"I don't understand. What sort of portfolio?"

"If you're eating dinner, I don't want to disturb you," continued Gavrilescu hurriedly. "I know where I left it. It's right next to the piano."

He made a move to enter, but the woman didn't budge from the doorway.

"Who is it you're looking for, sir?"

"For Mrs. Voitinovici. I'm Gavrilescu, Otilia's piano teacher. I don't think I've had the pleasure of meeting you," he added politely.

"You've got the wrong address," said the woman. "This is No. 18."

"Allow me," Gavrilescu began again, with a smile. "I've

known this apartment for five years. I might almost say I'm one of the family. I come here three times a week."

The young man had been leaning against the wall, listening to the conversation.

"What did you say her name is?" he asked.

"Mrs. Voitinovici. She's Otilia's aunt. Otilia Pandele."

"She doesn't live here," the young man interrupted him. "This is where *we* live, the Georgescus. This woman before you is my father's wife, née Petrescu."

"Please be polite," said the woman. "And don't bring all kinds of people home with you."

With that she turned her back and disappeared down the hall.

"I beg your pardon for this scene," said the young man, trying to smile. "She's my father's third wife, and she bears on her shoulders all the mistakes of the earlier marriages: five boys and a girl."

Gavrilescu was listening to him in embarrassment, fanning himself with his hat.

"I'm sorry," he began, "I'm very sorry. I didn't mean to make her angry. Of course it *is* a rather inconvenient time. It's dinnertime. But you see, tomorrow morning I have a lesson at Dealul Spirei.* I need my portfolio. I've got Czerny II and III in it. They're my scores, with my own interpretations noted in the margins. That's why I always carry them with me."

The young man continued to look at him with a smile. "I'm afraid I didn't make myself clear," he said. "What I'm trying to tell you is that this is where *we* live, the Georgescu family. We've been here four years."

* "Switchback Hill."—Trans.

"Impossible!" exclaimed Gavrilescu. "I was here just a few hours ago and gave Otilia her lesson from two to three. And then I got to talking with Mrs. Voitinovici."

"At Strada Preoteselor 18, first floor?" asked the young man in surprise, with an amused smile.

"Precisely. I know the house very well. I can tell you where the piano is. I'll take you there with my eyes closed. It's in the parlor, next to the window."

"We have no piano," said the young man. "Try another floor. Though, I can tell you, you won't find her on the second floor either. That's where Captain Zamfir and his family live. Try the third floor. I'm very sorry," he added, seeing that Gavrilescu was listening to him with alarm and fanning himself with his hat more and more agitatedly. "I really wish there was an Otilia in this house."

Gavrilescu hesitated, staring at him fixedly.

"Thank you," he said finally. "I *will* try the third floor. But I give you my word of honor that at three or maybe quarter past three I was *here*," and he pointed doggedly to the hall.

He began climbing the stairs, breathing heavily. When he reached the third floor, he spent a long time mopping his face with one of his handkerchiefs, then rang the bell. He heard a child's steps, and shortly the door was opened by a little boy perhaps five or six years old.

"Oh!" exclaimed Gavrilescu. "I'm afraid I've got the wrong floor. I was looking for Mrs. Voitinovici."

Then a young woman appeared at the door and greeted him with a smile.

"Mrs. Voitinovici used to live on the first floor," she said, "but she moved, she went off to the country."

"Did she move away very long ago?"

"Oh, yes, long ago. It will be eight years this fall. She left right after Otilia got married."

Gavrilescu put his hand to his forehead and began to rub it. Then he tried to catch her eye and smiled at her as pleasantly as he was able.

"I think you must be mistaken," he began. "It's Otilia Pandele I'm talking about, in the sixth class at the lyceum, Mrs. Voitinovici's niece."

"I knew them both quite well," said the woman. "When we first moved here, Otilia had just become engaged. You know, first there was that business with the major. Mrs. Voitinovici wouldn't give her consent, and she was right, the difference in age was too great. Otilia was still a girl, not yet nineteen. Fortunately she met Frâncu, Frâncu the engineer. You must have heard of him."

"Frâncu the engineer?" Gavrilescu repeated. "Frâncu?"

"Yes. The inventor. He's been written up in the newspapers."

"Frâncu the inventor," Gavrilescu repeated dreamily. "How strange . . ."

Then he extended his hand, stroked the little boy on the head, and bowing slightly from the waist he said:

"Please excuse me. I must have gotten the wrong floor."

The young man was waiting for him, leaning against the wall and smoking.

"Did you find out anything?" he asked.

"The lady upstairs claims she got married, but I assure you there's something wrong somewhere. Otilia isn't yet seventeen and she's in the sixth class at the lyceum. I had a long conversation with Mrs. Voitinovici today, and we talked about all sorts of things, but she never said a word about it."

"That's strange."

"Yes, it's very strange," said Gavrilescu, growing bolder. "And for that reason, I tell you, I don't believe a word of it. I give you my word of honor . . . But then, what's the use? There's something wrong somewhere. I'll just have to come back tomorrow morning."

And after saying good-by, he started down the stairs with a resolute air.

"Gavrilescu," he murmured, once he had reached the street, "watch out, you're getting decrepit. You're starting to lose your memory. You're getting the addresses all mixed up." He saw the streetcar coming and began walking faster. No sooner did he sit down by an open window than he began to feel a slight breeze.

"At last!" he exclaimed, addressing the woman across from him. "I think, I think that . . ."

But then he realized that he didn't know how to go on with his sentence, and he smiled with an embarrassed air.

"Yes," he began again after a short pause. "I was talking with a friend of mine not long ago. I think . . . I think I must have been in Arabia. Colonel Lawrence—perhaps you've heard of him."

The woman continued to look out of the window.

"Now, in another hour or two," Gavrilescu started again, "night will fall too. Darkness, I mean. The cool of night. At last! We'll be able to breathe again."

The conductor had stopped in front of him and was waiting there. Gavrilescu began rummaging through his pockets.

"After midnight we'll be able to breathe again," he said, addressing the conductor. "What a long day!" he added, a little nervously, since he hadn't managed to find his wallet. "So many things have happened! . . . Ah, at last!" he exclaimed, and opening his wallet quickly, he handed over a hundred-lei bill.

"This isn't good any more," said the conductor, handing him back the bill. "You'll have to change it at the bank."

"But what's wrong with it?" asked Gavrilescu in surprise, turning the bill over and over in his fingers.

"They were withdrawn from circulation a year ago. You'll have to change it at the bank."

"How strange!" said Gavrilescu, examining the bill very carefully. "It was good this morning. And they accept them at the gypsy girls'. I had three more just like this one, and they took them all at the gypsy girls'."

The woman paled slightly, and getting up ostentatiously went and sat down at the other end of the car.

"You shouldn't have mentioned the gypsy girls in front of a lady," said the conductor reproachfully.

"Everybody talks about them," Gavrilescu said defensively. "I ride this streetcar three times a week, and I give you my word of honor . . ."

"Yes, it's true," a passenger broke in. "We all talk about them, only not in front of ladies. It's a question of proper behavior. Especially now that the place is going to be illuminated. Oh, yes, and even the city government has given them permission: the garden is going to be illuminated. I am, may I say, a man without any prejudices, but illumination at the gypsy girls' I consider an outrage."

"How strange," remarked Gavrilescu. "I haven't heard anything about it."

"It's been in all the newspapers," put in another passenger. "It's a scandal!" he exclaimed, raising his voice. "It's a crime!"

Several people turned their heads, and under their reproachful gaze Gavrilescu lowered his eyes.

"Keep looking, perhaps you have some other money," said the conductor. "If not, you'll have to get off at the next stop."

Blushing and not daring to raise his eyes, Gavrilescu began searching in his pockets some more. Fortunately his change purse was right on top, among the handkerchiefs. Gavrilescu counted out a few coins and handed them to him.

"You've given me five lei," said the conductor, showing him the coins in his hand.

"Yes, I'm getting off at Vama Poştei."*

"I don't care where you're getting off, the ticket costs ten lei. Where in the world have you been keeping yourself?" added the conductor in a stern voice.

"I live in Bucureşti," said Gavrilescu, proudly raising his eyes, "and I ride on the streetcar three or four times a day, and I've been doing this for years on end, and I've always paid five lei."

Nearly everyone on the car was now listening to the conversation with interest. Several passengers moved closer and sat down nearby. The conductor tossed the coins in his hand several times and then spoke.

"If you won't give me the rest, you'll have to get off at the next stop."

"The fare went up three or four years ago," said someone.

* "Postal Toll House."—TRANS.

"Five years ago," the conductor corrected him.

"I give you my word of honor," began Gavrilescu pathetically.

"Then get off at the next stop," the conductor interrupted him.

"Better pay the difference," someone advised him, "because it's quite a ways to walk from here to Vama Poştei."

Gavrilescu looked in his purse and gave the conductor five lei more.

"Strange things are happening in this country," he muttered after the conductor had gone. "Decisions are made overnight. In twenty-four hours. More precisely, in six hours. I give you my word of honor . . . But then, what's the use? I've had a terrible day. And the worst thing about it is that we can't live without the streetcar. At least *I* can't. The life I lead obliges me to ride the streetcar three or four times a day. And at that, one piano lesson is only a hundred lei. One hundred-lei bill like this. And now even this bill isn't good any more. I have to go and get it changed at the bank."

"Give it to me," said an elderly gentleman. "I'll change it at the office tomorrow."

He took a bill out of his wallet and handed it to him. Gavrilescu took it gingerly and examined it closely.

"It's beautiful," he said. "How long ago did they put them into circulation?"

Several passengers exchanged glances, smiling.

"About three years ago," said one.

"It's strange that I've never seen one till now. Of course, I'm a bit absent-minded. I have the soul of an artist."

He put the bill in his wallet, then let his glance stray out of the window.

"Night has fallen," he said. "At last!"

He suddenly felt worn out and weary, and resting his head in his hand, he closed his eyes. He remained like that all the way to Vama Poştei.

He had tried in vain to unlock the door with his key, and then had pushed the bell button for a long time; after knocking several times on the dining-room windows as loudly as he could, he went back to the front door and began beating on it with his fist. Soon, at the open window of a neighboring house, there appeared in the darkness a man in a nightshirt, who called out hoarsely:

"What's all the commotion, man? What's got into you?"

"Excuse me," said Gavrilescu. "I don't know what's happened to my wife. She doesn't answer the door. And my key doesn't work either, so I can't get into the house."

"But what do you want to get in for? Who are you?"

Gavrilescu turned toward the window and introduced himself.

"Although we're neighbors," he began, "I don't believe I've had the pleasure of meeting you. My name is Gavrilescu and I live here with my wife, Elsa."

"You must have the wrong address. That's where *Dl* Stănescu lives. And he's not home, he's gone to the shore."

"Allow me," Gavrilescu interrupted him. "I'm sorry to contradict you, but I think you've got it all wrong. Elsa and I live here, No. 101. We've been here four years."

"Cut it out, gentlemen, we can't sleep!" someone called out. "Good God!"

"He claims he lives in *Dl* Stănescu's house."

"I don't *claim,*" Gavrilescu protested. "This is my house, and I won't allow anyone to . . . But above all I want to find out where Elsa is, what's happened to her."

"Inquire at the police station," put in someone on the next floor.

"Why the police station? What's happened?" he cried in agitation. "Do you know something?"

"No, I don't know anything, but I want to sleep. And if you're going to stand there all night chatting . . ."

"Allow me," said Gavrilescu. "I'm sleepy too; in fact, I may say I'm all worn out. I've had a terrible day. And the heat's been as bad as in Arabia . . . But I don't understand what's happened to Elsa; why doesn't she answer the door? Perhaps she felt sick and fainted."

And turning back to the door of No. 101, he started beating on it with his fist again, louder and louder.

"I told you he's not at home, sir, didn't I? *Dl* Stănescu has gone to the shore."

"Call the police!" he heard a woman cry in a shrill voice. "Call the police at once!"

Gavrilescu stopped instantly and leaned against the door, breathing heavily. Suddenly he felt very weary, and he sat down on the steps and leaned his head in his hands. "Gavrilescu," he murmured, "watch out, something very serious has happened, and they don't want to tell you. Get hold of yourself, try to remember."

"Mme. Trandafir!"* he exclaimed. "Why didn't I think of her before? Mme. Trandafir!" he called, standing up

* The name means "Rose."—Trans.

and turning toward the house across the street. "Mme. Trandafir!"

Someone who had stayed at the window said in a quieter voice, "Let her sleep, poor woman."

"It's quite urgent!"

"Let her sleep, God rest her soul, she died long ago."

"Impossible," said Gavrilescu, "I talked with her this morning."

"You must be confusing her with her sister, Ecaterina. Mme. Trandafir died five years ago."

Gavrilescu stood there a moment stupefied, then put his hands in his pockets and took out a number of handkerchiefs.

"How strange," he finally murmured.

He turned away slowly, and going up the three steps at No. 101, picked up his hat and put it on his head. He tried the door once more, then went back down the steps and started walking away, at a loss what to do now. He walked slowly, thinking of nothing, and mopping his forehead mechanically with a handkerchief. The tavern on the corner was still open, and after walking past it irresolutely, he decided to go in.

"We're only serving by the glass now," said the waiter. "We close at two."

"At two?" asked Gavrilescu in surprise. "What time is it now?"

"It's two. In fact, it's after two."

"It's terribly late," Gavrilescu murmured, as if to himself.

Going up to the counter, he thought the tavern keeper's face looked familiar, and his heart began to beat faster.

"Aren't you Mr. Costică?" he asked.

"Yes, I am," replied the tavern keeper, looking at him closely. "Don't I know you?" he added after a pause.

"I think, I think that . . . ," began Gavrilescu, but then he lost the train of his thought and fell silent, with an embarrassed smile on his face. "I used to come around here a long time ago," he began again. "I had friends here. Mme. Trandafir."

"Yes, God rest her soul."

"Mme. Gavrilescu, Elsa."

"Oh, yes, what a time she had," the tavern keeper interrupted. "To this very day no one knows what happened. The police searched for him for several months but were never able to find any trace of him, dead or alive. It was as if he'd been swallowed up by the earth. Poor Mme. Elsa, she waited and waited for him, and then finally went back to her family, in Germany. She sold everything she had and left. They didn't have much, they were penniless. I myself had some thought of buying their piano."

"So she left for Germany," said Gavrilescu pensively. "How long ago did she leave?"

"A long time ago. A few months after Gavrilescu's disappearance. In the fall it will be twelve years. It was all written up in the papers."

"How strange," murmured Gavrilescu, starting to fan himself with his hat. "And what if I should tell you . . . if I should tell you that this morning—and I give you my word of honor that I'm not exaggerating—this very morning I was talking to her. And what's more, we had lunch together. I can even tell you what we had to eat."

"Then she must have come back," said the tavern keeper, looking at him in perplexity.

"No, she hasn't come back. She never left. There's

something very wrong somewhere. Right now I'm quite tired, but tomorrow morning I'll find out what it's all about."

He bowed slightly and left.

He walked slowly, his hat in one hand and a handkerchief in the other, stopping to rest a while at every bench. It was a clear night, with no moon, and the coolness of the gardens was beginning to pour out into the streets. After some time a one-horse cab drove up beside him.

"Where are you going, sir?" asked the cab driver.

"To the gypsy girls'," replied Gavrilescu.

"Then get in. I'll take you there for forty lei," said the cab driver, stopping the cab.

"I'm sorry, but I haven't got much money. All I have left is a hundred lei and a little change. And I'll need a hundred to get in at the gypsy girls'."

"It'll take more than that," said the cab driver with a laugh. "A hundred lei won't do it."

"That's all I paid this afternoon. Good night," he added, setting off once more.

But the cab kept right with him, at a walk.

"That's the Queen of the Night," said the cab driver, taking a deep breath. "It's coming from the General's garden. That's why I like to drive this way at night. Whether I have passengers or not, I drive this way every night. I'm awfully fond of flowers."

"You have the soul of an artist," said Gavrilescu with a smile.

With that he sat down on a bench and waved him good-by. But the cab driver stopped the cab suddenly and pulled up alongside him, right next to the bench. He took out his tobacco box and began rolling a cigarette.

"I love flowers," he said. "Horses and flowers. When I was young I drove a hearse. And what a beauty! Six horses with black trappings and gold fittings, and flowers, flowers, masses of flowers! Alas, youth is past and they're all gone. I've grown old; I've become a night cab driver, with only one horse."

He lit his cigarette and took a long pull at it.

"Well now, you're going to the gypsy girls'," he said finally.

"Yes, it's a personal matter," Gavrilescu hastened to explain. "I was there this afternoon and somehow got involved in a terrible mix-up."

"Ah, the gypsy girls!" said the cab driver sadly. "If it wasn't for the gypsy girls," he added, lowering his voice. "If it wasn't for . . ."

"Yes," said Gavrilescu, "everybody talks about them. On the streetcar, I mean. When the streetcar goes past their garden, everybody talks about the gypsy girls."

He got up from the bench and set off once again, the cab staying right with him at a walk.

"Let's go this way," said the cab driver, pointing with his whip to an alley. "It's a shortcut. And this way we go past a church. The Queen of the Night is in bloom there too. Of course, it's not as fine as at the General's, but I don't think you'll be sorry."

"You have the soul of an artist," said Gavrilescu dreamily.

In front of the church they both stopped to breathe in the perfume from the flowers.

"I think there's something else there besides the Queen of the Night," said Gavrilescu.

"Oh, there are all kinds of flowers. If there was a funeral here today, lots of flowers were left. And now, toward morning, all these flower scents are freshening up again. I often used to come here with the hearse. How lovely it all was!"

He whistled to his horse and set off again at the same time as Gavrilescu.

"We don't have much farther to go now," he said. "Why don't you get in?"

"I'm sorry, but I don't have any money."

"Just give me some of your change. Get in."

Gavrilescu hesitated a couple of moments, then, with an effort, got in. But as soon as the cab started up, he put his head down on the cushion and fell asleep.

"It was lovely," began the cab driver. "It was a rich church, and none but the best people. Ah, youth!"

He turned his head; seeing Gavrilescu asleep, he began to whistle softly, and the horse began to trot.

"Here we are," he cried, climbing down from the box. "But the gates are closed."

He began to shake Gavrilescu, who awoke with a start.

"The gates are closed," the cab driver repeated. "You'll have to ring."

Gavrilescu picked up his hat, straightened his tie, and got out. Then he began to look for his change purse.

"Don't bother to look for it," said the cab driver. "You can give it to me some other time. I've got to wait here anyway," he added. "At this time of day, if I'm to get a passenger at all, this is where I'll find him."

Gavrilescu waved to the cab driver with his hat, then went up to the gate, found the bell, and pushed the button. The gate opened instantly; Gavrilescu entered the yard and headed toward the grove. A feeble light could still be seen at one of the windows. He knocked on the door timidly; seeing that no one came to answer, he opened the door and went in. The old woman had fallen asleep with her head on the little table.

"It's me, Gavrilescu," he said, tapping her on the shoulder. "You played some monstrous tricks on me," he added, seeing that she was waking up and starting to yawn.

"It's late," said the old woman, rubbing her eyes. "There's no one here."

But then, taking a long look at him, she recognized him and smiled.

"Oh, it's you again, the musician. The German girl might still be here. She never sleeps."

Gavrilescu felt his heart beat faster, and he began to tremble slightly.

"The German girl?" he repeated.

"A hundred lei," said the old woman.

Gavrilescu began looking for his wallet, but his hands were trembling more and more, and when at last he found it, among the handkerchiefs, he dropped it on the floor.

"Excuse me," he said, bending down with difficulty to pick it up. "I'm all worn out. I've had a terrible day."

The old woman took the hundred-lei bill, got up from her stool, and going to the door, waved her arm toward the big house.

"Now be careful you don't get lost," she told him. "Go straight down the corridor and count seven doors. And when you get to the seventh, knock three times and say: 'It's me, the old woman sent me.' "

Then she put her hand to her mouth to stifle a yawn, and closed the door after him. Scarcely daring to breathe, Gavrilescu walked slowly toward the building, which gleamed with a silvery light under the stars. He mounted the marble steps, opened the door, and paused a moment in indecision. In front of him stretched a feebly lighted corridor, and Gavrilescu again felt his heart begin to beat wildly, as if about to burst. He began walking along the corridor, excited, counting each door in a loud voice as he passed. But then he found himself counting, "Thirteen, fourteen . . ." and he stopped in confusion. "Gavrilescu," he murmured, "watch out, you've gotten all mixed up again. Not thirteen, not fourteen, but seven. That's what the old woman said, to count seven doors."

He started to go back to begin counting over again, but after a few steps he was overcome by exhaustion. Stopping at the first door he came to, he knocked three times and went in. The room was large but simple, and meagerly furnished. At the window he could see the silhouette of a young woman looking out into the garden.

"Excuse me," Gavrilescu began, with some difficulty. "I made a mistake counting the doors."

The figure left the window and came toward him with soft steps, and suddenly he recalled a forgotten perfume.

"Hildegard!" he exclaimed, dropping his hat.

"I've been waiting for you such a long time!" said the girl, coming closer to him. "I looked for you everywhere."

"I went to a beer hall," murmured Gavrilescu. "If I hadn't gone to the beer hall with her, nothing would have happened. Or if I'd had any money on me . . . But as it was, *she* paid—Elsa paid—and, you understand, I felt obliged . . . And now it's late, isn't it? It's very late."

"What does that matter now?" asked the girl. "Come on, let's go!"

"But I don't even have a house any more, I don't have anything. I've had a terrible day. I stopped to chat with Mrs. Voitinovici and I forgot the portfolio with my scores."

"You always were absent-minded," the girl interrupted him. "Let's go."

"But where? Where?" asked Gavrilescu, trying to shout. "Somebody has moved into my house. I forget his name, but it's somebody I don't know. And he's not even at home so that I can explain it all to him. He's gone to the shore."

"Come with me," said the girl, taking his hand and pulling him gently toward the corridor.

"But I don't even have any money," continued Gavrilescu in a low voice. "Right now when they've changed the currency and the streetcar fare has gone up!"

"You're just the same as ever," said the girl, starting to laugh. "You're afraid."

"And nobody's left of all my acquaintances," continued Gavrilescu. "Everybody's at the shore. And Mrs. Voitinovici, from whom I could have borrowed something, they say she's moved to the country . . . Oh, my hat!" he exclaimed, and was about to go back to get it.

"Leave it there," replied the girl. "You won't need it any more now."

"You never can tell, you never can tell," Gavrilescu insisted, trying desperately to free his hand from the girl's grasp. "It's a very good hat, and almost new."

"Can it be true?" asked the girl in amazement. "You still don't understand? You don't understand what's happened to you, now, a short while ago, a very short while ago? Is it true that you don't understand?"

Gavrilescu looked deep into her eyes, then heaved a sigh.

"I'm all worn out," he said. "Forgive me. I've had a terrible day . . . But now I think I'm starting to feel better."

The girl pulled him gently along after her. They crossed the yard and went out without even opening the gate. The cab driver was waiting for them, dozing, he saw; and the girl pulled him ever so gently into the cab with her.

"But I swear," began Gavrilescu in a whisper, "I give you my word of honor that I haven't got a cent."

"Where to, lady?" asked the cab driver. "And how do you want me to drive? At a walk, or faster?"

"Drive us to the woods, and go the longest way," said the girl. "And drive slowly. We're in no hurry."

"Ah, youth!" said the cab driver, whistling softly to his horse.

She was holding his hand between her hands, leaning back with her head on the cushion, looking at the sky. Gavrilescu gazed at her intently, lost in thought.

"Hildegard," he began finally. "Something's happening to me, and I don't quite understand what. If I hadn't heard you speak to the cab driver, I would think I was dreaming."

The girl turned her head toward him and smiled.

"We're all dreaming," she said. "That's how it begins. As if in a dream . . ."

Translated from the Romanian
by William Ames Coates

CARLOS FUENTES

AURA

Man hunts and struggles.
Woman intrigues and dreams;
she is the mother of fantasy,
the mother of the gods.
She has second sight,
the wings that enable her to fly
to the infinite of
desire and the imagination . . .
The gods are like men:
they are born and they die
on a woman's breast . . .

—*Jules Michelet*

1

You're reading the advertisement: an offer like this isn't made every day. You read it and reread it. It seems to be addressed to you and nobody else. You don't even notice when the ash from your cigarette falls into the cup of tea you ordered in this cheap, dirty café. You read it again. "Wanted, young historian, conscientious, neat. Perfect knowledge colloquial French." Youth . . . knowledge of French, preferably after living in France for a while . . . "Four thousand pesos a month, all meals, comfortable bedroom-study." All that's missing is your name. The advertisement should have two more words, in bigger, blacker type: Felipe Montero. Wanted, Felipe Montero, formerly on scholarship at the Sorbonne, historian full of useless facts, accustomed to digging among yellowed documents, part-time teacher in private schools, nine hundred pesos a month. But if you read that, you'd be suspicious, and take it as a joke. "Address, Donceles 815." No telephone. Come in person.

You leave a tip, reach for your briefcase, get up. You wonder if another young historian, in the same situation you are, has seen the same advertisement, has got ahead of you and taken the job already. You walk down to the corner, trying to forget this idea. As you wait for the bus, you run over the dates you must have on the tip of your tongue so that your sleepy pupils will respect you. The bus is coming now, and you're staring at the tips of your black shoes. You've got to be prepared. You put your hand in your pocket, search among the coins, and finally take out thirty centavos. You've got to be prepared. You grab the handrail —the bus slows down but doesn't stop—and jump aboard. Then you shove your way forward, pay the driver the thirty centavos, squeeze yourself in among the passengers already standing in the aisle, hang onto the overhead rail, press your briefcase tighter under your left arm, and automatically put your left hand over the back pocket where you keep your billfold.

This day is just like any other day, and you don't remember the advertisement until the next morning, when you sit down in the same café and order breakfast and open your newspaper. You come to the advertising section and there it is again: *young historian.* The job is still open. You reread the advertisement, lingering over the final words: four thousand pesos.

It's surprising to know that anyone lives on Donceles Street. You always thought that nobody lived in the old center of the city. You walk slowly, trying to pick out the number 815 in that conglomeration of old colonial mansions, all of them converted into repair shops, jewelry shops, shoe stores, drugstores. The numbers have been changed, painted over, confused. A 13 next to a 200. An old plaque reading 47 over a scrawl in blurred charcoal: *Now 924*. You look up at the second stories. Up there, everything is the same as it was. The jukeboxes don't disturb them. The mercury streetlights don't shine in. The cheap merchandise on sale along the street doesn't have any effect on that upper level; on the baroque harmony of the carved stones; on the battered stone saints with pigeons clustering on their shoulders; on the latticed balconies, the copper gutters, the sandstone gargoyles; on the greenish curtains that darken the long windows; on that window from which someone draws back when you look at it. You gaze at the fanciful vines carved over the doorway, then lower your eyes to the peeling wall and discover *815, formerly 69*.

You rap vainly with the knocker, that copper head of a dog, so worn and smooth that it resembles the head of a canine foetus in a museum of natural science. It seems as if the dog is grinning at you and you let go of the cold metal. The door opens at the first light push of your fingers, but before going in you give a last look over your shoulder, frowning at the long line of stalled cars that growl, honk, and belch out the unhealthy fumes of their impatience. You try to retain some single image of that indifferent outside world.

You close the door behind you and peer into the darkness of a roofed alleyway. It must be a patio of some sort, because you can smell the mold, the dampness of the plants, the rotting roots, the thick drowsy aroma. There isn't any light to guide you, and you're searching in your coat pocket for the box of matches when a sharp, thin voice tells you, from a distance: "No, it isn't necessary. Please. Walk thirteen steps forward and you'll come to a stairway at your right. Come up, please. There are twenty-two steps. Count them."

Thirteen. To the right. Twenty-two.

The dank smell of the plants is all around you as you count out your steps, first on the paving-stones, then on the creaking wood, spongy from the dampness. You count to twenty-two in a low voice and then stop, with the matchbox in your hand, and the briefcase under your arm. You knock on a door that smells of old pine. There isn't any knocker. Finally you push it open. Now you can feel a carpet under your feet, a thin carpet, badly laid. It makes you trip and almost fall. Then you notice the grayish filtered light that reveals some of the humps.

"Señora," you say, because you seem to remember a woman's voice. "Señora . . ."

"Now turn to the left. The first door. Please be so kind."

You push the door open: you don't expect any of them to be latched, you know they all open at a push. The scattered lights are braided in your eyelashes, as if you were seeing them through a silken net. All you can make out are the dozens of flickering lights. At last you can see that they're votive lights, all set on brackets or hung between unevenly spaced panels. They cast a faint glow on the silver objects, the crystal flasks, the gilt-framed mirrors.

Then you see the bed in the shadows beyond, and the feeble movement of a hand that seems to be beckoning to you.

But you can't see her face until you turn your back on that galaxy of religious lights. You stumble to the foot of the bed, and have to go around it in order to get to the head of it. A tiny figure is almost lost in its immensity. When you reach out your hand, you don't touch another hand, you touch the ears and thick fur of a creature that's chewing silently and steadily, looking up at you with its glowing red eyes. You smile and stroke the rabbit that's crouched beside her hand. Finally you shake hands, and her cold fingers remain for a long while in your sweating palm.

"I'm Felipe Montero. I read your advertisement."

"Yes, I know. I'm sorry, there aren't any chairs."

"That's all right. Don't worry about it."

"Good. Please let me see your profile. No, I can't see it well enough. Turn toward the light. That's right. Excellent."

"I read your advertisement . . ."

"Yes, of course. Do you think you're qualified? *Avez-vous fait des études?*"

"*A Paris, madame.*"

"*Ah, oui, ça me fait plaisir, toujours, toujours, d'entendre . . . oui . . . vous savez . . . on était tellement habitué . . . et après . . .*"

You move aside so that the light from the candles and the reflections from the silver and crystal show you the silk coif that must cover a head of very white hair, and that frames a face so old it's almost childlike. Her whole body is covered by the sheets and the feather pillows and the high, tightly buttoned white collar, all except for her arms, which are wrapped in a shawl, and her pallid hands resting on her stomach. You can only stare at her face until a movement of the rabbit lets you glance furtively at the crusts and bits of bread scattered on the worn-out red silk of the pillows.

"I'll come directly to the point. I don't have many years ahead of me, Señor Montero, and therefore I decided to break a life-long rule and place an advertisement in the newspaper."

"Yes, that's why I'm here."

"Of course. So you accept."

"Well, I'd like to know a little more."

"Yes. You're wondering."

She sees you glance at the night table, the different-colored bottles, the glasses, the aluminum spoons, the row of pillboxes, the other glasses—all stained with whitish liquids—on the floor within reach of her hand. Then you notice that the bed is hardly raised above the level of the floor. Suddenly the rabbit jumps down and disappears in the shadows.

"I can offer you four thousand pesos."

"Yes, that's what the advertisement said today."

"Ah, then it came out."

"Yes, it came out."

"It has to do with the memoirs of my husband, General Llorente. They must be put in order before I die. I want them to be published. I decided that a short time ago."

"But the General himself? Wouldn't he be able to . . ."

"He died sixty years ago, Señor. They're his unfinished memoirs. They have to be completed before I die."

"But . . ."

"I can tell you everything. You'll learn to write in my husband's own style. You'll only have to arrange and read his manuscripts to become fascinated by his style . . . his clarity . . . his . . ."

"Yes, I understand."

"Saga, Saga. Where are you? *Ici*, Saga!"

"Who?"

"My companion."

"The rabbit?"

"Yes. She'll come back."

When you raise your eyes, which you've been keeping lowered, her lips are closed but you can hear her words again—"She'll come back"—as if the old lady were pronouncing them at that instant. Her lips remain still. You look in back of you and you're almost blinded by the gleam from the religious objects. When you look at her again you see that her eyes have opened very wide, and that they're clear, liquid, enormous, almost the same color as the yellowish whites around them, so that only the black dots of the pupils mar that clarity. It's lost a moment later in the heavy folds of her lowered eyelids, as if she wanted to protect that glance which is now hiding at the back of its dry cave.

"Then you'll stay here. Your room is upstairs. It's sunny there."

"It might be better if I didn't trouble you, Señora. I can go on living where I am and work on the manuscripts there."

"My conditions are that you have to live here. There isn't much time left."

"I don't know if . . ."

"Aura . . ."

The old woman moves for the first time since you entered her room. As she reaches out her hand again, you sense that agitated breathing beside you, and another hand reaches out to touch the Señora's fingers. You look around and a girl is standing there, a girl whose whole body you can't see because she's standing so close to you and her arrival was so unexpected, without the slightest sound—not even those sounds that can't be heard but are real anyway because they're remembered immediately afterwards, because in spite of everything they're louder than the silence that accompanies them.

"I told you she'd come back."

"Who?"

"Aura. My companion. My niece."

"Good afternoon."

The girl nods and at the same instant the old lady imitates her gesture.

"This is Señor Montero. He's going to live with us."

You move a few steps so that the light from the candles won't blind you. The girl keeps her eyes closed, her hands at her sides. She doesn't look at you at first, then little by little she opens her eyes as if she were afraid of the light. Finally you can see that those eyes are sea green and that they surge, break to foam, grow calm again, then surge again like a wave. You look into them and tell yourself it isn't true, because they're beautiful green eyes just like all the beautiful green eyes you've ever known. But you can't deceive yourself: those eyes do surge, do change, as if offering you a landscape that only you can see and desire.

"Yes. I'm going to live with you."

2

The old woman laughs sharply and tells you that she is grateful for your kindness and that the girl will show you to your room. You're thinking about the salary of four thousand pesos, and how the work should be pleasant because you like these jobs of careful research that don't include physical effort or going from one place to another or meeting people you don't want to meet. You're thinking about this as you follow her out of the room, and you discover that you've got to follow her with your ears instead of your eyes: you follow the rustle of her skirt, the rustle of taffeta, and you're anxious now to look into her eyes again. You climb the stairs behind that sound in the darkness, and you're still unused to the obscurity. You remember it must be about six in the afternoon, and the flood of light surprises you when Aura opens the door to your bedroom—another door without a latch—and steps aside to tell you: "This is your room. We'll expect you for supper in an hour."

She moves away with that same faint rustle of taffeta, and you weren't able to see her face again.

You close the door and look up at the skylight that serves as a roof. You smile when you find that the evening light is blinding compared with the darkness in the rest of the house, and smile again when you try out the mattress on the gilded metal bed. Then you glance around the room: a red wool rug, olive and gold wallpaper, an easy chair covered in red velvet, an old walnut desk with a green leather top, an old Argand lamp with its soft glow for your nights of research, and a bookshelf over the desk in reach of your hand. You walk over to the other door, and on pushing it open you discover an outmoded bathroom: a four-legged bathtub with little flowers painted on the porcelain, a blue hand basin, an old-fashioned toilet. You look at yourself in the large oval mirror on the door of the wardrobe—it's also walnut—in the bathroom hallway. You move your heavy eyebrows and wide thick lips, and your breath fogs the mirror. You close your black eyes, and when you open them again the mirror has cleared. You stop holding your breath and run your hand through your dark, limp hair; you touch your fine profile, your lean cheeks; and when your breath hides your face again you're repeating her name: "Aura."

After smoking two cigarettes while lying on the bed, you get up, put on your jacket, and comb your hair. You push the door open and try to remember the route you followed coming up. You'd like to leave the door open so that the lamplight could guide you, but that's impossible because the springs close it behind you. You could enjoy playing with that door, swinging it back and forth. You don't do it. You could take the lamp down with you. You don't do it. This house will always be in darkness, and you've got to learn it and relearn it by touch. You grope your way like a blind man, with your arms stretched out wide, feeling your way along the wall, and by accident you turn on the light-switch. You stop and blink in the bright middle of that long, empty hall. At the end of it you can see the bannister and the spiral staircase.

You count the stairs as you go down: another custom you've got to learn in Señora Llorente's house. You take a step backward when you see the reddish eyes of the rabbit, which turns its back on you and goes hopping away.

You don't have time to stop in the lower hallway because Aura is waiting for you at a half-open stained-glass door, with a candelabrum in her hand. You walk toward her, smiling, but you stop when you hear the painful yowling of a number of cats—yes, you stop to listen, next to Aura, to be sure that they're cats—and then follow her to the parlor.

"It's the cats," Aura tells you. "There are lots of rats in this part of the city."

You go through the parlor: furniture upholstered in faded silk; glass-fronted cabinets containing porcelain figurines, musical clocks, medals, glass balls; carpets with Persian designs; pictures of rustic scenes; green velvet curtains. Aura is dressed in green.

"Is your room comfortable?"

"Yes. But I have to get my things from the place where . . ."

"It won't be necessary. The servant has already gone for them."

"You shouldn't have bothered."

You follow her into the dining room. She places the candelabrum in the middle of the table. The room feels damp and cold. The four walls are paneled in dark wood, carved in Gothic style, with fretwork arches and large rosettes. The cats have stopped yowling. When you sit down, you notice that four places have been set. There are two large, covered plates and an old, grimy bottle.

Aura lifts the cover from one of the plates. You breathe in the pungent odor of the liver and onions she serves you, then you pick up the old bottle and fill the cut-glass goblets with that thick red liquid. Out of curiosity you try to read the label on the wine bottle, but the grime has obscured it. Aura serves you some whole broiled tomatoes from the other plate.

"Excuse me," you say, looking at the two extra places, the two empty chairs, "but are you expecting someone else?"

Aura goes on serving the tomatoes. "No. Señora Consuelo feels a little ill tonight. She won't be joining us."

"Señora Consuelo? Your aunt?"

"Yes. She'd like you to go in and see her after supper."

You eat in silence. You drink that thick wine, occasionally shifting your glance so that Aura won't catch you in the hypnotized stare that you can't control. You'd like to fix the girl's features in your mind. Every time you look away you forget them again, and an irresistible urge forces you to look at her once more. As usual, she has her eyes lowered. While you're searching for the pack of cigarettes in your coat pocket, you run across that big key, and remember, and say to Aura: "Ah! I forgot that one of the drawers in my desk is locked. I've got my papers in it."

And she murmurs: "Then you want to go out?" She says it as a reproach.

You feel confused, and reach out your hand to her with the key dangling from one finger.

"It isn't important. The servant can go for them tomorrow."

But she avoids touching your hand, keeping her own hands on her lap. Finally she looks up, and once again you question your senses, blaming the wine for your bewilderment, for the dizziness brought on by those shining, clear green eyes, and you stand up after Aura does, running your hand over the wooden back of the Gothic chair, without daring to touch her bare shoulder or her motionless head.

You make an effort to control yourself, diverting your attention away from her by listening to the imperceptible movement of a door behind you—it must lead to the kitchen—or by separating the two different elements that make up the room: the compact circle of light around the candelabrum, illuminating the table and one carved wall, and the larger circle of darkness surrounding it. Finally you have the courage to go up to her, take her hand, open it, and place your key-ring in her smooth palm as a token.

She closes her hand, looks up at you, and murmurs, "Thank you." Then she rises and walks quickly out of the room.

You sit down in Aura's chair, stretch your legs, and light a cigarette, feeling a pleasure you've never felt before, one that you knew was part of you but that only now you're experiencing fully, setting it free, bringing it out because this time you know it'll be answered and won't be lost . . . And Señora Consuelo is waiting for you, as Aura said. She's waiting for you after supper . . .

You leave the dining room, and with the candelabrum in your hand you walk through the parlor and the hallway. The first door you come to is the old lady's. You rap on it with your knuckles, but there isn't any answer. You knock again. Then you push the door open because she's waiting for you. You enter cautiously, murmuring: "Señora . . . Señora . . ."

She doesn't hear you, for she's kneeling in front of that wall of religious objects, with her head resting on her clenched fists. You see her from a distance: she's kneeling there in her coarse woolen nightgown, with her head sunk into her narrow shoulders; she's thin, even emaciated, like a medieval sculpture; her legs are like two sticks, and they're inflamed with erysipelas. While you're thinking of the continual rubbing of that rough wool against her skin, she suddenly raises her fists and strikes feebly at the air, as if she were doing battle against the images you can make out as you tiptoe closer: Christ, the Virgin, St. Sebastian, St. Lucia, the Archangel Michael, and the grinning demons in an old print, the only happy figures in that iconography of sorrow and wrath, happy because they're jabbing their pitchforks into the flesh of the damned, pouring cauldrons of boiling water on them, violating the women, getting drunk, enjoying all the liberties forbidden to the saints. You approach that central image, which is surrounded by the tears of Our Lady of Sorrows, the blood of Our Crucified Lord, the delight of Lucifer, the anger of the Archangel, the viscera preserved in bottles of alcohol, the silver heart: Señora Consuelo, kneeling, threatens them with her fists, stammering the words you can hear as you move even closer: "Come, City of God! Gabriel, sound your trumpet! Ah, how long the world takes to die!"

She beats her breast until she collapses in front of the images and candles in a spasm of coughing. You raise her by the elbow, and as you gently help her to the bed you're surprised at her smallness: she's almost a little girl, bent over almost double. You realize that without your assistance she would have had to get back to bed on her hands and knees. You help her into that wide bed with its bread crumbs and old feather pillows, and cover her up, and wait until her breathing is back to normal, while the involuntary tears run down her parchment cheeks.

"Excuse me . . . excuse me, Señor Montero. Old ladies have nothing left but . . . the pleasures of devotion . . . Give me my handkerchief, please."

"Señorita Aura told me . . ."

"Yes, of course. I don't want to lose any time. We should . . . we should begin working as soon as possible. Thank you."

"You should try to rest."

"Thank you . . . Here . . ."

The old lady raises her hand to her collar, unbuttons it, and lowers her head to remove the frayed purple ribbon that she hands to you. It's heavy because there's a copper key hanging from it.

"Over in that corner . . . Open that trunk and bring me the papers at the right, on top of the others . . . They're tied with a yellow ribbon."

"I can't see very well . . ."

"Ah, yes . . . it's just that I'm so accustomed to the darkness. To my right . . . Keep going till you come to the trunk. They've walled us in, Señor Montero. They've built up all around us and blocked off the light. They've tried to force me to sell, but I'll die first. This house is full of memories for us. They won't take me out of here till I'm dead! Yes, that's it. Thank you. You can begin reading this part. I will give you the others later. Good night, Señor Montero. Thank you. Look, the candelabrum has gone out. Light it outside the door, please. No, no, you can keep the key. I trust you."

"Señora, there's a rat's nest in that corner."

"Rats? I never go over there."

"You should bring the cats in here."

"The cats? What cats? Good night. I'm going to sleep. I'm very tired."

"Good night."

3

That same evening you read those yellow papers written in mustard-colored ink, some of them with holes where a careless ash had fallen, others heavily fly-specked. General Llorente's French doesn't have the merits his wife attributed to it. You tell yourself you can make considerable improvements in the style, can tighten up his rambling account of past events: his childhood on a hacienda in Oaxaca, his military studies in France, his friendship with the duc de Morny and the intimates of Napoleon III, his return to Mexico on the staff of Maximilian, the imperial ceremonies and gatherings, the battles, the defeat in 1867, his exile in France. Nothing that hasn't been described before. As you undress you think of the old lady's distorted notions, the value she attributes to these memoirs. You smile as you get into bed, thinking of the four thousand pesos.

You sleep soundly until a flood of light wakes you up at six in the morning: that glass roof doesn't have any curtain. You bury your head under the pillow and try to go back to sleep. Ten minutes later you give it up and walk into the bathroom, where you find all your things neatly arranged on a table and your few clothes hanging in the wardrobe. Just as you finish shaving the early morning silence is broken by that painful, desperate yowling.

You try to find out where it's coming from: you open the door to the hallway, but you can't hear anything from there: those cries are coming from up above, from the skylight. You jump up on the chair, from the chair onto the desk, and by supporting yourself on the bookshelf you can reach the skylight. You open one of the windows and pull yourself up to look out at that side garden, that square of yew trees and brambles where five, six, seven cats—you can't count them, can't hold yourself up there for more than a second—are all twined together, all writhing in flames and giving off a dense smoke that reeks of burnt fur. As you get down again you wonder if you really saw it: perhaps you only imagined it from those dreadful cries that continue, grow less, and finally stop.

You put on your shirt, brush off your shoes with a piece of paper, and listen to the sound of a bell that seems to run through the passageways of the house until it arrives at your door. You look out into the hallway. Aura is walking along it with a bell in her hand. She turns her head to look at you and tells you that breakfast is ready. You try to detain her but she goes down the spiral staircase, still ringing that black-painted bell as if she were trying to wake up a whole asylum, a whole boarding-school.

You follow her in your shirt-sleeves, but when you reach the downstairs hallway you can't find her. The door of the old lady's bedroom opens behind you and you see a hand that reaches out from behind the partly opened door, sets a chamberpot in the hallway and disappears again, closing the door.

In the dining room your breakfast is already on the table, but this time only one place has been set. You eat quickly, return to the hallway, and knock at Señora Consuelo's door. Her sharp, weak voice tells you to come in. Nothing has changed: the perpetual shadows, the glow of the votive lights and the silver objects.

"Good morning, Señor Montero. Did you sleep well?"

"Yes. I read till quite late."

The old lady waves her hand as if in a gesture of dismissal. "No, no, no. Don't give me your opinion. Work on those pages and when you've finished I'll give you the others."

"Very well. Señora, would I be able to go into the garden?"

"What garden, Señor Montero?"

"The one that's outside my room."

"This house doesn't have any garden. We lost our garden when they built up all around us."

"I think I could work better outdoors."

"This house has only got that dark patio where you came in. My niece is growing some shade plants there. But that's all."

"It's all right, Señora."

"I'd like to rest during the day. But come to see me tonight."

"Very well, Señora."

You spend all morning working on the papers, copying out the passages you intend to keep, rewriting the ones you think are especially bad, smoking one cigarette after another and reflecting that you ought to space your work so that the job lasts as long as possible. If you can manage to save at least twelve thousand pesos, you can spend a year on nothing but your own work, which you've postponed and almost forgotten. Your great, inclusive work on the Spanish discoveries and conquests in the New World. A work that sums up all the scattered chronicles, makes them intelligible, and discovers the resemblances among all the undertakings and adventures of Spain's Golden Age, and all the human prototypes and major accomplishments of the Renaissance. You end up by putting aside the General's tedious pages and starting to compile the dates and summaries of your own work. Time passes and you don't look at your watch until you hear the bell again. Then you put on your coat and go down to the dining room.

Aura is already seated. This time Señora Llorente is at the head of the table, wrapped in her shawl and nightgown and coif, hunching over her plate. But the fourth place has also been set. You note it in passing. It doesn't bother you any more. If the price of your future creative liberty is to put up with all the manias of this old woman, you can pay it easily. As you watch her eating her soup you try to figure out her age. There's a time after which it's impossible to detect the passing of the years, and Señora Consuelo crossed that frontier a long time ago. The General hasn't mentioned her in what you've already read of the memoirs. But if the General was forty-two at the time of the French invasion, and died in 1901, forty years later, he must have died at the age of eighty-two. He must have married the Señora after the defeat at Querétaro and his exile. But she would only have been a girl at that time . . .

The dates escape you because now the Señora is talking in that thin, sharp voice of hers, that bird-like chirping. She's talking to Aura and you listen to her as you eat, hearing her long list of complaints, pains, suspected illnesses, more complaints about the cost of medicines, the dampness of the house and so forth. You'd like to break in on this domestic conversation to ask about the servant who went for your things yesterday, the servant you've never even glimpsed and who never waits on table. You're going to ask about him but you're suddenly surprised to realize that up to this moment Aura hasn't said a word and is eating with a sort of mechanical fatality, as if she were waiting for some outside impulse before picking up her knife and fork, cutting a piece of liver—yes, it's liver again, apparently the favorite dish in this house—and carrying it to her mouth. You glance quickly from the aunt to the niece, but at that moment the Señora becomes motionless, and at the same moment Aura puts her knife on her plate and also becomes motionless, and you remember that the Señora put down her knife only a fraction of a second earlier.

There are several minutes of silence: you finish eating while they sit there rigid as statues, watching you. At last the Señora says, "I'm very tired. I ought not to eat at the table. Come, Aura, help me to my room."

The Señora tries to hold your attention: she looks directly at you so that you'll keep looking at her, although what she's saying is aimed at Aura. You have to make an effort in order to evade that look, which once again is wide, clear, and yellowish, free of the veils and wrinkles that usually obscure it. Then you look at Aura, who is staring fixedly at nothing and silently moving her lips. She gets up with a motion like those you associate with dreaming, takes the arm of the bent old lady, and slowly helps her from the dining room.

Alone now, you help yourself to the coffee that has been there since the beginning of the meal, the cold coffee you sip as you wrinkle your brow and ask yourself if the Señora doesn't have some secret power over her niece: if the girl, your beautiful Aura in her green dress, isn't kept in this dark old house against her will. But it would be so easy for her to escape while the Señora was asleep in her shadowy room. You tell yourself that her hold over the girl must be terrible. And you consider the way out that occurs to your imagination: perhaps Aura is waiting for you to release her from the chains in which the perverse, insane old lady, for some unknown reason, has bound her. You remember Aura as she was a few moments ago, spiritless, hypnotized by her terror, incapable of speaking in front of the tyrant, moving her lips in silence as if she were silently begging you to set her free; so enslaved that she imitated every gesture of the Señora, as if she were permitted to do only what the Señora did.

You rebel against this tyranny. You walk toward the other door, the one at the foot of the staircase, the one next to the old lady's room: that's where Aura must live, because there's no other room in the house. You push the door open and go in. This room is dark also, with whitewashed walls, and the only decoration is an enormous black Christ. At the left there's a door that must lead into the widow's bedroom. You go up to it on tiptoe, put your hands against it, then decide not to open it: you should talk with Aura alone.

And if Aura wants your help she'll come to your room. You go up there for a while, forgetting the yellowed manuscripts and your own notebooks, thinking only about the beauty of your Aura. And the more you think about her, the more you make her yours, not only because of her beauty and your desire, but also because you want to set her free: you've found a moral basis for your desire, and you feel innocent and self-satisfied. When you hear the bell again you don't go down to supper because you can't bear another scene like the one at the middle of the day. Perhaps Aura will realize it, and come up to look for you after supper.

You force yourself to go on working on the papers.

When you're bored with them you undress slowly, get into bed, and fall asleep at once, and for the first time in years you dream, dream of only one thing, of a fleshless hand that comes toward you with a bell, screaming that you should go away, everyone should go away; and when that face with its empty eye-sockets comes close to yours, you wake up with a muffled cry, sweating, and feel those gentle hands caressing your face, those lips murmuring in a low voice, consoling you and asking you for affection. You reach out your hands to find that other body, that naked body with a key dangling from its neck, and when you recognize the key you recognize the woman who is lying over you, kissing you, kissing your whole body. You can't see her in the black of the starless night, but you can smell the fragrance of the patio plants in her hair, can feel her smooth, eager body in your arms; you kiss her again and don't ask her to speak.

When you free yourself, exhausted, from her embrace, you hear her first whisper: "You're my husband." You agree. She tells you it's daybreak, then leaves you, saying that she'll wait for you that night in her room. You agree again, and then fall asleep, relieved, unburdened, emptied of desire, still feeling the touch of Aura's body, her trembling, her surrender.

It's hard for you to wake up. There are several knocks on the door, and at last you get out of bed, groaning and still half-asleep. Aura, on the other side of the door, tells you not to open it: she says that Señora Consuelo wants to talk with you, is waiting for you in her room.

Ten minutes later you enter the widow's sanctuary. She's propped up against the pillows, motionless, her eyes hidden by those drooping, wrinkled, dead-white lids; you notice the puffy wrinkles under her eyes, the utter weariness of her skin.

Without opening her eyes she asks you, "Did you bring the key to the trunk?"

"Yes, I think so . . . Yes, here it is."

"You can read the second part. It's in the same place. It's tied with a blue ribbon."

You go over to the trunk, this time with a certain disgust: the rats are swarming around it, peering at you with their glittering eyes from the cracks in the rotted floorboards, galloping toward the holes in the rotted walls. You open the trunk and take out the second batch of papers, then return to the foot of the bed. Señora Consuelo is petting her white rabbit. A sort of croaking laugh emerges from her buttoned-up throat, and she asks you, "Do you like animals?"

"No, not especially. Perhaps because I've never had any."

"They're good friends. Good companions. Above all when you're old and lonely."

"Yes, they must be."

"They're always themselves, Señor Montero. They don't have any pretensions."

"What did you say his name is?"

"The rabbit? She's Saga. She's very intelligent. She follows her instincts. She's natural and free."

"I thought it was a male rabbit."

"Oh? Then you still can't tell the difference."

"Well, the important thing is that you don't feel all alone."

"They want us to be alone, Señor Montero, because they tell us that solitude is the only way to achieve saintliness. They forget that in solitude the temptation is even greater."

"I don't understand, Señora."

"Ah, it's better that you don't. Get back to work now, please."

You turn your back on her, walk to the door, leave her room. In the hallway you clench your teeth. Why don't you have courage enough to tell her that you love the girl? Why don't you go back and tell her, once and for all, that you're planning to take Aura away with you when you finish the job? You approach the door again and start pushing it open, still uncertain, and through the crack you see Señora Consuelo standing up, erect, transformed, with a military tunic in her arms: a blue tunic with gold buttons, red epaulettes, bright medals with crowned eagles—a tunic the old lady bites ferociously, kisses tenderly, drapes over her shoulders as she performs a few teetering dance steps. You close the door.

"She was fifteen years old when I met her," you read in the second part of the memoirs. "*Elle avait quinze ans lorsque je l'ai connue et, si j'ose le dire, ce sont ses yeux verts qui ont fait ma perdition.*" Consuelo's green eyes, Consuelo who was only fifteen in 1867, when General Llorente married her and took her with him into exile in Paris. "*Ma jeune poupée,*" he wrote in a moment of inspiration, "*ma jeune poupée aux yeux verts; je t'ai comblée d'amour.*" He described the house they lived in, the outings, the dances, the carriages, the world of the Second Empire, but all in a dull enough way. "*J'ai même supporté ta haine des chats, moi qu'aimais tellement les jolies bêtes . . .*" One day he found her torturing a cat: she had it clasped between her legs, with her crinoline skirt pulled up, and he didn't know how to attract her attention because it seemed to him that "*tu faisais ca d'une façon si innocent, par pur enfantillage,*" and in fact it excited him so much that if you can believe what he wrote, he made love to her that night with extraordinary passion, "*parce que tu m'avais dit que torturer les chats était ta manière a toi de rendre notre amour favorable, par un sacrifice symbolique . . .*" You've figured it up: Señora Consuelo must be 109. Her husband died fifty-nine years ago. "*Tu sais si bien t'habiller, ma douce Consuelo, toujours drappé dans de velours verts, verts comme tes yeux. Je pense que tu seras toujours belle, même dans cent ans . . .*" Always dressed in green. Always beautiful, even after a hundred years. "*Tu es si fière de ta beauté; que ne ferais-tu pas pour rester toujours jeune?*"

4

Now you know why Aura is living in this house: to perpetuate the illusion of youth and beauty in that poor, crazed old lady. Aura, kept here like a mirror, like one more icon on that votive wall with its clustered offerings, preserved hearts, imagined saints and demons.

You put the manuscript aside and go downstairs, suspecting there's only one place Aura could be in the morning—the place that greedy old woman has assigned to her.

Yes, you find her in the kitchen, at the moment she's beheading a kid: the vapor that rises from the open throat, the smell of spilt blood, the animal's glazed eyes, all give you nausea. Aura is wearing a ragged, blood-stained dress and her hair is disheveled; she looks at you without recognition and goes on with her butchering.

You leave the kitchen: this time you'll really speak to the old lady, really throw her greed and tyranny in her face. When you push open the door she's standing behind the veil of lights, performing a ritual with the empty air, one hand stretched out and clenched, as if holding something up, and the other clasped around an invisible object, striking again and again at the same place. Then she wipes her hands against her breast, sighs, and starts cutting the air again, as if—yes, you can see it clearly—as if she were skinning an animal . . .

You run through the hallway, the parlor, the dining room, to where Aura is slowly skinning the kid, absorbed in her work, heedless of your entrance or your words, looking at you as if you were made of air.

You climb up to your room, go in, and brace yourself against the door as if you were afraid someone would follow you: panting, sweating, victim of your horror, of your certainty. If something or someone should try to enter, you wouldn't be able to resist, you'd move away from the door, you'd let it happen. Frantically you drag the armchair over to that latchless door, push the bed up against it, then fall onto the bed, exhausted, drained of your will-power, with your eyes closed and your arms wrapped around your pillow—the pillow that isn't yours. Nothing is yours.

You fall into a stupor, into the depths of a dream that's your only escape, your only means of saying No to insanity. "She's crazy, she's crazy," you repeat again and again to make yourself sleepy, and you can see her again as she skins the imaginary kid with an imaginary knife. "She's crazy, she's crazy . . ."

in the depths of the dark abyss, in your silent dream with its mouths opening in silence, you see her coming toward you from the blackness of the abyss, you see her crawling toward you.

in silence,

moving her fleshless hand, coming toward you until her face touches yours and you see the old lady's bloody gums, her toothless gums, and you scream and she goes away again, moving her hand, sowing the abyss with the yellow teeth she carries in her blood-stained apron:

your scream is an echo of Aura's, she's standing in front of you in your dream, and she's screaming because someone's hands have ripped her green taffeta skirt in two, and then

she turns her head toward you

with the torn folds of the skirt in her hands, turns toward you and laughs silently, with the old lady's teeth superimposed on her own, while her legs, her naked legs, shatter into bits and fly toward the abyss . . .

There's a knock at the door, then the sound of the bell, the supper bell. Your head aches so much that you can't make out the hands on the clock, but you know it must be late: above your head you can see the night clouds beyond the skylight. You get up painfully, dazed and hungry. You hold the glass pitcher under the faucet, wait for the water to run, fill the pitcher, then pour it into the basin. You wash your face, brush your teeth with your worn toothbrush that's clogged with greenish paste, dampen your hair—you don't notice you're doing all this in the wrong order—and comb it meticulously in front of the oval mirror on the walnut wardrobe. Then you tie your tie, put on your jacket and go down to the empty dining room, where only one place has been set—yours.

Beside your plate, under your napkin, there's an object you start caressing with your fingers: a clumsy little rag doll, filled with a powder that trickles from its badly sewn shoulder; its face is drawn with India ink, and its body is naked, sketched with a few brush strokes. You eat the cold supper—liver, tomatoes, wine—with your right hand while holding the doll in your left.

You eat mechanically, without noticing at first your own hypnotized attitude, but later you glimpse a reason for your oppressive sleep, your nightmare, and finally identify your sleep-walking movements with those of Aura and the old lady. You're suddenly disgusted by that horrible little doll, in which you begin to suspect a secret illness, a contagion. You let it fall to the floor. You wipe your lips with the napkin, look at your watch, and remember that Aura is waiting for you in her room.

You go cautiously up to Señora Consuelo's door, but there isn't a sound from within. You look at your watch again: it's barely nine o'clock. You decide to feel your way down to that dark, roofed patio you haven't been in since you came through it, without seeing anything, on the day you arrived here.

You touch the damp, mossy walls, breathe the perfumed air, and try to isolate the different elements you're breathing, to recognize the heavy, sumptuous aromas that surround you. The flicker of your match lights up the narrow, empty patio, where various plants are growing on each side in the loose, reddish earth. You can make out the tall, leafy forms that cast their shadows on the walls in the light of the match. But it burns down, singeing your fingers, and you have to light another one to finish seeing the flowers, fruits and plants you remember reading about in old chronicles, the forgotten herbs that are growing here so fragrantly and drowsily: the long, broad, downy leaves of the henbane; the twining stems with flowers that are yellow outside, red inside; the pointed, heart-shaped leaves of the nightshade; the ash-colored down of the grape-mullein with its clustered flowers; the bushy gatheridge with its white blossoms; the belladonna. They come to life in the flare of your match, swaying gently with their shadows, while you recall the uses of these herbs that dilate the pupils, alleviate pain, reduce the pangs of childbirth, bring consolation, weaken the will, induce a voluptuous calm.

You're all alone with the perfumes when the third match burns out. You go up to the hallway slowly, listen again at Señora Consuelo's door, then tiptoe on to Aura's. You push it open without knocking and go into that bare room, where a circle of light reveals the bed, the huge Mexican crucifix, and the woman who comes toward you when the door is closed. Aura is dressed in green, in a green taffeta robe from which, as she approaches, her moon-pale thighs reveal themselves. The woman, you repeat as she comes close, the woman, not the girl of yesterday: the girl of yesterday—you touch Aura's fingers, her waist—couldn't have been more than twenty; the woman of today—you caress her loose black hair, her pallid cheeks—seems to be forty. Between yesterday and today, something about her green eyes has turned hard; the red of her lips has strayed beyond their former outlines, as if she wanted to fix them in a happy grimace, a troubled smile; as if, like that plant in the patio, her smile combined the taste of honey and the taste of gall. You don't have time to think of anything more.

"Sit down on the bed, Felipe."

"Yes."

"We're going to play. You don't have to do anything. Let me do everything myself."

Sitting on the bed, you try to make out the source of that diffuse, opaline light that hardly lets you distinguish the objects in the room, and the presence of Aura, from the golden atmosphere that surrounds them. She sees you looking up, trying to find where it comes from. You can tell from her voice that she's kneeling down in front of you.

"The sky is neither high nor low. It's over us and under us at the same time."

She takes off your shoes and socks and caresses your bare feet.

You feel the warm water that bathes the soles of your feet, while she washes them with a heavy cloth, now and then casting furtive glances at that Christ carved from black wood. Then she dries your feet, takes you by the hand, fastens a few violets in her loose hair, and begins to hum a melody, a waltz, to which you dance with her, held by the murmur of her voice, gliding around to the slow, solemn rhythm she's setting, very different from the light movements of her hands, which unbutton your shirt, caress your chest, reach around to your back and grasp it. You also murmur that wordless song, that melody rising naturally from your throat: you glide around together, each time closer to the bed, until you muffle the song with your hungry kisses on Aura's mouth, until you stop the dance with your crushing kisses on her shoulders and breasts.

You're holding the empty robe in your hands. Aura, squatting on the bed, places an object against her closed thighs, caressing it, summoning you with her hand. She caresses that thin wafer, breaks it against her thighs, oblivious of the crumbs that roll down her hips: she offers you half of the wafer and you take it, place it in your mouth at the same time she does, and swallow it with difficulty. Then you fall on Aura's naked body, you fall on her naked arms, which are stretched out from one side of the bed to the other like the arms of the crucifix hanging on the wall, the black Christ with that scarlet silk wrapped around his thighs, his spread knees, his wounded side, his crown of thorns set on a tangled black wig with silver spangles. Aura opens up like an altar.

You murmur her name in her ear. You feel the woman's full arms against your back. You hear her warm voice in your ear: "Will you love me forever?"

"Forever, Aura. I'll love you forever."

"Forever? Do you swear it?"

"I swear it."

"Even though I grow old? Even though I lose my beauty? Even though my hair turns white?"

"Forever, my love, forever."

"Even if I die, Felipe? Will you love me forever, even if I die?"

"Forever, forever. I swear it. Nothing can separate us."

"Come, Felipe, come . . ."

When you wake up, you reach out to touch Aura's

shoulder, but you only touch the still-warm pillow and the white sheet that covers you.

You murmur her name.

You open your eyes and see her standing at the foot of the bed, smiling but not looking at you. She walks slowly toward the corner of the room, sits down on the floor, places her arms on the knees that emerge from the darkness you can't peer into, and strokes the wrinkled hand that comes forward from the lessening darkness: she's sitting at the feet of the old lady, of Señora Consuelo, who is seated in an armchair you hadn't noticed earlier: Señora Consuelo smiles at you, nodding her head, smiling at you along with Aura, who moves her head in rhythm with the old lady's: they both smile at you, thanking you. You lie back, without any will, thinking that the old lady has been in the room all the time;

you remember her movements, her voice, her dance,
though you keep telling yourself she wasn't there.

The two of them get up at the same moment, Consuelo from the chair, Aura from the floor. Turning their backs on you, they walk slowly toward the door that leads to the widow's bedroom, enter that room where the lights are forever trembling in front of the images, close the door behind them, and leave you to sleep in Aura's bed.

5

Your sleep is heavy and unsatisfying. In your dreams you had already felt the same vague melancholy, the weight on your diaphragm, the sadness that won't stop oppressing your imagination. Although you're sleeping in Aura's room, you're sleeping all alone, far from the body you believe you've possessed.

When you wake up, you look for another presence in the room, and realize it's not Aura who disturbs you but rather the double presence of something that was engendered during the night. You put your hands on your forehead, trying to calm your disordered senses: that dull melancholy is hinting to you in a low voice, the voice of memory and premonition, that you're seeking your other half, that the sterile conception last night engendered your own double.

And you stop thinking, because there are things even stronger than the imagination: the habits that force you to get up, look for a bathroom off this room without finding one, go out into the hallway rubbing your eyelids, climb the stairs tasting the thick bitterness of your tongue, enter your own room feeling the rough bristles on your chin, turn on the bath faucets and then slide into the warm water, letting yourself relax into forgetfulness.

But while you're drying yourself, you remember the old lady and the girl as they smiled at you before leaving the room arm in arm; you recall that whenever they're together they always do the same things: they embrace, smile, eat, speak, enter, leave, at the same time, as if one were imitating the other, as if the will of one depended on the existence of the other . . . You cut yourself lightly on one cheek as you think of these things while you shave; you make an effort to get control of yourself. When you finish shaving you count the objects in your traveling case, the bottles and tubes which the servant you've never seen brought over from your boarding house: you murmur the names of these objects, touch them, read the contents and instructions, pronounce the names of the manufacturers, keeping to these objects in order to forget that other one, the one without a name, without a label, without any rational consistency. What is Aura expecting of you? you ask yourself, closing the traveling case. What does she want, what does she want?

In answer you hear the dull rhythm of her bell in the corridor telling you breakfast is ready. You walk to the door without your shirt on. When you open it you find Aura there: it must be Aura because you see the green taffeta she always wears, though her face is covered with a green veil. You take her by the wrist, that slender wrist which trembles at your touch . . .

"Breakfast is ready," she says, in the faintest voice you've ever heard.

"Aura, let's stop pretending."

"Pretending?"

"Tell me if Señora Consuelo keeps you from leaving, from living your own life. Why did she have to be there when you and I . . . Please tell me you'll go with me when . . ."

"Go away? Where?"

"Out of this house. Out into the world, to live together. You shouldn't feel bound to your aunt forever . . . Why all this devotion? Do you love her that much?"

"Love her?"

"Yes. Why do you have to sacrifice yourself this way?"

"Love her? She loves me. She sacrifices herself for me."

"But she's an old woman, almost a corpse. You can't . . ."

"She has more life than I do. Yes, she's old and repulsive . . . Felipe, I don't want to become . . . to be like her . . . another . . ."

"She's trying to bury you alive. You've got to be reborn, Aura."

"You have to die before you can be reborn . . . No, you don't understand. Forget about it, Felipe. Just have faith in me."

"If you'd only explain."

"Just have faith in me. She's going to be out today for the whole day."

"She?"

"Yes, the other."

"She's going out? But she never . . ."

"Yes, sometimes she does. She makes a great effort and goes out. She's going out today. For all day. You and I could . . ."

"Go away?"

"If you want to."

"Well . . . perhaps not yet. I'm under contract. But as soon as I can finish the work, then . . ."

"Ah, yes. But she's going to be out all day. We could do something."

"What?"

"I'll wait for you this evening in my aunt's bedroom. I'll wait for you as always."

She turns away, ringing her bell like the lepers who use a bell to announce their approach, telling the unwary: "Out of the way, out of the way." You put on your shirt and coat and follow the sound of the bell calling you to the dining room. In the parlor the widow Llorente comes toward you, bent over, leaning on a knobby cane; she's dressed in an old white gown with a stained and tattered gauze veil. She goes by without looking at you, blowing her nose into a handkerchief, blowing her nose and spitting. She murmurs, "I won't be at home today, Señor Montero. I have complete confidence in your work. Please keep at it. My husband's memoirs must be published."

She goes away, stepping across the carpets with her tiny feet, which are like those of an antique doll, and supporting herself with her cane, spitting and sneezing as if she wanted to clear something from her congested lungs. It's only by an effort of the will that you keep yourself from following her with your eyes, despite the curiosity you feel at seeing the yellowed bridal gown she's taken from the bottom of that old trunk in her bedroom.

You scarcely touch the cold coffee that's waiting for you in the dining room. You sit for an hour in the tall, arch-back chair, smoking, waiting for the sounds you never hear, until finally you're sure the old lady has left the house and can't catch you at what you're going to do. For the last hour you've had the key to the trunk clutched in your hand, and now you get up and silently walk through the parlor into the hallway, where you wait for another fifteen minutes —your watch tells you how long—with your ear against Señora Consuelo's door. Then you slowly push it open until you can make out, beyond the spider's web of candles, the empty bed on which her rabbit is gnawing at a carrot: the bed that's always littered with scraps of bread, and that you touch gingerly as if you thought the old lady might be hidden among the rumples of the sheets. You walk over to the corner where the trunk is, stepping on the tail of one of those rats; it squeals, escapes from your foot, and scampers off to warn the others. You fit the copper key into the rusted padlock, remove the padlock, and then raise the lid, hearing the creak of the old, stiff hinges. You take out the third portion of the memoirs—it's tied with a red ribbon—and under it you discover those photographs, those old, brittle, dog-eared photographs. You pick them up without looking at them, clutch the whole treasure to your breast, and hurry out of the room without closing the trunk, forgetting the hunger of the rats. You close the door, lean against the wall in the hallway till you catch your breath, then climb the stairs to your room.

Up there you read the new pages, the continuation, the events of an agonized century. In his florid language General Llorente describes the personality of Eugenia de Montijo, pays his respects to Napoleon the Little, summons up his most martial rhetoric to proclaim the Franco-Prussian War, fills whole pages with his sorrow at the defeat, harangues all men of honor about the Republican monster, sees a ray of hope in General Boulanger, sighs for Mexico, believes that in the Dreyfus affair the honor—always that word "honor"—of the army has asserted itself again.

The brittle pages crumble at your touch: you don't respect them now, you're only looking for a reappearance of the woman with green eyes. "I know why you weep at times, Consuelo. I have not been able to give you children, although you are so radiant with life . . ." And later: "Consuelo, you should not tempt God. We must reconcile ourselves. Is not my affection enough? I know that you love me; I feel it. I am not asking you for resignation, because that would offend you. I am only asking you to see, in the great love which you say you have for me, something sufficient, something that can fill both of us, without the need of turning to sick imaginings . . ." On another page: "I told

Consuelo that those medicines were utterly useless. She insists on growing her own herbs in the garden. She says she is not deceiving herself. The herbs are not to strengthen the body, but rather the soul." Later: "I found her in a delirium, embracing the pillow. She cried, 'Yes, yes, yes, I've done it, I've re-created her! I can invoke her, I can give her life with my own life!' It was necessary to call the doctor. He told me he could not quiet her, because the truth was that she was under the effects of narcotics, not of stimulants." And finally: "Early this morning I found her walking barefooted through the hallways. I wanted to stop her. She went by without looking at me, but her words were directed to me. 'Don't stop me,' she said. 'I'm going toward my youth, and my youth is coming toward me. It's coming in, it's in the garden, it's come back . . .' Consuelo, my poor Consuelo! Even the devil was an angel once."

There isn't any more. The memoirs of General Llorente end with that sentence: *"Consuelo, le démon aussi était un ange, avant . . ."*

And after the last page, the portraits. The portrait of an elderly gentleman in a military uniform, an old photograph with these words in one corner: *"Moulin, Photographe, 35 Boulevard Haussmann"* and the date *"1894."* Then the photograph of Aura, of Aura with her green eyes, her black hair gathered in ringlets, leaning against a Doric column with a painted landscape in the background: the landscape of a Lorelei in the Rhine. Her dress is buttoned up to the collar, there's a handkerchief in her hand, she's wearing a bustle: Aura, and the date *"1876"* in white ink, and on the back of the daguerreotype, in spidery handwriting: *"Fait pour notre dixième anniversaire de mariage,"* and a signature in the same hand, *"Consuelo Llorente."*

In the third photograph you see both Aura and the old gentleman, but this time they're dressed in outdoor clothes, sitting on a bench in a garden. The photograph has become a little blurred: Aura doesn't look as young as she did in the other picture, but it's she, it's he, it's . . . it's you. You stare and stare at the photographs, then hold them up to the skylight. You cover General Llorente's beard with your finger, and imagine him with black hair, and you only discover yourself: blurred, lost, forgotten, but you, you, you.

Your head is spinning, overcome by the rhythms of that distant waltz, by the odor of damp, fragrant plants: you fall exhausted on the bed, touching your cheeks, your eyes, your nose, as if you were afraid that some invisible hand had ripped off the mask you've been wearing for twenty-seven years, the cardboard features that hid your true face, your real appearance, the appearance you once had but then forgot. You bury your face in the pillow, trying to keep the wind of the past from tearing away your own features, because you don't want to lose them. You lie there with your face in the pillow, waiting for what has to come, for what you can't prevent. You don't look at your watch again, that useless object tediously measuring time in accordance with human vanity, those little hands marking out the long hours that were invented to disguise the real passage of time, which races with a mortal and insolent swiftness no clock could ever measure. A life, a century, fifty years: you can't imagine those lying measurements any longer, you can't hold that bodiless dust within your hands.

When you look up from the pillow, you find you're in darkness. Night has fallen.

Night has fallen. Beyond the skylight the swift black clouds are hiding the moon, which tries to free itself, to reveal its pale, round, smiling face. It escapes for only a moment, then the clouds hide it again. You haven't got any hope left. You don't even look at your watch. You hurry down the stairs, out of that prison cell with its old papers and faded daguerreotypes, and stop at the door of Señora Consuelo's room, and listen to your own voice, muted and transformed after all those hours of silence: "Aura . . ."

Again: "Aura . . ."

You enter the room. The votive lights have gone out. You remember that the old lady has been away all day: without her faithful attention the candles have all burned up. You grope forward in the darkness to the bed.

And again: "Aura . . ."

You hear a faint rustle of taffeta, and the breathing that keeps time with your own. You reach out your hand to touch Aura's green robe.

"No. Don't touch me. Lie down at my side."

You find the edge of the bed, swing up your legs, and remain there stretched out and motionless. You can't help feeling a shiver of fear: "She might come back any minute."

"She won't come back."

"Ever?"

"I'm exhausted. She's already exhausted. I've never been able to keep her with me for more than three days."

"Aura . . ."

You want to put your hand on Aura's breasts. She turns her back: you can tell by the difference in her voice.

"No . . . Don't touch me . . ."

"Aura . . . I love you."

"Yes. You love me. You told me yesterday that you'd always love me."

"I'll always love you, always. I need your kisses, your body . . ."

"Kiss my face. Only my face."

You bring your lips close to the head that's lying next to yours. You stroke Aura's long black hair. You grasp that fragile woman by the shoulders, ignoring her sharp complaint. You tear off her taffeta robe, embrace her, feel her small and lost and naked in your arms, despite her moaning resistance, her feeble protests, kissing her face without thinking, without distinguishing, and you're touching her withered breasts when a ray of moonlight shines in and surprises you, shines in through a chink in the wall that the rats have chewed open, an eye that lets in a beam of silvery moonlight. It falls on Aura's eroded face, as brittle and yellowed as the memoirs, as creased with wrinkles as the photographs. You stop kissing those fleshless lips, those toothless gums: the ray of moonlight shows you the naked body of the old lady, of Señora Consuelo, limp, spent, tiny, ancient, trembling because you touch her. You love her, you too have come back . . .

You plunge your face, your open eyes, into Consuelo's silver-white hair, and you'll embrace her again when the clouds cover the moon, when you're both hidden again, when the memory of youth, of youth re-embodied, rules the darkness.

"She'll come back, Felipe. We'll bring her back together. Let me recover my strength and I'll bring her back . . ."

Translated from the Spanish
by Lysander Kemp

ITALO CALVINO

ADAM, ONE AFTERNOON

The new gardener's boy had long hair kept in place by a piece of cloth tied around his head with a little bow. He was walking along the path with his watering can filled to the brim and his other arm stretched out to balance the load. Slowly, carefully, he watered the nasturtiums as if pouring out coffee and milk, until the earth at the foot of each plant dissolved into a soft black patch; when it was large and moist enough he lifted the watering can and passed on to the next plant. Maria-nunziata was watching him from the kitchen window, and thinking what a nice calm job gardening must be. He was a young man, she noticed, though he still wore shorts and that long hair made him look like a girl. She stopped washing the dishes and tapped on the window.

"Hey, boy," she called.

The gardener's boy raised his head, saw Maria-nunziata

and smiled. She laughed back at him, partly because she had never seen a boy with such long hair and a bow like that on his head. The gardener's boy beckoned to her with one hand, and Maria-nunziata went on laughing at the funny gesture he'd made, and began gesturing back to explain that she had the dishes to wash. But the boy beckoned again, and pointed at the pots of dahlias with his other hand. Why was he pointing at those dahlias? Maria-nunziata opened the window and stuck her head out.

"What's up?" she asked, and began laughing again.

"D'you want to see something nice?"

"What's that?"

"Something nice. Come and see. Quickly."

"Tell me what."

"I'll give it to you. I'll give you something very nice."

"But I've got the dishes to wash, and the signora'll come along and not find me."

"Do you want it or don't you? Come on, now."

"Wait a second," said Maria-nunziata, and shut the window.

When she came out through the kitchen door the gardener's boy was still there, watering the nasturtiums.

"Hello," said Maria-nunziata.

Maria-nunziata seemed taller than she was because of her high-heeled shoes, which were awful to work in, but she loved wearing them. Her little face looked like a child's amid its mass of black curls, and her legs were thin and childlike too, though her body, under the folds of her apron, was already round and ripe. She was always laughing: either at what others or she herself said.

"Hello," said the gardener's boy. The skin on his face,

neck and chest was dark brown; perhaps because he was always half naked, as now.

"What's your name?" asked Maria-nunziata.

"Libereso," said the gardener's boy.

Maria-nunziata laughed and repeated: "Libereso . . . Libereso . . . what a funny name, Libereso."

"It's a name in Esperanto," he said. "In Esperanto it means 'liberty.' "

"Esperanto," said Maria-nunziata. "Are you Esperanto?"

"Esperanto's a language," explained Libereso. "My father speaks Esperanto."

"I'm Calabrian," exclaimed Maria-nunziata.

"What's your name?"

"Maria-nunziata," she said and laughed.

"Why are you always laughing?"

"Why are you called Esperanto?"

"Not Esperanto, Libereso."

"Why?"

"Why are you called Maria-nunziata?"

"It is the Madonna's name. I'm named after the Madonna, and my brother after Saint Joseph."

"Senjosef?"

Maria-nunziata burst out laughing: "Senjosef! Saint Joseph, not Senjosef, Libereso!"

"My brother," said Libereso, "is named 'Germinal' and my sister 'Omnia.' "

"That nice thing you mentioned," said Maria-nunziata, "show it to me."

"Come on, then," said Libereso. He put down the watering can and took her by the hand.

Maria-nunziata hesitated. "Tell me what it is first."

"You'll see," he said, "but you must promise me to take care of it."

"Will you give it to me?"

"Yes, I'll give it to you." He had led her to a corner of the garden wall. There the dahlias standing in pots were as tall as the two of them.

"It's there."

"What is?"

"Wait."

Maria-nunziata peeped over his shoulder. Libereso bent down to move a pot, lifted another by the wall, and pointed to the ground.

"There," he said.

"What is it?" asked Maria-nunziata. She could not see anything; the corner was in shadow, full of wet leaves and garden mold.

"Look, it's moving," said the boy. Then she saw something that looked like a moving stone or leaf, something wet, with eyes and feet; a toad.

"*Mammamia!*"

Maria-nunziata went skipping away among the dahlias in her high-heeled shoes. Libereso squatted down by the toad and laughed, showing the white teeth in the middle of his brown face.

"Are you frightened? It's only a toad! Why are you frightened?"

"A toad!" gasped Maria-nunziata.

"Of course it's a toad. Come here," said Libereso.

She pointed at it with a trembling finger. "Kill it."

He put out his hands, as if to protect it. "I don't want to. It's so nice."

"A nice toad?"

"All toads are nice. They eat the worms."

"Oh!" said Maria-nunziata, but she did not come any nearer. She was chewing the edge of her apron and trying to watch out of the corners of her eyes.

"Look how pretty it is," said Libereso and put a hand on it.

Maria-nunziata approached, no longer laughing, and looked on open-mouthed. "No! No! Don't touch it!"

With one finger Libereso was stroking the toad's gray-green back, which was covered with slimy warts.

"Are you mad? Don't you know they burn when you touch them, and make your hand swell up?"

The boy showed her his big brown hands, the palms covered with a layer of yellow calluses.

"Oh, it won't hurt me," he said. "And it's so pretty."

Now he'd taken the toad by the scruff of the neck like a cat and put it in the palm of his hand. Maria-nunziata, still chewing the edge of her apron, came nearer and crouched down beside him.

"*Mammamia!*" she exclaimed.

They were both crouching down behind the dahlias, and Maria-nunziata's rosy knees were grazing the brown, scratched ones of Libereso. Libereso cupped his other hand over the back of the toad, and caught it every now and again as it tried to slip out.

"You stroke it, Maria-nunziata," he said.

The girl hid her hands in her apron.

"No," she said firmly.

"What?" he said. "You don't want it?"

Maria-nunziata lowered her eyes, glanced at the toad, and lowered them again quickly.

"No," she said.

"But it's yours. I'm giving it to you."

Maria-nunziata's eyes clouded over. It was sad to refuse a present, no one ever gave her presents, but the toad really did revolt her.

"You can take it home if you like. It'll keep you company."

"No," she said.

Libereso put the toad back on the ground, and it quickly hopped away and squatted under the leaves.

"Good-bye, Libereso."

"Wait a minute."

"But I must go and finish washing the dishes. The signora doesn't like me to come out in the garden."

"Wait. I want to give you something. Something really nice. Come with me."

She began following him along the gravel paths. What a strange boy this Libereso was, with that long hair, and picking up toads in his hands.

"How old are you, Libereso?"

"Fifteen. And you?"

"Fourteen."

"Now, or on your next birthday?"

"On my next birthday. Assumption Day."

"Has that passed yet?"

"What, don't you know when Assumption Day is?" She began laughing.

"No."

"Assumption Day, when there's the procession. Don't you go to the procession?"

"Me? No."

"Back home there are lovely processions. It's not like

here, back home. There are big fields full of bergamots, nothing but bergamots, and everyone picks bergamots from morning till night. I've fourteen brothers and sisters and they all pick bergamots; five died when they were babies, and then my mother got tetanus, and we were in a train for a week to go to Uncle Carmelo's, and eight of us all slept in a garage there. Tell me, why do you have such long hair?"

They had stopped.

"Because it grows like that. You've got long hair, too."

"I'm a girl. If you wear long hair, you're like a girl."

"I'm not like a girl. You don't tell a boy from a girl by the hair."

"Not by the hair?"

"No, not by the hair."

"Why not by the hair?"

"Would you like me to give you something nice?"

"Oh, yes."

Libereso began moving among the arum lilies, budding white trumpets silhouetted against the sky. Libereso looked into each, groped around with two fingers, and then hid something in his fist. Maria-nunziata had not gone into the flower bed, and was watching him, with silent laughter. What was he up to now? When Libereso had looked into all the lilies, he came up to her, holding one hand over the other.

"Open your hands," he said. Maria-nunziata cupped her hands but was afraid to put them under his.

"What have you got in there?"

"Something very nice. You'll see."

"Show me first."

Libereso opened his hands and let her look inside. His palm was full of multicolored rose chafers, red and black and even purple ones, but the green were the prettiest. They were buzzing and slithering over one another and waving little black legs in the air. Maria-nunziata hid her hands under her apron.

"Here," said Libereso. "Don't you like them?"

"Yes," said Maria-nunziata uncertainly, still keeping her hands under her apron.

"When you hold them tight they tickle; would you like to feel?"

Maria-nunziata held out her hands timidly, and Libereso poured a cascade of rose chafers of every color into them.

"Don't be frightened; they won't bite you."

"*Mammamia!*" It hadn't occurred to her that they might bite her. She opened her hands and the rose chafers spread their wings and the beautiful colors vanished and there was nothing to be seen but a swarm of black insects flying about and settling.

"What a pity. I try to give you a present and you don't want it."

"I must go wash the dishes. The signora will be cross if she can't find me."

"Don't you want a present?"

"What are you going to give me now?"

"Come and see."

He took her hand again and led her through the flower beds.

"I must get back to the kitchen soon, Libereso. There's a chicken to pluck, too."

"Pooh!"

"Why pooh?"

"We don't eat the flesh of dead birds or animals."

"Why, are you always in Lent?"

"What do you mean?"

"Well, what do you eat then?"

"Oh, all sorts of things, artichokes, lettuce, tomatoes. My father doesn't like us to eat the flesh of dead animals. Or coffee or sugar, either."

"What d'you do with your sugar ration, then?"

"Sell it on the black market."

They had reached some climbing plants, starred all over with red flowers.

"What lovely flowers," said Maria-nunziata. "D'you ever pick them?"

"What for?"

"To take to the Madonna. Flowers are for the Madonna."

"Mesembryanthemum."

"What's that?"

"This plant's called Mesembryanthemum in Latin. All flowers have Latin names."

"The Mass is in Latin too."

"I wouldn't know about that."

Libereso was now peering closely between the winding branches on the wall.

"There it is," he said.

"What is?"

It was a lizard, green with black markings, basking in the sun.

"I'll catch it."

"No."

But he inched toward the lizard, very slowly, with both hands open; a jump, and he'd caught it. He laughed happily, showing his white teeth. "Look out, it's escaping!" First a stunned-looking head, then a tail, slithered out between his closed fingers. Maria-nunziata was laughing, too; but every time she saw the lizard she skipped back and pulled her skirt tight about her knees.

"So you really don't want me to give you anything at all?" said Libereso, rather sadly, and very carefully he put the lizard back on the wall; off it shot. Maria-nunziata kept her eyes lowered.

"Come on," said Libereso, and took her hand again.

"I'd like to have a lipstick and paint my lips red on Sundays to go out dancing. And a black veil to put on my head afterward for Benediction."

"On Sundays," said Libereso, "I go out to the woods with my brother, and we fill two sacks with pine cones. Then, in the evening, my father reads out loud from Kropotkin. My father has hair down to his shoulders and a beard right down to his chest. And he wears shorts in summer and winter. And I do drawings for the Anarchist Federation windows. The figures in top hats are businessmen, those in caps are generals, and those in round hats are priests; then I paint them in water colors."

They came to a pond with round water-lily leaves floating on it.

"Quiet, now," commanded Libereso.

Under the water a frog could be seen swimming up with sharp little strokes of its green legs. It suddenly surfaced, jumped onto a water-lily leaf, and sat down in the middle.

"There," cried Libereso and put out a hand to catch it,

but Maria-nunziata let out a cry—"Ugh!"—and the frog jumped back into the water. Libereso began searching for it, his nose almost touching the surface.

"There it is."

He thrust in a hand and pulled it out in his closed fist.

"Two of them together," he cried. "Look. Two of them, on top of each other."

"Why?" asked Maria-nunziata.

"Male and female stuck together," said Libereso. "Look what they're doing." And he tried to put the frogs into Maria-nunziata's hand. Maria-nunziata wasn't sure whether she was frightened because they were frogs, or because they were male and female stuck together.

"Leave them alone," she said. "You mustn't touch them."

"Male and female," repeated Libereso. "They're making tadpoles." A cloud passed over the sun. Suddenly Maria-nunziata began to feel anxious.

"It's late. The signora must be looking for me."

But she did not go. Instead they went on wandering around though the sun did not come out again. And then he found a snake, a tiny little snake, behind a hedge of bamboo. Libereso wound it around his arm and stroked its head.

"Once I used to train snakes. I had a dozen of them; one was long and yellow, a water snake, but it shed its skin and escaped. Look at this one opening its mouth, look how its tongue is forked. Stroke it—it won't bite."

But Maria-nunziata was frightened of snakes, too. Then they went to the rock pool. First he showed her the fountains and opened all the jets, which pleased her very much.

Then he showed her the goldfish. It was a lonely old goldfish, and its scales were already whitening. At last: Maria-nunziata liked the goldfish. Libereso began to move his hands around in the water to catch it; it was very difficult but when he'd caught it Maria-nunziata could put it in a bowl and keep it in the kitchen. He managed to catch it, but didn't take it out of the water in case it suffocated.

"Put your hands down here; stroke it," said Libereso. "You can feel it breathing; it has fins like paper and scales that prickle. Not much, though."

But Maria-nunziata did not want to stroke the fish either.

In the petunia bed the earth was very soft, and Libereso dug about with his fingers and pulled out some long, soft worms.

But Maria-nunziata ran away with little shrieks.

"Put your hand here," said Libereso, pointing to the trunk of an old peach tree. Maria-nunziata did not understand why, but she put her hand there; then she screamed and ran to dip it in the pool. For when she had pulled her hand away it was covered with ants. The peach tree was a mass of them, tiny black "Argentine" ants.

"Look," said Libereso and put a hand on the trunk. The ants could be seen crawling over his hand, but he didn't brush them off.

"Why?" asked Maria-nunziata. "Why are you letting yourself get covered with ants?"

His hand was now quite black, and they were crawling up his wrist.

"Take your hand away," moaned Maria-nunziata. "You'll get them all over you."

The ants were crawling up his naked arm, and had already reached his elbow.

Now his whole arm was covered with a veil of moving black dots; they reached his armpit but he did not brush them off.

"Get rid of them, Libereso. Put your arm in water!"

Libereso laughed, while some ants now even crawled from his neck onto his face.

"Libereso! I'll do whatever you like! I'll accept all those presents you gave me."

She threw her arms around his neck and started to brush off the ants.

Smiling his brown-and-white smile, Libereso took his hand away from the tree and began nonchalantly dusting his arm. But he was obviously touched.

"Very well, then, I'll give you a really big present, I've decided. The biggest present I can."

"What's that?"

"A hedgehog."

"*Mammamia!* The signora! The signora's calling me!"

Maria-nunziata had just finished washing the dishes when she heard a pebble beat against the window. Underneath stood Libereso with a large basket.

"Maria-nunziata, let me in. I want to give you a surprise."

"No, you can't come up. What have you got there?"

But at that moment the signora rang the bell, and Maria-nunziata vanished.

When she returned to the kitchen, Libereso was no longer to be seen. Neither inside the kitchen nor underneath the window. Maria-nunziata went up to the sink. Then she saw the surprise.

On every plate she had left to dry there was a crouching frog; a snake was coiled up inside a saucepan, there was a soup bowl full of lizards, and slimy snails were making iridescent streaks all over the glasses. In the basin full of water swam the lonely old goldfish.

Maria-nunziata stepped back, but between her feet she saw a great big toad. And behind it were five toads in a line, taking little hops toward her across the black-and-white-tiled floor.

Translated from the Italian
by Archibald Colquhoun and Peggy Wright

ILSE AICHINGER

STORY IN A MIRROR

If somebody comes and pushes your bed out of the ward and you see the sky turning green and you want to spare the curate his graveside homily, then it's time for you to creep out of bed, quietly, like children creep out of bed when the morning light shines through the shutters; you must take care that nurse doesn't see you, and you must be quick.

But the curate has already started his homily: you can hear his young and earnest voice in full spate. Let him go on; let the blind rain swallow up his pious words. Your grave is open. Leave him with nothing on which to exercise his ready trust, and help yourself. If you go, he'll be left without the slightest idea whether he has started yet or not, and so he'll make a sign to the bearers. They won't ask many questions, but pick your coffin up again, and hand back the wreath that's on the lid to the young man standing with bowed head by the graveside. The young man will take back his wreath, and be embarrassed, and smooth out the ribbons, and for a moment he'll raise his brow, and the rain will cause a few tears to trickle down his cheeks. Then the funeral procession will make its way back again along the walls. The candles in the hideous little chapel will be lit again, and the curate will say the prayers for the dead, to enable you to live. He will vigorously shake the young man's hand, and out of embarrassment wish him the best of luck. This is his first funeral service, and he will blush right under his collar. Before he can correct himself the young man will have disappeared. What is he to do next? After the officiating priest has wished a mourner the best of luck, what can he possibly do but send the corpse back to where it came from?

A few moments later the hearse with your coffin will be driving back again down the long street. There are yellow daffodils in the windows of all the houses on both sides of the road, the same kind of daffodils that the wreaths are made of, but it can't be helped. Children press their faces against the windows, which are closed because of the rain, but in spite of that a small boy comes running out of a front-door and hitches himself onto the back of the hearse. But he is told to get off and is left behind. He puts both hands over his eyes and looks after you angrily. What chance of a lift has a boy who lives on the road to the cemetery except on a hearse?

The hearse has to stop at the crossroads and wait for the green light. It's not raining so heavily now, and the drops are dancing on the hearse roof. There is a distant smell of hay. The streets have been newly christened, and heaven has laid its hand on all the roofs. For a time your hearse drives side by side with a tram. Two small boys on the curb bet which will overtake the other, but the boy who backed the tram is bound to lose. You could have warned him, but no one has ever yet climbed out of a coffin for such a purpose.

Be patient. It is early summer, and at this season morning reaches far into the night. Before it gets dark and all the children have vanished from the streets the hearse turns into the hospital yard, and a strip of moon appears just over the entrance gate. Men immediately appear and lift your coffin from the hearse, which drives cheerfully away.

They carry your coffin through the second gate and across the yard to the mortuary, where the empty slab is waiting, black and high and bare. They put your coffin on it and open it again, and one of them curses, because the nails have been hammered in so firmly. That cursed thoroughness!

Soon afterwards the young man appears, bringing his wreath back; and high time too. The men tidy the bows on the wreath, and place it neatly again on the coffin. There's no need to worry about the wreath. Overnight the faded blooms will have freshened and closed up into buds again. All night you'll be left alone, with the cross in your hands, and during the day you'll have plenty of rest too. It will be a long time before you manage to lie so still again.

In the morning the young man turns up again; because there's no rain to give him tears he stares into the void and twists his cap in his hands. Only when they come and pick the coffin up again does he cover his face with his hands and weep. You're leaving the mortuary now, so why should he weep? The coffin lid is loose, it is broad daylight and the sparrows are chirping merrily. They do not know that it is forbidden to wake the dead. The young man walks in front of your coffin; he walks as if he were afraid of treading on glass. The wind is cool and unruly, a child not yet of age.

They carry you back into the hospital and up the stairs, and lift you out of the coffin. Your bed is freshly made. The young man stares through the window down into the yard, where two pigeons are mating and cooing loudly, and he turns away in disgust.

Now they have put you back into bed and covered your face again, which makes you look so strange. The young man starts shrieking, and flings himself on top of you. They lead him gently away. There are notices on the walls saying: "Quiet, please," and all the hospitals are overcrowded nowadays, and the dead must not be wakened too soon.

The ship's sirens sound in the harbor. Is it an arrival or a departure? There's no way of telling. Quiet, please! Don't wake the dead too soon, for they sleep lightly. But the ships' sirens howl again. Soon they will have to uncover your face, whether they want to or not; and they will wash you and change your nightgown, and one of them will quickly bend over you to listen to your heart—that is, while you are still dead. There's not much time left, and that's the ships' fault. The morning is getting darker. They open your eyes, in which there is a white gleam. They no longer say that you look peaceful, thank heaven, the words die in their mouth. Wait a bit! Soon they will all go away.

Nobody wants to be a witness of what is happening, because they would be burned at the stake for it, even today.

They leave you alone. They leave you so alone that you open your eyes and see the green sky. They leave you so alone that you start breathing, deeply and heavily and with a rattling sound, like an anchor chain when it is let down. You start struggling, and shrieking for your mother. How green the sky is!

"The fever dreams are slackening and the death struggle is beginning," says a voice behind you.

Don't listen to them! What do they know about it?

Now is the time to go. Now is your chance. They have all been called away. Slip away before they come back and start whispering again. Go down the stairs and slip past the hall porter, and out into the morning that is turning into night. The birds are shrieking in the dark, as if your pains had started to rejoice. Go home and get back into your own bed, even if it's unmade and creaks in all its joints. In your own bed you'll get well quicker. In your own bed you'll rave against yourself for only three days and drink your fill of the green sky, and for three days you'll refuse the soup that the woman from upstairs brings you, and on the fourth day you'll drink it.

And on the seventh day, which is the day of rest, you go out. Your pains drive you, and you find the way. First left, and then right, and then left again, and through the alleys down by the harbor, which are so dreadful that they can't help leading to the sea. If only the young man were with you, but he's not here now—in your coffin you were much more beautiful. Now your face is twisted with pain, your pains have stopped rejoicing and there's continual perspiration on your brow. No, you were more beautiful in your coffin.

All the way children are playing marbles. You make your way through them, it's as if you were walking backwards among them, but none of the children is your child. How could any of them be your child if you're going to the old woman who lives next door to the tavern? The whole harbor knows how the old woman earns the money to pay for her drink.

She's standing at the open door, holding out her hand towards you. It's a filthy hand, and the whole place is filthy. There are yellow flowers on the mantelpiece, the flowers they make wreaths of, the same flowers again; the old woman is much too friendly, and the stairs creak here too, and the ships' sirens howl. Wherever you go you hear the ships howling, and they howl here too. Your pains shake you, but you're not allowed to shriek. The ships are allowed to howl, but you are not. Give the old woman the money for her drink! When she has got her money she'll keep her mouth shut. She's perfectly sober from all the brandy she has drunk, and she doesn't dream about the unborn. Innocent children don't dare complain about her to the saints, nor do the guilty ones. But you dare.

"Bring my child back to life!" you shriek at her.

No one has ever dared ask her that before, but you dare. The cracked, worn-out, unreflecting mirror gives you strength. The unseeing mirror with the fly marks on it gives you strength to ask for something for which nobody has ever asked before.

"Bring my child back to life, or I'll knock your yellow flowers over, I'll scratch your eyes out, I'll fling open the window and tell the whole street what they know already, I'll scream. . . ."

That terrifies the old woman, and in her terror she carries out your wish in the unseeing mirror. She doesn't know what she's doing, but in the unseeing mirror she manages to do it. The fear becomes terrible, and at last the pains begin to rejoice again. And before you scream you remember the lullaby: "Sleep, baby, sleep!" And before you scream the mirror throws you downstairs again and lets you go, lets you walk. Don't walk too quickly!

You had better not look down at the ground, or you might collide with a man, a young man who twists his cap in his hands, down there by the fence round the vacant building plot. You recognize him by the way he twists his cap. He did it just now beside your coffin, and here he is again. Here he is, leaning against the fence, as if he had never gone away. You fall into his arms. He has no tears in his eyes this time either, so give him some of yours. And say good-bye to him before you take his arm. Say good-bye to him! You won't forget it, even if he does; one says good-bye at the beginning. Before you walk away with him you must say good-bye for ever by the fence round the vacant building plot.

Then you walk away together. There is a path there that leads past the coal dump down to the sea. Neither of you speak. You wait for him to speak first, you wait for him to start, so that you won't have to speak last. What is he going to say? Quick! Before you reach the sea, which makes you reckless. What does he say? What is the first thing he says? Can what he wants to say really be so difficult that it makes him stammer and afraid to look up? Or is it the huge heaps of coal rearing up behind the fence that give him rings under his eyes and dazzle him with their blackness? The first thing he says—at last he has come out with it—is the name of a street, the street the old woman lives on. How can that be possible? He mentions the old woman to you before he knows you're expecting a child, before telling you even that he loves you. Calm yourself! He doesn't know that you've been to the old woman already, he couldn't know, he knows nothing about the mirror. But no sooner has he said it than he has forgotten it. You tell the mirror everything you want to forget. No sooner have you said that you are expecting a child than you have told him nothing. The mirror reflects everything. The piles of coal disappear behind you, because you have reached the shore and can see white sails like question-marks on the horizon. Keep quiet, because the sea takes the answers out of your mouth, swallows up what you were going to say.

From the sea you walk many times up the beach, as if you were leaving it behind and going home.

What are they whispering in their white headdresses? "This is the death struggle." Let them whisper!

One day the sky will be pale enough, so pale that its very pallor will shine brightly. Is there any brightness other than that of the last pallor?

Today the doomed house is reflected in the blind mirror. People call a house that is being pulled down doomed, but that's because they know no better. There's no cause to be afraid. The sky is pale enough now. After much laughter tears come easily. You have wept enough. Take back your wreath. Soon you'll be able to loosen your plaits again. Everything is in the mirror. And the sea lies green behind everything you do. If you leave the house it is standing in front of you. If you step out through the sunk windows you have forgotten. In the mirror one does everything so that it may be forgiven.

At his point he starts pleading with you to go inside with him. But in the excitement you leave the house behind you and turn away from the beach. Neither of you turns round, and you leave the doomed house behind you. You go up the river, and your own fever flows downstream against you, past you. His pleading becomes less urgent, and you are no longer ready, both of you are shyer. It's the ebb, which withdraws the sea from the coast, at the ebb even the rivers sink. And over on the other side treetops at last take the place of cranes. White shingle roofs sleep under them.

Listen, because soon he'll start talking about the future, about long life and many children, and his enthusiasm will set his cheeks aflame, and yours too. You will argue whether you want boys or girls, and you would prefer boys. He'd prefer a tiled roof, and you . . . but you have gone much too far up the river. Fright seizes both of you. The shingle roofs on the other side have disappeared, and there's nothing there now but damp meadows. On this side you must watch carefully where you are going. It's twilight—the sober twilight of dawn. The future is over. The future is a path along the river ending in the meadows. Go back!

What is to happen next?

Another three days and he'll no longer dare put his arm round your shoulders; and three days later he'll ask you your name, and you'll ask his. After that you won't even know each other's names, and you won't even ask. It's better like that. Haven't you both become a secret to each other?

Now at last you're walking silently side by side again. If he asks you anything now, it will be something like whether it is going to rain or not. As if anyone could know! You grow stranger and stranger to each other, and have long since given up talking about the future. You see each other less and less often, but you're still not strangers enough to each other. Wait, be patient, because it will come to that yet. He will be such a stranger to you that one day in a dark street in front of an open gateway you will start falling in love with him.

Everything in its own time. Now it has come.

"It's near the end," they say behind you. "It won't be long now!"

What do they know about it? Isn't it really only the beginning?

The day will come when you see him for the first time, and he sees you. The first time means the last; it means that you'll never see him again. But don't be frightened. You don't have to say good-bye to each other, for you've done that long ago. What a good thing it is that you have said good-bye already!

It will be an autumn day, full of anticipation of all the fruits turning into blossom again, a real autumn day, with light smoke and shadows that lie so sharply between your feet that you could almost cut your feet on them, and you fall when you're sent to market to fetch apples, you fall out of sheer joy and exuberance. A young man comes and helps you. His jacket hangs loosely over his shoulders, and he smiles and twists his cap in his hands and doesn't know what to say. But you are both very happy in that last light. You thank him, and throw your head back a little, and the plaits twisted round your ears fall down. "Oh," he says, "do you still go to school?" He turns and goes away whistling. That is how you part, without even turning to look at each other, entirely painlessly, and without knowing that this is your parting.

Now you can play with your little brothers again, and take them for walks along the river, along the path under the alder trees, and the shingle roofs are still on the opposite bank. What does the future bring? No sons, but brothers, and plaits to dance about, and balls to throw in the air. Don't be angry with the future, it has given you the best it has. It's time to go to school.

You're not old enough yet, so during the long break you still have to walk in crocodile, whispering and blushing and giggling between your fingers. But wait another year, and you'll be able to kick over the traces and clutch at the branches that hang over the wall. You have learned foreign languages, but you are not out of trouble yet, because learning your own language is much harder. Learning to read and write is harder still, but forgetting everything is hardest of all. If at your first exam you had to know everything, at the very end you have to know nothing at all. Will you be able to pass that test? Will you be quiet enough? If you have enough fear not to open your mouth, it will be all right.

You hang the blue hat that all school girls wear on the hook and leave the school. It is autumn again. The blossoms have long since turned into buds, the buds into nothing, and nothing into fruit. Everywhere small children who have passed their exams like you are going home. All of you know nothing any longer. You go home, father is waiting for you, and your little brothers make as much noise as they can, and pull your hair. You quieten them, and console your father.

Soon summer with its long days comes again, and your mother dies. You and your father fetch her from the cemetery. For three days she lies in the flickering candlelight, as you did once. Blow out all the candles before she wakes up! But she smells the wax, and raises herself on her elbows, and quietly grumbles about the expense. Then she gets up and changes her clothes.

It's as well that your mother died, because you wouldn't have been able to manage your little brothers much longer by yourself. But now she is here. Now she looks after everything, and teaches you all sorts of things about playing, because that is something one can never know enough about. It's no easy art. But the hardest is still to come.

The hardest is to forget how to talk, and to unlearn walking, to babble hopelessly and crawl about on the floor, and finally to be back in swaddling clothes. The hardest is to put up with all the tenderness, and only to look. Be patient. Soon everything will be all right. God knows the day on which you will be weak enough.

It's the day of your birth. You are born, and you open your eyes and shut them again because of the strong light. The light warms your limbs, you move in the sunlight, you are there, you are alive. Father bends over you.

"It's over," they say behind you. "She's dead!"

Quiet! Let them talk!

Translated from the German
by Eric Mosbacher

J. G. BALLARD

THE DROWNED GIANT

On the morning after the storm the body of a drowned giant was washed ashore on the beach five miles to the northwest of the city. The first news was brought by a nearby farmer and subsequently confirmed by the local newspaper reporters and the police. Despite this the majority of people, myself among them, remained sceptical, but the return of more and more eyewitnesses attesting to the vast size of the giant was finally too much for our curiosity. The library where my colleagues and I were carrying out our research was almost deserted when we set off for the coast shortly after two o'clock, and throughout the day people continued to leave their offices and shops as accounts of the giant circulated around the city.

By the time we reached the dunes above the beach a substantial crowd had gathered, and we could see the body lying in the shallow water two hundred yards away. At first the estimates of its size seemed greatly exaggerated. It was then at low tide, and almost all the giant's body was exposed, but he appeared to be a little larger than a basking shark. He lay on his back with his arms at his sides, in an attitude of repose, as if asleep on the mirror of wet sand, the reflection of his blanched skin fading as the water receded. In the clear sunlight his body glistened like the white plumage of a sea bird.

Puzzled by this spectacle, and dissatisfied with the matter-of-fact explanations of the crowd, my friends and I stepped down from the dunes onto the shingle. Everyone seemed reluctant to approach the giant, but half an hour later two fishermen in wading boots walked out across the sand. As their diminutive figures neared the recumbent body a sudden hubbub of conversation broke out among the spectators. The two men were completely dwarfed by the giant. Although his heels were partly submerged in the sand, the feet rose to at least twice the fishermen's height, and we immediately realized that this drowned leviathan had the mass and dimensions of the largest sperm whale.

Three fishing smacks had arrived on the scene and with keels raised remained a quarter of a mile offshore, the crews watching from the bows. Their discretion deterred the spectators on the shore from wading out across the sand. Impatiently everyone stepped down from the dunes and waited on the shingle slopes, eager for a closer view. Around the margins of the figure the sand had been washed away, forming a hollow, as if the giant had fallen out of the sky. The two fishermen were standing between the immense plinths of the feet, waving to us like tourists among the columns of some water-lapped temple on the Nile. For a moment I feared that the giant was merely asleep and might suddenly stir and clap his heels together, but his glazed eyes stared skyward, unaware of the minuscule replicas of himself between his feet.

The fishermen then began a circuit of the corpse, strolling past the long white flanks of the legs. After a pause to examine the fingers of the supine hand, they disappeared from sight between the arm and chest, then re-emerged to survey the head, shielding their eyes as they gazed up at its Grecian profile. The shallow forehead, straight high-bridged nose and curling lips reminded me of a Roman copy of Praxiteles, and the elegantly formed cartouches of the nostrils emphasized the resemblance to monumental sculpture.

Abruptly there was a shout from the crowd, and a hundred arms pointed toward the sea. With a start I saw that one of the fishermen had climbed onto the giant's chest and was now strolling about and signaling to the shore. There was a roar of surprise and triumph from the crowd, lost in a rushing avalanche of shingle as everyone surged forward across the sand.

As we approached the recumbent figure, which was lying in a pool of water the size of a field, our excited chatter fell away again, subdued by the huge physical dimensions of this moribund colossus. He was stretched out at a slight angle to the shore, his legs carried nearer the beach, and this foreshortening had disguised his true length. Despite the two fishermen standing on his abdomen, the crowd formed itself into a wide circle, groups of three or four people tentatively advancing toward the hands and feet.

My companions and I walked around the seaward side of the giant, whose hips and thorax towered above us like the hull of a stranded ship. His pearl-colored skin, distended by immersion in salt water, masked the contours of the enormous muscles and tendons. We passed below the left knee, which was flexed slightly, threads of damp seaweed clinging to its sides. Draped loosely across the midriff, and preserving a tenuous propriety, was a shawl of heavy open-weaved material, bleached to a pale yellow by the water. A strong odor of brine came from the garment as it steamed in the sun, mingled with the sweet but potent scent of the giant's skin.

We stopped by his shoulder and gazed up at the motionless profile. The lips were parted slightly, the open eye cloudy and occluded, as if injected with some blue milky liquid, but the delicate arches of the nostrils and eyebrows invested the face with an ornate charm that belied the brutish power of the chest and shoulders.

The ear was suspended in mid-air over our heads like a sculptured doorway. As I raised my hand to touch the pendulous lobe someone appeared over the edge of the forehead and shouted down at me. Startled by this apparition, I stepped back, and then saw that a group of youths had climbed up onto the face and were jostling each other in and out of the orbits.

People were now clambering all over the giant, whose reclining arms provided a double stairway. From the palms they walked along the forearms to the elbow and then crawled over the distended belly of the biceps to the flat promenade of the pectoral muscles which covered the upper half of the smooth hairless chest. From here they climbed up onto the face, hand over hand along the lips and nose, or forayed down the abdomen to meet others who had straddled the ankles and were patrolling the twin columns of the thighs.

We continued our circuit through the crowd, and stopped to examine the outstretched right hand. A small pool of water lay in the palm, like the residue of another world, now being kicked away by the people ascending the arm. I tried to read the palm-lines that grooved the skin, searching for some clue to the giant's character, but the distension of the tissues had almost obliterated them, carrying away all trace of the giant's identity and his last tragic predicament. The huge muscles and wrist bones of the hand seemed to deny any sensitivity to their owner, but the delicate flexion of the fingers and the well-tended nails, each cut symmetrically to within six inches of the quick, argued a certain refinement of temperament, illustrated in the Grecian features of the face, on which the townsfolk were now sitting like flies.

One youth was even standing, arms wavering at his sides, on the very tip of the nose, shouting down at his companions, but the face of the giant retained its massive composure.

Returning to the shore, we sat down on the shingle, and watched the continuous stream of people arriving from the city. Some six or seven fishing boats had collected offshore, and their crews waded in through the shallow water for a closer look at this enormous storm-catch. Later a party of police appeared and made a half-hearted attempt to cordon off the beach, but after walking up to the recumbent figure any such thoughts left their minds, and they went off together with bemused backward glances.

An hour later there were a thousand people on the

beach, at least two hundred of them were standing or sitting on the giant, crowded along his arms and legs or circulating in a ceaseless melee across his chest and stomach. A large gang of youths occupied the head, toppling each other off the cheeks and sliding down the smooth planes of the jaw. Two or three straddled the nose, and another crawled into one of the nostrils, from which he emitted barking noises like a dog.

That afternoon the police returned, and cleared a way through the crowd for a party of scientific experts—authorities on gross anatomy and marine biology—from the university. The gang of youths and most of the people on the giant climbed down, leaving behind a few hardy spirits perched on the tips of the toes and on the forehead. The experts strode around the giant, heads nodding in vigorous consultation, preceded by the policemen who pushed back the press of spectators. When they reached the outstretched hand the senior officer offered to assist them up onto the palm, but the experts hastily demurred.

After they returned to the shore, the crowd once more climbed onto the giant, and was in full possession when we left at five o'clock, covering the arms and legs like a dense flock of gulls sitting on the corpse of a large fish.

I next visited the beach three days later. My friends at the library had returned to their work, and delegated to me the task of keeping the giant under observation and preparing a report. Perhaps they sensed my particular interest in the case, and it was certainly true that I was eager to return to the beach. There was nothing necrophilic about this, for to all intents the giant was still alive for me, indeed more alive than many of the people watching him. What I found so fascinating was partly his immense scale, the huge volumes of space occupied by his arms and legs, which seemed to confirm the identity of my own miniature limbs, but above all the mere categorical fact of his existence. Whatever else in our lives might be open to doubt, the giant, dead or alive, existed in an absolute sense, providing a glimpse into a world of similar absolutes of which we spectators on the beach were such imperfect and puny copies.

When I arrived at the beach the crowd was considerably smaller, and some two or three hundred people sat on the shingle, picnicking and watching the groups of visitors who walked out across the sand. The successive tides had carried the giant nearer the shore, swinging his head and shoulders toward the beach, so that he seemed doubly to gain in size, his huge body dwarfing the fishing boats beached beside his feet. The uneven contours of the beach had pushed his spine into a slight arch, expanding his chest and tilting back the head, forcing him into a more expressly heroic posture. The combined effects of seawater and the tumefaction of the tissues had given the face a sleeker and less youthful look. Although the vast proportions of the features made it impossible to assess the age and character of the giant, on my previous visit his classically modeled mouth and nose suggested that he had been a young man of discreet and modest temper. Now, however, he appeared to be at least in early middle age. The puffy cheeks, thicker nose and temples and narrowing eyes gave him a look of well-fed maturity that even now hinted at a growing corruption to come.

This accelerated post-mortem development of the giant's character, as if the latent elements of his personality had gained sufficient momentum during his life to discharge themselves in a brief final résumé, continued to fascinate me. It marked the beginning of the giant's surrender to that all-demanding system of time in which the rest of humanity finds itself, and of which, like the million twisted ripples of a fragmented whirlpool, our finite lives are the concluding products. I took up my position on the shingle directly opposite the giant's head, from where I could see the new arrivals and the children clambering over the legs and arms.

Among the morning's visitors were a number of men in leather jackets and cloth caps, who peered up critically at the giant with a professional eye, pacing out his dimensions and making rough calculations in the sand with spars of driftwood. I assumed them to be from the public works department and other municipal bodies, no doubt wondering how to dispose of this gargantuan piece of jetsam.

Several rather more smartly attired individuals, circus proprietors and the like, also appeared on the scene, and strolled slowly around the giant, hands in the pockets of their long overcoats, saying nothing to one another. Evidently its bulk was too great even for their matchless enterprise. After they had gone the children continued to run up and down the arms and legs, and the youths wrestled with each other over the supine face, the damp sand from their feet covering the white skin.

The following day I deliberately postponed my visit until the late afternoon, and when I arrived there were fewer than fifty or sixty people sitting on the shingle. The giant had been carried still closer to the shore, and was now little more than seventy-five yards away, his feet crushing the palisade of a rotting breakwater. The slope of the firmer sand tilted his body toward the sea, and the bruised face was averted in an almost conscious gesture. I sat down on a large metal winch which had been shackled to a concrete caisson above the shingle, and looked down at the recumment figure.

His blanched skin had now lost its pearly translucence and was spattered with dirty sand which replaced that washed away by the night tide. Clumps of seaweed filled the intervals between the fingers and a collection of litter and cuttlebones lay in the crevices below the hips and knees. But despite this, and the continuous thickening of his features, the giant still retained his magnificent Homeric stature. The enormous breadth of the shoulders, and the huge columns of the arms and legs, still carried the figure into another dimension, and the giant seemed a more authentic image of one of the drowned Argonauts or heroes of the Odyssey than the conventional human-sized portrait previously in my mind.

I stepped down onto the sand, and walked between the pools of water toward the giant. Two small boys were sitting in the well of the ear, and at the far end a solitary youth stood perched high on one of the toes, surveying me as I approached. As I had hoped when delaying my visit, no one else paid any attention to me, and the people on the shore remained huddled beneath their coats.

The giant's supine right hand was covered with broken shells and sand, in which a score of footprints were visible.

The rounded bulk of the hip towered above me, cutting off all sight of the sea. The sweetly acrid odor I had noticed before was now more pungent, and through the opaque skin I could see the serpentine coils of congealed blood vessels. However repellent it seemed, this ceaseless metamorphosis, a visible life in death, alone permitted me to set foot on the corpse.

Using the jutting thumb as a stair rail, I climbed up onto the palm and began my ascent. The skin was harder than I expected, barely yielding to my weight. Quickly I walked up the sloping forearm and the bulging balloon of the biceps. The face of the drowned giant loomed to my right, the cavernous nostrils and huge flanks of the cheeks like the cone of some freakish volcano.

Safely rounding the shoulder, I stepped out onto the broad promenade of the chest, across which the bony ridges of the rib cage lay like huge rafters. The white skin was dappled by the darkening bruises of countless footprints, in which the patterns of individual heel marks were clearly visible. Someone had built a small sandcastle on the center of the sternum, and I climbed onto this partly demolished structure to give myself a better view of the face.

The two children had now scaled the ear and were pulling themselves into the right orbit, whose blue globe, completely occluded by some milk-colored fluid, gazed sightlessly past their miniature forms. Seen obliquely from below, the face was devoid of all grace and repose, the drawn mouth and raised chin propped up by its gigantic slings of muscles resembling the torn prow of a colossal wreck. For the first time I became aware of the extremity of this last physical agony of the giant, no less painful for his unawareness of the collapsing musculature and tissues. The absolute isolation of the ruined figure, cast like an abandoned ship upon the empty shore, almost out of sound of the waves, transformed his face into a mask of exhaustion and helplessness.

As I stepped forward, my foot sank into a trough of soft tissue, and a gust of fetid gas blew through an aperture between the ribs. Retreating from the fouled air, which hung like a cloud over my head, I turned toward the sea to clear my lungs. To my surprise I saw that the giant's left hand had been amputated.

I stared with bewilderment at the blackening stump, while the solitary youth reclining on his aerial perch a hundred feet away surveyed me with a sanguinary eye.

This was only the first of a sequence of depredations. I spent the following two days in the library, for some reason reluctant to visit the shore, aware that I had probably witnessed the approaching end of a magnificent illusion. When I next crossed the dunes and set foot on the shingle the giant was little more than twenty yards away, and with this close proximity to the rough pebbles all traces had vanished of the magic which once surrounded his distant wave-washed form. Despite his immense size, the bruises and dirt that covered his body made him appear merely human in scale, his vast dimensions only increasing his vulnerability.

His right hand and foot had been removed, dragged up the slope and trundled away by cart. After questioning the small group of people huddled by the breakwater, I gathered that a fertilizer company and a cattle food manufacturer were responsible.

The giant's remaining foot rose into the air, a steel hawser fixed to the large toe, evidently in preparation for the following day. The surrounding beach had been disturbed by a score of workmen, and deep ruts marked the ground where the hands and foot had been hauled away. A dark brackish fluid leaked from the stumps, and stained the sand and the white cones of the cuttlefish. As I walked down the shingle I noticed that a number of jocular slogans, swastikas and other signs had been cut into the gray skin, as if the mutilation of this motionless colossus had released a sudden flood of repressed spite. The lobe of one of the ears was pierced by a spear of timber, and a small fire had burned out in the center of the chest, blackening the surrounding skin. The fine wood ash was still being scattered by the wind.

A foul smell enveloped the cadaver, the undisguisable signature of putrefaction, which had at last driven away the usual gathering of youths. I returned to the shingle and climbed up onto the winch. The giant's swollen cheeks had now almost closed his eyes, drawing the lips back in a monumental gape. The once straight Grecian nose had been twisted and flattened, stamped into the ballooning face by countless heels.

When I visited the beach the following day I found, almost with relief, that the head had been removed.

Some weeks elapsed before I made my next journey to the beach, and by then the human likeness I had noticed earlier had vanished again. On close inspection the recumbent thorax and abdomen were unmistakably manlike, but as each of the limbs was chopped off, first at the knee and elbow, and then at shoulder and thigh, the carcass resembled that of any headless sea animal—whale or whale-shark. With this loss of identity, and the few traces of personality that had clung tenuously to the figure, the interest of the spectators expired, and the foreshore was deserted except for an elderly beachcomber and the watchman sitting in the doorway of the contractor's hut.

A loose wooden scaffolding had been erected around the carcass, from which a dozen ladders swung in the wind, and the surrounding sand was littered with coils of rope, long metal-handled knives and grappling irons, the pebbles oily with blood and pieces of bone and skin.

I nodded to the watchman, who regarded me dourly over his brazier of burning coke. The whole area was pervaded by the pungent smell of huge squares of blubber being simmered in a vat behind the hut.

Both the thigh bones had been removed, with the assistance of a small crane draped in the gauzelike fabric which had once covered the waist of the giant, and the open sockets gaped like barn doors. The upper arms, collarbones and pudenda had likewise been dispatched. What remained of the skin over the thorax and abdomen had been marked out in parallel strips with a tar brush, and the first five or six sections had been pared away from the midriff, revealing the great arch of the rib cage.

As I left a flock of gulls wheeled down from the sky and alighted on the beach, picking at the stained sand with ferocious cries.

Several months later, when the news of his arrival had been generally forgotten, various pieces of the body of the dismembered giant began to reappear all over the city. Most of these were bones, which the fertilizer manufacturers had found too difficult to crush, and their massive size, and the huge tendons and discs of cartilage attached to their joints, immediately identified them. For some reason, these disembodied fragments seemed better to convey the essence of the giant's original magnificence than the bloated appendages that had been subsequently amputated. As I looked across the road at the premises of the largest wholesale merchants in the meat market, I recognized the two enormous thighbones on either side of the doorway. They towered over the porters' heads like the threatening megaliths of some primitive druidical religion, and I had a sudden vision of the giant climbing to his knees upon these bare bones and striding away through the streets of the city, picking up the scattered fragments of himself on his return journey to the sea.

A few days later I saw the left humerus lying in the entrance to one of the shipyards (its twin for several years lay on the mud among the piles below the harbor's principal commercial wharf). In the same week the mummified right hand was exhibited on a carnival float during the annual pageant of the guilds.

The lower jaw, typically, found its way to the museum of natural history. The remainder of the skull has disappeared, but is probably still lurking in the waste grounds or private gardens of the city—quite recently, while sailing down the river, I noticed two ribs of the giant forming a decorative arch in a waterside garden, possibly confused with the jawbones of a whale. A large square of tanned and tattooed skin, the size of an Indian blanket, forms a backcloth to the dolls and masks in a novelty shop near the amusement park, and I have no doubt that elsewhere in the city, in the hotels or golf clubs, the mummified nose or ears of the giant hang from the wall above a fireplace. As for the immense pizzle, this ends its days in the freak museum of a circus which travels up and down the northwest. This monumental apparatus, stunning in its proportions and sometime potency, occupies a complete booth to itself. The irony is that it is wrongly identified as that of a whale, and indeed most people, even those who first saw him cast up on the shore after the storm, now remember the giant, if at all, as a large sea beast.

The remainder of the skeleton, stripped of all flesh, still rests on the seashore, the clutter of bleached ribs like the timbers of a derelict ship. The contractor's hut, the crane and the scaffolding have been removed, and the sand being driven into the bay along the coast has buried the pelvis and backbone. In the winter the high curved bones are deserted, battered by the breaking waves, but in the summer they provide an excellent perch for the sea-wearying gulls.

DONALD BARTHELME

THE EMERALD

Hey buddy what's your name?
My name is Tope. What's your name?
My name is Sallywag. You after the emerald?
Yeah I'm after the emerald you after the emerald too?
I am. What are you going to do with it if you get it?
Cut it up into little emeralds. What are you going to do with it?
I was thinking of solid emerald armchairs. For the rich.
That's an idea. What's your name, you?
Wide Boy.
You after the emerald?
Sure as shootin'.
How you going to get in?
Blast.
That's going to make a lot of noise isn't it?
You think it's a bad idea?

Well . . . What's your name, you there?

Taptoe.

You after the emerald?

Right as rain. What's more, I got a plan.

Can we see it?

No it's my plan I can't be showing it to every—

Okay okay. What's that guy's name behind you?

My name is Sometimes.

You here about the emerald, Sometimes?

I surely am.

Have you got an approach?

Tunneling. I've took some test borings. Looks like a stone cinch.

If this is the right place.

You think this may not be the right place?

The last three places haven't been the right place.

You tryin' to bring me down?

Why would I want to do that? What's that guy's name, the one with the shades?

My name is Brother. Who are all these people?

Businessmen. What do you think of the general situation, Brother?

I think it's crowded. This is my pal, Wednesday.

What say, Wednesday. After the emerald, I presume?

Thought we'd have a go.

Two heads better than one, that the idea?

Yep.

What are you going to do with the emerald, if you get it?

Facet. Facet and facet and facet.

Moll talking to a member of the news media.

Tell me, as a member of the news media, what do you do?

Well we sort of figure out what the news is, then we go out and talk to people, the newsmakers, those who have made the news—

These having been identified by certain people very high up in your organization.

The editors. The editors are the ones who say this is news, this is not news, maybe this is news, damned if I know whether this is news or not—

And then you go out and talk to people and they tell you everything.

They tell you a surprising number of things, if you are a member of the news media. Even if they have something to hide, questionable behavior or one thing and another, or having killed their wife, that sort of thing, still they tell you the most amazing things. Generally.

About themselves. The newsworthy.

Yes. Then we have our experts in the various fields. They are experts in who is a smart cookie and who is a dumb cookie. They write pieces saying which kind of cookie these various cookies are, so that the reader can make informed choices. About things.

Fascinating work I should think.

Your basic glamour job.

I suppose you would have to be very well-educated to get that kind of job.

Extremely well-educated. Typing, everything.

Admirable.

Yes. Well, back to the pregnancy. You say it was a seven-year pregnancy.

Yes. When the agency was made clear to me—

The agency was, you contend, extraterrestrial.

It's a fact. Some people can't handle it.

The father was—

He sat in that chair you're sitting in. The red chair. Naked and wearing a morion.

That's all?

Yes he sat naked in the chair wearing only a morion, and engaged me in conversation.

The burden of which was—

Passion.

What was your reaction?

I was surprised. My reaction was surprise.

Did you declare your unworthiness?

Several times. He was unmoved.

Well I don't know, all this sounds a little unreal, like I mean unreal, if you know what I mean.

Qui, je sais.

What role were you playing?

Well obviously I was playing myself. Mad Moll.

What's a morion?

Steel helmet with a crest.

You considered his offer.

More in the nature of a command.

Then, the impregnation. He approached your white or pink as yet undistended belly with his hideously engorged member—

It was more fun than that.

I find it hard to believe, if you'll forgive me, that you, although quite beautiful in your own way, quite lush of figure and fair of face, still the beard on your chin and that black mark like a furry caterpillar crawling in the middle of your forehead—

It's only a small beard after all.

That's true.

And he seemed to like the black mark on my forehead. He caressed it.

So you did in fact enjoy the . . . event. You understand I wouldn't ask these questions, some of which I admit verge on the personal, were I not a duly credentialed member of the press. Custodian as it were of the public's right to know. Everything. Every last little slippy-dippy thing.

Well okay yes I guess that's true strictly speaking. I suppose that's true. Strictly speaking. I could I suppose tell you to buzz off but I respect the public's right to know. I think. An informed public is, I suppose, one of the basic bulwarks of—

Yes I agree but of course I would wouldn't I, being I mean in my professional capacity my professional role—

Yes I see what you mean.

But of course I exist aside from that role, as a person I mean, as a woman like you—

You're not like me.

Well no in the sense that I'm not a witch.

You must forgive me if I insist on this point. You're not like me.

Well, yes, I don't disagree, I'm not arguing, I have not after all produced after a pregnancy of seven years a gigantic emerald weighing seven thousand and thirty-five carats— Can I, could I, by the way, see the emerald?

No not right now it's sleeping.

The emerald is sleeping?

Yes it's sleeping right now. It sleeps.

It sleeps?

Yes didn't you hear me it's sleeping right now it sleeps just like any other—

What do you mean the emerald is sleeping?

Just what I said. It's asleep.

Do you talk to it?

Of course, sure I talk to it, it's mine, I mean I *gave birth* to it, I cuddle it and polish it and talk to it, what's so strange about that?

Does it talk to you?

Well I mean it's only one month old. How could it talk?

Hello?

Yes?

Is this Mad Moll?

Yes this is Mad Moll who are you?

You the one who advertised for somebody to stand outside the door and knock down anybody tries to come in?

Yes that's me are you applying for the position?

Yes I think so what does it pay?

Two hundred a week and found.

Well that sounds pretty good but tell me lady who is it I have to knock down for example?

Various parties. Some of them not yet known to me. I mean I have an inkling but no more than that. Are you big?

Six eight.

How many pounds?

Two forty-nine.

IQ?

One forty-six.

What's your best move?

I got a pretty good shove. A not-bad bust in the mouth. I can trip. I can fall on 'em. I can gouge. I have a good sense of where the ears are. I know thumbs and kneecaps.

Where did you get your training?

Just around. High school, mostly.

What's your name?

Soapbox.

That's not a very tough name if you'll forgive me.

You want me to change it? I've been called different things in different places.

No I don't want you to change it. It's all right. It'll do.

Okay do you want to see me or do I have the job?

You sound okay to me Soapbox. You can start tomorrow.

What time?

Dawn?

Understand, ye sons of the wise, what this exceedingly precious Stone crieth out to you! Seven years, close to tears. Slept for the first two, dreaming under four blankets, black, blue, brown, brown. Slept and pissed, when I wasn't dreaming I was pissing, I was a fountain. After the first year I knew something irregular was in progress, but not what. I thought, moonstrous! Salivated like a mad dog, four quarts or more a day, when I wasn't pissing I was spitting. Chawed moose steak, moose steak and morels, and fluttered with new men—the butcher, baker, candlestick maker, especially the butcher, one Shatterhand, he was neat. Gobbled a lot of iron, liver and rust from the bottoms of boats, I had serial nosebleeds every day of the seventeenth trimester. Mood swings of course, heigh-de-ho, instances of false labor in years six and seven, palpating the abdominal wall I felt edges and thought, edges? Then on a cold February night the denouement, at six sixty-six in the evening, or a bit past seven, they sent a Miss Leek to do the delivery, one of us but not the famous one, she gave me scopolamine and a little swan-sweat, that helped, she turned not a hair when the emerald presented itself but placed it in my arms with a kiss or two and a pat or two and drove away, in a coach pulled by a golden pig.

Vandermaster has the Foot.

Yes.

The Foot is very threatening to you.

Indeed.

He is a mage and goes around accompanied by a black bloodhound.

Yes. Tarbut. Said to have been raised on human milk.

Could you give me a little more about the Foot. Who owns it?

Monks. Some monks in a monastery in Merano or outside of Merano. That's in Italy. It's their Foot.

How did Vandermaster get it?

Stole it.

Do you by any chance know what order that is?

Let me see if I can remember—Carthusian.

Can you spell that for me?

C-a-r-t-h-u-s-i-a-n. I think.

Thank you. How did Vandermaster get into the monastery?

They hold retreats, you know, for pious laymen or people who just want to come to the monastery and think about their sins or be edified, for a week or a few days . . .

Can you describe the Foot? Physically?

The Foot proper is encased in silver. It's about the size of a foot, maybe slightly larger. It's cut off just above the ankle. The toe part is rather flat, it's as if people in those days had very flat toes. The whole is quite graceful. The Foot proper sits on top of this rather elaborate base, three levels, gold, little claw feet . . .

And you are convinced that this, uh, reliquary contains the true Foot of Mary Magdalene.

Mary Magdalene's Foot. Yes.

He's threatening you with it.

It has a history of being used against witches, throughout history, to kill them or mar them—

He wants the emerald.

My emerald. Yes.

You won't reveal its parentage. Who the father was.

Oh well hell. It was the man in the moon. Deus Lunus.

The man in the moon ha-ha.

No I mean it, it was the man in the moon. Deus Lunus as he's called, the moon god. Deus Lunus. Him.

You mean you want me to believe—

Look woman I don't give dandelions what you believe you asked me who the father was. I told you. I don't give a zipper whether you believe me or don't believe me.

You're actually asking me to—

Sat in that chair, that chair right there. The red chair.

Oh for heaven's sake all right that's it I'm going to blow this pop stand I know I'm just a dumb ignorant media person but if you think for one minute that . . . I respect your uh conviction but this has got to be a delusionary belief. The man in the moon. A delusionary belief.

Well I agree it sounds funny but there it is. Where else

would I get an emerald that big, seven thousand and thirty-five carats? A poor woman like me?

Maybe it's not a real emerald?

If it's not a real emerald why is Vandermaster after me?

You going to the hog wrassle?

No I'm after the emerald.

What's your name?

My name is Cold Cuts. What's that machine?

That's an emerald cutter.

How's it work?

Laser beam. You after the emerald too?

Yes I am.

What's your name?

My name is Pro Tem.

That a dowsing rod you got there?

No it's a giant wishbone.

Looks like a dowsing rod.

Well it dowses like a dowsing rod but you also get the wish.

Oh. What's his name?

His name is Plug.

Can't he speak for himself?

He's deaf and dumb.

After the emerald?

Yes. He has special skills.

What are they?

He knows how to diddle certain systems.

Playing it close to the vest is that it?

That's it.

Who's that guy there?

I don't know, all I know about him is he's from Antwerp.

The Emerald Exchange?
That's what I think.
What are all those little envelopes he's holding?
Sealed bids?

Look here, Soapbox, look here.
What's your name, man?
My name is Dietrich von Dietersdorf.
I don't believe it.
You don't believe my name is my name?
Pretty fancy name for such a pissant-looking fellow as you.
I will not be balked. Look here.
What you got?
Silver thalers, my friend, thalers big as onion rings.
That's money, right?
Right.
What do I have to do?
Fall asleep.
Fall asleep at my post here in front of the door?
Right. Will you do it?
I could. But should I?
Where does this "should" come from?
My mind. I have a mind, stewing and sizzling.
Well deal with it, man, deal with it. Will you do it?
Will I? Will I? *I don't know!*

Where is my daddy? asked the emerald. My da?
Moll dropped a glass, which shattered.
Your father.
Yes, said the emerald, amn't I supposed to have one?
He's not here.

Noticed that, said the emerald.

I'm never sure what you know and what you don't know. I ask in true perplexity.

He was Deus Lunus. The moon god. Sometimes thought of as the man in the moon.

Bosh! said the emerald. I don't believe it.

Do you believe I'm your mother?

I do.

Do you believe you're an emerald?

I am an emerald.

Used to be, said Moll, women wouldn't drink from a glass into which the moon had shone. For fear of getting knocked up.

Surely this is superstition?

Hoo, hoo, said Moll. I like superstition.

I thought the moon was female.

Don't be culture-bound. It's been female in some cultures at some times, and in others, not.

What did it feel like? The experience.

Not a proper subject for discussion with a child.

The emerald sulking. Green looks here and there.

Well it wasn't the worst. Wasn't the worst. I had an orgasm that lasted for three hours. I judge that not the worst.

What's an orgasm?

Feeling that shoots through one's electrical system giving you little jolts, *spam spam*, many little jolts, *spam spam spam spam* . . .

Teach me something. Teach me something, mother of mine, about this gray world of yours.

What have I to teach? The odd pitiful spell. Most of them won't even put a shine on a pair of shoes.

Teach me one.

"To achieve your heart's desire, burn in water, wash in fire."

What does that do?

French-fries. Anything you want French-fried.

That's all?

Well.

I have buggered up your tranquillity.

No no no no no.

I'm valuable, said the emerald. I am a thing of value. Over and above my personhood, if I may use the term.

You are a thing of value. A value extrinsic to what I value.

How much?

Equivalent I would say to a third of a sea.

Is that much?

Not inconsiderable.

People want to cut me up and put little chips of me into rings and bangles.

Yes. I'm sorry to say.

Vandermaster is not of this ilk.

Vandermaster is an ilk unto himself.

The more threatening for so being.

Yes.

What are you going to do?

Make me some money. Whatever else is afoot, this delight is constant.

Now the Molljourney the Molltrip into the ferocious Out with a wire shopping cart what's that sucker there doing? tips his hat bends his middle shuffles his feet why he's doing courtly not seen courtly for many a month he does a quite decent courtly I'll smile, briefly, out of my way there citizen sirens shrieking on this swarm summer's day here an idiot there an idiot that one's eyeing me eyed me on the corner and eyed me round the corner as the Mad Moll song has it and that one standing with his cheek crushed against the warehouse wall and that one browsing in a trash basket and that one picking that one's pocket and that one with the gotch eye and his hands on his I'll twoad 'ee bastard I'll—

Hey there woman come and stand beside me.

Buzz off buster I'm on the King's business and have no time to trifle.

You don't even want to stop a moment and look at this thing I have here?

What sort of thing is it?

Oh it's a rare thing, a beautiful thing, a jim-dandy of a thing, a thing any woman would give her eyeteeth to look upon.

Well yes okay but what is it?

Well I can't tell you. I have to show you. Come stand over here in the entrance to this dark alley.

Naw man I'm not gonna go into no alley with you what do you think I am a nitwit?

I think you're a beautiful woman even if you do have that bit of beard there on your chin like a piece of burnt toast or something, most becoming. And that mark like a dead insect on your forehead gives you a certain—

Cut the crap daddy and show me what you got. Standing right here. Else I'm on my way.

No it's too rich and strange for the full light of day we have to have some shadow, it's too—

If this turns out to be an ordinary—

No no no nothing like that. You mean you think I might be a what-do-you-call-'em, one of those guys who—

Your discourse sir strongly suggests it.

And your name?

Moll. Mad Moll. Sometimes Moll the Poor Girl.

Beautiful name. Your mother's name or the name of some favorite auntie?

Moll totals him with a bang in the balls.

Jesus Christ these creeps what can you do?

She stops at a store and buys a can of gem polish.

Polish my emerald so bloody bright it will bloody blind you.

Sitting on the street with a basket of dirty faces for sale. The dirty faces are all colors, white black yellow tan rosy-red.

Buy a dirty face! Slap it on your wife! Buy a dirty face! Complicate your life!

But no one buys.

A boy appears pushing a busted bicycle.

Hey lady what are those things there they look like faces.

That's what they are, faces.

Lady, Halloween is not until—

Okay kid move along you don't want to buy a face move along.

But those are actual faces lady Christ I mean they're *actual faces*—

Fourteen ninety-five kid you got any money on you?

I don't even want to *touch* one, look like they came off dead people.

Would you feel better if I said they were plastic?

Well I hope to God they're not—

Okay they're plastic. What's the matter with your bike?

Chain's shot.

Give it here.

The boy hands over the bicycle chain.

Moll puts the broken ends in her mouth and chews for a moment.

Okay here you go.

The boy takes it in his hands and yanks on it. It's fixed.

Shit how'd you do that, lady?

Moll spits and wipes her mouth on her sleeve.

Run along now kid beat it I'm tired of you.

Are you magic, lady?

Not enough.

Moll at home playing her oboe.

I love the oboe. The sound of the oboe.

The noble, noble oboe!

Of course it's not to every taste. Not everyone swings with the oboe.

Whoops! Goddamn oboe let me take that again.

Not perhaps the premier instrument of the present age. What would that be? The bullhorn, no doubt.

Why did he interfere with me? Why?

Maybe has to do with the loneliness of the gods. Oh thou great one whom I adore beyond measure, oh thou bastard and fatherer of bastards—

Tucked-away gods whom nobody speaks to anymore. Once so lively.

Polish my emerald so bloody bright it will bloody blind you.

Good God what's that?

Vandermaster used the Foot!

Oh my God look at that hole!

It's awful and tremendous!

What in the name of God?

Vandermaster used the Foot!

The Foot did that? I don't believe it!

You don't believe it? What's your name?

My name is Coddle. I don't believe the Foot could have done that. I one hundred percent don't believe it.

Well it's right there in front of your eyes. Do you think Moll and the emerald are safe?

The house seems structurally sound. Smoke-blackened, but sound.

What happened to Soapbox?

You mean Soapbox who was standing in front of the house poised to bop any mother's son who—

Good Lord Soapbox is nowhere to be seen!

He's not in the hole!

Let me see there. What's your name?

My name is Mixer. No, he's not in the hole. Not a shred of him in the hole.

Good, true Soapbox!

You think Moll is still inside? How do we know this is the right place after all?

Heard it on the radio. What's your name by the way?

My name is Ho Ho. Look at the ground smoking!

The whole thing is tremendous, demonstrating the awful power of the Foot!

I am shaking with awe right now! Poor Soapbox!

Noble, noble Soapbox!

Mr. Vandermaster.

Madam.

You may be seated.

I thank you.

The red chair.

Thank you very much.

May I offer you some refreshment?

Yes I will have a splash of something thank you.

It's Scotch I believe.

Yes Scotch.

And I will join you I think, as the week has been a most fatiguing one.

Care and cleaning I take it.

Yes, care and cleaning and in addition there was a media person here.

How tiresome.

Yes it was tiresome in the extreme her persistence in her peculiar vocation is quite remarkable.

Wanted to know about the emerald I expect.

She was most curious about the emerald.

Disbelieving.

Yes disbelieving but perhaps that is an attribute of the profession?

So they say. Did she see it?

No it was sleeping and I did not wish to—

Of course. How did this person discover that you had as it were made yourself an object of interest to the larger public?

Indiscretion on the part of the midwitch I suppose, some people cannot maintain even minimal discretion.

Yes that's the damned thing about some people. Their discretion is out to lunch.

Blabbing things about would be an example.

Popping off to all and sundry about matters.

Ah well.

Ah well. Could we, do you think, proceed?

If we must.

I have the Foot.

Right.

You have the emerald.

Correct.

The Foot has certain properties of special interest to witches.

So I have been told.

There is a distaste, a bad taste in the brain, when one is forced to put the boots to someone.

Must be terrible for you, terrible. Where is my man Soapbox by the way?

That thug you had in front of the door?

Yes, Soapbox.

He is probably reintegrating himself with the basic matter of the universe, right now. Fascinating experience I should think.

Good to know.

I intend only the best for the emerald, however.

What is the best?

There are as you are aware others not so scrupulous in the field. Chislers, in every sense.

And you? What do you intend for it?

I have been thinking of emerald dust. Emerald dust with soda, emerald dust with tomato juice, emerald dust with a dash of bitters, emerald dust with Ovaltine.

I beg your pardon?

I want to live twice.

Twice?

In addition to my present life, I wish another, future life.

A second life. Incremental to the one you are presently enjoying.

As a boy, I was very poor. Poor as pine.

And you have discovered a formula.

Yes.

Plucked from the arcanum.

Yes. Requires a certain amount of emerald. Powdered emerald.

Ugh!

Carat's weight a day for seven thousand thirty-five days.

Coincidence.

Not at all. Only *this* emerald will do. A moon's emerald born of human witch.

No.

I have been thinking about bouillon. Emerald dust and bouillon with a little Tabasco.

No.

No?

No.

My mother is eighty-one, said Vandermaster. I went to my mother and said, Mother, I want to be in love.

And she replied?

She said, me too.

Lily the media person standing in the hall.

I came back to see if you were ready to confess. The hoax.

It's talking now. It talks.

It what?

Lovely complete sentences. Maxims and truisms.

I don't want to hear this. I absolutely—

Look kid this is going to cost you. Sixty dollars.

Sixty dollars for what?

For the interview.

That's checkbook journalism!

Sho' nuff.

It's against the highest traditions of the profession!

You get paid, your boss gets paid, the stockholders get their slice, why not us members of the raw material? Why shouldn't the raw material get paid?

It talks?

Most assuredly it talks.

Will you take a check?

If I must.

You're really a witch.

How many times do I have to tell you?

You do tricks or anything?

Consulting, you might say.

You have clients? People who come to see you regularly on a regular basis?

People with problems, yes.

What kind of problems, for instance?

Some of them very simple, really, things that just need a specific, bit of womandrake for example—

What's womandrake?

Black bryony. Called the herb of beaten wives. Takes away black-and-blue marks.

You get beaten wives?

Stick a little of that number into the old man's pork and beans, he retches. For seven days and seven nights. It near to kills him.

I have a problem.

What's the problem?

The editor, or editor-king, as he's called around the shop.

What about him?

He takes my stuff and throws it on the floor. When he doesn't like it.

On the floor?

I know it's nothing to you but it *hurts me*. I cry. I know I shouldn't cry but I cry. When I see my stuff on the floor. Pages and pages of it, so carefully typed, *every word spelled right*—

Don't you kids have a union?

Yes but he won't speak to it.

That's this man Lather, right?

Mr. Lather. Editor-imperator.

Okay I'll look into it that'll be another sixty you want to pay now or you want to be billed?

I'll give you another check. *Can* Vandermaster live twice?

There are two theories, the General Theory and the Special Theory. I take it he is relying on the latter. Requires ingestion of a certain amount of emerald. Powdered emerald.

Can you defend yourself?

I have a few things in mind. A few little things.

Can I see the emerald now?

You may. Come this way.

Thank you. Thank you at last. My that's impressive what's that?

That's the thumb of a thief. Enlarged thirty times. Bronze. I use it in my work.

Impressive if one believed in that sort of thing ha-ha I don't mean to—

What care I? What care I? In here. Little emerald, this is Lily Lily, this is the emerald.

Enchanté, said the emerald. What a pretty young woman you are!

This emerald is young, said Lily. Young, but good. I do not believe what I am seeing with my very eyes!

But perhaps that is a sepsis of the profession? said the emerald.

Vandermaster wants to live twice!

Oh, most foul, most foul!

He was very poor, as a boy! Poor as pine!

Hideous presumption! Cheeky hubris!

He wants to be in love! In love! Presumably with another person!

Unthinkable insouciance!

We'll have his buttons for dinner!

We'll clean the gutters with his hair!

What's your name, buddy?

My name is Tree and I'm smokin' mad!

My name is Bump and I'm just about ready to bust!

I think we should break out the naked-bladed pikes!

I think we should lay hand to torches and tar!

To live again! From the beginning! *Ab ovo!* This concept riles the very marrow of our minds!

We'll flake the white meat from his bones!

And that goes for his damned dog, too!

Hello is this Mad Moll?

Yes who is this?

My name is Lather.

The editor?

Editor-king, actually.

Yes Mr. Lather what is the name of your publication I don't know that Lily ever—

World. I put it together. When *World* is various and beautiful, it's because I am various and beautiful. When *World* is sad and dreary, it's because I am sad and dreary. When *World* is not thy friend, it's because *I* am not thy friend. And if I am not thy friend, baby—

I get the drift.

Listen, Moll, I am not satisfied with what Lily's been giving me. She's not giving me potato chips. I have decided that I am going to handle this story personally, from now on.

She's been insufficiently insightful and comprehensive?

Gore, that's what we need, actual or psychological gore, and this twitter she's been filing—anyhow, I have sent her to Detroit.

Not Detroit!

She's going to be second night-relief paper clipper in the Detroit bureau. She's standing here right now with her bags packed and ashes in her hair and her ticket in her mouth.

Why in her mouth?

Because she needs her hands to rend her garments with.

All right Mr. Lather send her back around. There is new bad news. Bad, bad, new bad news.

That's wonderful!

Moll hangs up the phone and weeps every tear she's capable of weeping, one, two, three.

Takes up a lump of clay, beats it flat with a Bible.

Let me see what do I have here?

I have Ya Ya Oil, that might do it.

I have Anger Oil, Lost & Away Oil, Confusion Oil, Weed of Misfortune, and War Water.

I have graveyard chips, salt, and coriander—enough coriander to freight a ship. Tasty coriander. Magical, magical coriander!

I'll eye-bite the son of a bitch. Have him in worm's hall by teatime.

Understand, ye sons of the wise, what this exceedingly precious Stone crieth out to you!

I'll fold that sucker's tent for him. If my stuff works. One never knows for sure, dammit. And where is Papa?

Throw in a little dwale now, a little orris . . .

Moll shapes the clay into the figure of a man.

So mote it be!

What happened was that they backed a big van up to the back door.

Yes.

There were four of them or eight of them.

Yes.

It was two in the morning or three in the morning or four in the morning—I'm not sure.

Yes.

They were great big hairy men with cudgels and ropes and pads like movers have and a dolly and come-alongs made of barbed wire—that's a loop of barbed wire big enough to slip over somebody's head, with a handle—

Yes.

They wrapped the emerald in the pads and placed it on the dolly and tied ropes around it and got it down the stairs through the door and into the van.

Did they use the Foot?

No they didn't use the Foot they had four witches with them.

Which witches?

The witches Aldrin, Endrin, Lindane, and Dieldrin. Bad-ass witches.

You knew them.

Only by repute. And Vandermaster was standing there with clouds of 1, 1, 2, 2-tetrachloroethylene seething from his nostrils.

That's toxic.

Extremely. I was staggering around bumping into things, tried to hold on to the walls but the walls fell away from me and I fell after them trying to hold on.

These other witches, they do anything to you?

Kicked me in the ribs when I was on the floor. With their pointed shoes. I woke up emeraldless.

Right. Well I guess we'd better get the vast resources of our organization behind this. *World*. From sea to shining sea to shining sea. I'll alert all the bureaus in every direction.

What good will that do?

It will harry them. When a free press is on the case, you can't get away with anything really terrible.

But look at this.

What is it?

A solid silver louse. They left it.

What's it mean?

Means that the devil himself has taken an interest.

A free press, madam, is not afraid of the devil himself.

Who cares what's in a witch's head? Pretty pins for sticking pishtoshio redthread for sewing names to shrouds gallant clankers I'll twoad 'ee and the gollywobbles to give away and the trinkum-trankums to give away with a generous hand pricksticks for the eye damned if I do and damned if I don't what's that upon her forehead? said my father it's a mark said my mother black mark like a furry caterpillar I'll scrub it away with the Ajax and what's that upon her chin? said my father it's a bit of a beard said my mother I'll pluck it away with the tweezers and what's that upon her mouth? said my father it must be a smirk said my mother I'll wipe it away with the heel of my hand she's got hair down there already said my father is that natural? I'll shave it said my mother no one will ever know and those said my father pointing *those?* just what they look like said my mother I'll make a bandeau with this nice clean dish towel she'll be flat as a jack of diamonds in no time and where's the belly button? said my father flipping me about I don't see one anywhere must be coming along later said my mother I'll just pencil one in here with the Magic Marker this child is a bit of a mutt said my father recall to me if you will the circumstances of her conception it was a dark and stormy night said my mother . . . But who cares what's in a witch's head caskets of cankers shelves of twoads for twoading paxwax scalpel polish people with scares sticking to their faces memories of God who held me up and sustained me until I fell from His hands into the world . . .

Twice? Twice? Twice? Twice?

Hey Moll.
Who's that?
It's me.
Me who?
Soapbox.

Soapbox!

I got it!

Got what?

The Foot! I got it right here!

I thought you were blown up!

Naw I pretended to be bought so I was out of the way. Went with them back to their headquarters, or den. Then when they put the Foot back in the refrigerator I grabbed it and beat it back here.

They kept it in the refrigerator?

It needs a constant temperature or else it gets restless. It's hot-tempered. They said.

It's elegant. Weighs a ton though.

Be careful you might—

Soapbox, I am not totally without—it's warm to the hand.

Yes it is warm I noticed that, look what else I got.

What are those?

Thalers. Thalers big as onion rings. Forty-two grand worth.

What are you going to do with them?

Conglomerate!

It is wrong to want to live twice, said the emerald. If I may venture an opinion.

I was very poor, as a boy, said Vandermaster. Nothing to eat but gruel. It was gruel; gruel, gruel. I was fifteen before I ever saw an onion.

These are matters upon which I hesitate to pronounce, being a new thing in the world, said the emerald. A latecomer to the welter. But it seems to me that, having weltered, the wish to *re*welter might be thought greedy.

Gruel today, gruel yesterday, gruel tomorrow. Sometimes gruel substitutes. I burn to recoup.

Something was said I believe about love.

The ghostfish of love has eluded me these forty-five years.

That Lily person is a pleasant person I think. And pretty too. Very pretty. Good-looking.

Yes she is.

I particularly like the way she is dedicated. She's extremely dedicated. Very dedicated. To her work.

Yes I do not disagree. Admirable. A free press is, I believe, an essential component of—

She is true-blue. Probably it would be great fun to talk to her and get to know her and kiss her and sleep with her and everything of that nature.

What are you suggesting?

Well, there's then, said the emerald, that is to say, your splendid second life.

Yes?

And then there's now. Now is sooner than then.

You have a wonderfully clear head, said Vandermaster, for a rock.

Okay, said Lily. I want you to tap once for yes and twice for no. Do you understand that?

Tap.

You are the true Foot of Mary Magdalene?

Tap.

Vandermaster stole you from a monastery in Italy?

Tap.

A Carthusian monastery in Merano or outside Merano?

Tap.

Are you uncomfortable in that reliquary?

Tap tap.

Have you killed any witches lately? In the last year or so?

Tap tap.

Are you morally neutral or do you have opinions?

Tap.

You have opinions?

Tap.

In the conflict we are now witnessing between Moll and Vandermaster, which of the parties seems to you to have right and justice on her side?

Tap tap tap tap.

That mean Moll? One tap for each letter?

Tap.

Is it warm in there?

Tap.

Too warm?

Tap tap.

So you have been, in a sense, an unwilling partner in Vandermaster's machinations.

Tap.

And you would not be averse probably to using your considerable powers on Moll's behalf.

Tap.

Do you know where Vandermaster is right now?

Tap tap.

Have you any idea what his next move will be?

Tap tap.

What is your opinion of the women's movement?

Tap tap tap tap tap tap tap tap tap tap tap tap tap tap.

I'm sorry I didn't get that. Do you have a favorite color

what do you think of cosmetic surgery should children be allowed to watch television after ten P.M. how do you feel about aging is nuclear energy in your opinion a viable alternative to fossil fuels how do you deal with stress are you afraid to fly and do you have a chili recipe you'd care to share with the folks?

Tap tap.

The first interview in the world with the true Foot of Mary Magdalene and no chili recipe!

Mrs. Vandermaster.

Yes.

Please be seated.

Thank you.

The red chair.

You're most kind.

Can I get you somthing, some iced tea or a little hit of Sanka?

A Ghost Dance is what I wouldn't mind if you can do it.

What's a Ghost Dance?

That's one part vodka to one part tequila with half an onion. Half a regular onion.

Wow wow wow wow wow.

Well when you're eighty-one, you know, there's not so much. Couple of Ghost Dances, I begin to take an interest.

I believe I can accommodate you.

Couple of Ghost Dances, I begin to look up and take notice.

Mrs. Vandermaster, you are aware are you not that your vile son has, with the aid of various parties, abducted my emerald? My own true emerald?

I mighta heard about it.

Well have you or haven't you?

'Course I don't pay much attention to that boy myself. He's bent.

Bent?

Him and his dog. He goes off in a corner and talks to the dog. Looking over his shoulder to see if I'm listening. As if I'd care.

The dog doesn't—

Just listens. *Intently.*

That's Tarbut.

Now I don't mind somebody who just addresses an occasional remark to the dog, like "Attaboy, dog," or something like that, or "Get the ball, dog," or something like that, but he *confides* in the dog. Bent.

You know what Vandermaster's profession is.

Yes, he's a mage. Think that's a little bent.

Is there anything you can do, or would do, to help me get my child back? My sweet emerald?

Well I don't have that much say-so.

You don't.

I don't know too much about what-all he's up to. He comes and goes.

I see.

The thing is, he's bent.

You told me.

Wants to live twice.

I know.

I think it's a sin and a shame.

You do.

And your poor little child.

Yes.
A damned scandal.
Yes.
I'd witch his eyes out if I were you.
The thought's appealing.
His eyes like onions . . .

A black bloodhound who looks as if he might have been fed on human milk. Bloodhounding down the center of the street, nose to the ground.

You think this will work?
Soapbox, do you have a better idea?
Where did you find him?
I found him on the doorstep. Sitting there. In the moonlight.
In the moonlight?
Aureoled all around with moonglow.
You think that's significant?
Well I don't think it's happenstance.
What's his name?
Tarbut.
There's something I have to tell you.
What?
I went to the refrigerator for a beer?
Yes?
The Foot's walked.

Dead! Kicked in the heart by the Foot!
That's incredible!
Deep footprint right over the breastbone!
That's ghastly and awful!

After Lily turned him down he went after the emerald with a sledge!

Was the emerald hurt?

Chipped! The Foot got there in the nick!

And Moll?

She's gluing the chips back with grume!

What's grume?

Clotted blood!

And was the corpse claimed?

Three devils showed up! Lily's interviewing them right now!

A free press is not afraid of a thousand devils!

There are only three!

What do they look like?

Like Lather, the editor!

And the Foot?

Soapbox is taking it back to Italy! He's starting a security-guard business! Hired Sallywag, Wide Boy, Taptoe, and Sometimes!

What's your name by the way?

My name is Knucks. What's your name?

I'm Pebble. And the dog?

The dog's going to work for Soapbox too!

Curious, the dog showing up on Moll's doorstep that way!

Deus Lunus works in mysterious ways!

Deus Lunus never lets down a pal!

Well how 'bout a drink!

Don't mind if I do! What'll we drink to?

We'll drink to living once!

Hurrah for the here and now!

Tell me, said the emerald, what are diamonds like?

I know little of diamonds, said Moll.

Is a diamond better than an emerald?

Apples and oranges I would say.

Would you have *preferred* a diamond?

Nope.

Diamond-hard, said the emerald, that's an expression I've encountered.

Diamonds are a little ordinary. Decent, yes. Quiet, yes. But *gray*. Give me step-cut zicrons, square-cut spodumenes, jasper, sardonyx, bloodstones, Baltic amber, cursed opals, peridots of your own hue, the padparadscha sapphire, yellow chrysoberyls, the shifty tourmaline, cabochons . . . But best of all, an emerald.

But what is the *meaning* of the emerald? asked Lily. I mean overall? If you can say.

I have some notions, said Moll. You may credit them or not.

Try me.

It means, one, that the gods are not yet done with us.

Gods not yet done with us.

The gods are still trafficking with us and making interventions of this kind and that kind and are not dormant or dead as has often been proclaimed by dummies.

Still trafficking. Not dead.

Just as in former times a demon might enter a nun on a piece of lettuce she was eating so even in these times a simple Mailgram might be the thin edge of the wedge.

Thin edge of the wedge.

Two, the world may congratulate itself that desire can

still be raised in the dulled hearts of the citizens by the rumor of an emerald.

Desire or cupidity?

I do not distinguish qualitatively among the desires, we have referees for that, but he who covets not at all is a lump and I do not wish to have him to dinner.

Positive attitude toward desire.

Yes. Three, I do not know what this Stone portends, whether it portends for the better or portends for the worse or merely portends a bubbling of the in-between but you are in any case rescued from the sickliness of same and a small offering in the hat on the hall table would not be ill regarded.

And what now? said the emerald. What now, beautiful mother?

We resume the scrabble for existence, said Moll. We resume the scrabble for existence, in the sweet of the here and now.

JOYCE CAROL OATES

FURTHER CONFESSIONS

I

On the morning of October third I boarded the *Cap Arcona* and, in my opulent stateroom, where my steamer trunk and my innumerable pieces of luggage were already waiting, I chanced to look out one of the portholes and saw a hellish sight.

A half-dozen gulls were fighting. Their wings flapping, their beaks furious, their cries demented and alarming—they were fighting over something that floated in the water, bobbing and plunging with the waves. Though I knew better, I could not resist staring. I threw the porthole window open and actually leaned forward to take in that ugly sight.

(It will be sufficient for my purposes to report that the thing that floated in the harbor, eyeless and trailing its guts, was not human: was not of our species.)

Shocked, sickened, I slammed the window shut.

And then a vision came upon me, seemed to open within my affrighted head. I lost all awareness of my surroundings—lost my interest in the other estimable passengers—in the identity of a particularly handsome woman who had boarded the ship unaccompanied—and I found myself, inspired by the ungainly splashing and cries of the gulls outside my window, recalling with disturbing vividness a dream I had had shortly before dawn.

I am not one to linger in the realm of dreams. If I may speak of myself frankly, I must say that I am, far more than most, *attuned* to the world—to its splendid demands and its even more splendid rewards. *He who really loves the world shapes himself to please it*—so I have known from earliest adolescence, though it is only in the past few years that I have felt confident enough in my own destiny to articulate that truth. As one loves the world and serves it, by being, not least of all, one of its more graceful creations, so the world will respond in kind—will offer evidence of its respect; will offer evidence, upon occasion, of its adulation. And so the world of dreams, claustrophobic and overheated, has never interested me. I sleep well—like all healthy animals I sleep intensely—and I have always enjoyed sleep, as a physiological pleasure; but dreams have struck me as merely distracting and in my case indecipherable.

Very early in the morning of October third, however, I had been visited by a ghastly dream that could not so easily be brushed aside. It was utterly silent—except for the stray, seemingly accidental, and very faint cries of seabirds: a dream of my own death, my own corpse, laid in state in an enormous coffin that was at the same time a kind of boat, pushing out to sea. Hideous . . . ! At each of the four corners of the darkly gleaming coffin was a bird of death which flapped its wings solemnly; its eyes were agates, cloudy and opaque. The corpse—my corpse—lay with its head resting upon a pillow of white satin, eyes shut, lips firmly closed, an expression of sorrow giving the face a grayish cast: aging it by ten years at least. But the face showed not merely sorrow; it showed, as well, a certain resentment, a look of vexation, almost, as if the death that had come was really a most unpleasant surprise. I stared and stared upon that extraordinary sight. I awaited a flicker of life, a movement of the eyelids—a glance of recognition. Could I really be dead? I, Felix, so young, so handsome, hardly across the threshold of a life that promised great riches of all kinds? Incredible that the adventure might be so abruptly halted: yet the corpse was my own. Those fair brown curls arranged about the waxen, peevish face were my own, "arranged" just as artificially as they would be, no doubt, if a stranger were given license to dress them for the grave.

The horror of gazing upon one's own corpse can well be imagined. I stared, sickened with a sense of outrage as well—a sense that something had gone wrong, some mistake had occurred. But the corpse did not stir. The eyelids did not flutter. There was no sound except that of the ugly, ungainly birds of death, their high-pitched, random cries that blended with the sounds of the sea and the wind, and the vast indifferent spaces of the world itself—the "world" as it exists emptied of the human and of all human values.

I cried aloud, stricken with anguish. It was not simply "my" death I mourned but the fact of death itself—and most egregious of all, the fact that so graceful, so very nearly beautiful a creature as I might be brought to a premature end. I crief aloud and turned away and awoke, heart pounding; and the vision came to a merciful conclusion.

Of course I managed to forget it almost at once. After a few agitated minutes I feel asleep again, and did not wake until seven-thirty. From that point on I was exceptionally busy—settling my accounts with the Savoy Palace, bestowing generous though not lavish tips on its employees (for, having been a hotel employee myself at one time, I can well testify to the demoralizing consequences of unreasonably lavish tips), arranging for my considerable amount of luggage to be transported to the *Cap Arcona*. I did note that the day was overcast and humid. There is something melancholy about white, impassive skies—they are like ceilings that press too closely upon us, from which we cannot escape.

Once at the harbor I was, of course, distracted by the general atmosphere of festivity, busyness, and anticipation. I have always rejoiced in ceremonial occasions—in those occasions, at least, when the more attractive aspects of human nature are called forth. All about me my fellow passengers were saying good-by to relatives and friends. I halfway regretted my decision to leave Lisbon without informing certain acquaintances of mine (of whom I do not choose to speak at the moment); at the same time, being alone in the midst of so much commotion gave me the opportunity to study the others closely. I took notice of the very attractive woman of whom I spoke—took notice first of all of the phaeton from which she alighted; it was elegant, upholstered in dove-gray silk, almost too luxurious for my taste. And the woman herself!—beautifully dressed in scarlet and creamy-white and black. She must have been about thirty-five years old, with a pale, narrow face, very dark eyes and hair; seeing her off were an older couple, no doubt her parents, and an elderly white-haired woman, probably her grandmother. I could not overhear their conversation yet I seemed to sense, or to actually know, that the woman was a widow. (I knew also that we would become acquainted, well before the ship docked in Buenos Aires.) And there were other fascinating passengers boarding the ship: twin boys of about eight, strikingly beautiful, dark-complexioned, almost swarthy, accompanied by an older woman who must have been a governess, and by an enormous whippetlike dog; and a couple in their forties, the gentleman in earnest conversation with his rather plain but agreeable wife—I was certain I had seen him a few days ago in the Museu Sciências Naturaes in the Rua da Prata, studying with great interest a display of fossil remains; and an elderly white-haired gentleman with a fine Spanish face who leaned heavily on the arm of a smartly dressed young man about my age; and . . . and also . . .

But it is pointless to recount these sights and to record the excited impressions I received that morning. For I was fated not to sail on the *Cap Arcona* after all.

As soon as my vision cleared I left my stateroom. I took no luggage with me, not even a handbag; in my panic I thought of nothing except escape. No doubt people stared —I did not see—my eyes were blinded with tears—I could not remain on the ship another moment—I had to get back to land. It did not occur to me at the time that I might be acting unwisely, or crazily, or that I would reget my impulsive behavior once the ship sailed.

The death warning could not be ignored. Its vividness,

its incredible authenticity could not be ignored. And so I fled . . . I fled . . . leaving behind my handsome leather suitcases filled with clothes and costly possessions, and my detailed plans for an itinerary that was to have included South America, North America, the South Seas, Japan, India, Egypt, Constantinople, Greece, Italy, and France. I fled like a frightened child, unashamed, unself-conscious; knowing only the necessity of immediate flight. I did not want to die. I did not want to be transformed into that corpse! And so there was nothing to do but escape, carrying only the money I had in my wallet, and sacrificing forever the small fortune I would have acquired had I been in a position to draw upon the letters of credit awaiting me in banks in the principal ports of call around the world. . . .

What good is the promise of wealth, if one has gazed upon the face of his own corpse? Life calls to life, wishing only to sustain itself. And so I made a rather ungracious exit and thwarted my destiny.

II

I spent the rest of that day and the night in a nondescript hotel near the Tagus, where no one knew me, and then, with the aid of my halting Portuguese, I managed to secure a small but altogether charming, and very clean, apartment along the side of the Praça de São Pedro de Alcántara. The steep street pleased me; I seemed to feel that I might be safer on a hillside. Fate could not so easily approach me.

For some days I was not really aware of the apartment's modest furnishings, or the heavy tolling of a cathedral's bells every quarter hour, or the fine, warm autumnal rain that fell every morning. I was still in a dazed condition. The dream-vision had shaken me as violently as if I had, in my own person, only barely escaped death. (Indeed a death of some sort had taken place in my soul. From that morning on I could no longer think of myself as a young man: not as *young*. My features grew more serious, more somber; I even discovered a few bone-white hairs at my temples. Sleep, which had always been so pleasurable, and so effortless, became now an uncertain venture from which I might wake at any time, disturbed and perspiring. Life itself became an uncertain venture.) Never a religious person, and certainly not superstitious, I nevertheless found myself in the habit of closing my eyes at odd, incidental moments of the day, and offering thanks that my life was saved. I did not know to whom or to what I offered thanks, but the compulsion had to be honored; it was an instinct as direct as that which forced me to leave the doomed ship.

(For the *Cap Arcona* did indeed meet with disaster, five days out. A hurricane struck, most of the passengers and seamen were killed, the battered ship itself sank. A horrible tragedy that shocked all of Europe, but especially Lisbon. I read again and again news articles about the disaster, my eyes welling with tears at the thought of the passengers who had died so senselessly. The woman in the handsome scarlet dress, the elderly white-haired gentleman, the twins with the dog— It had been in my power to save them but I had done nothing: I had been concerned only with my own safety.)

The days became a week, the week two weeks, and then a month. It was now November. Not only because I wished to make my money stretch as far as possible but also because

I wished to disguise my appearance, I bought quite ordinary clothes, a dark woollen overcoat for the winter, cotton shirts in place of linen. I made a conscious effort to minimize my German accent; my speech became less impassioned and flowery and self-consciously poetic; fortunately there had always been a Mediterranean cast to my features. While I did not exactly disappear into the populace, I did not stand out as remarkably foreign.

(I have no intention of going into my personal history—for it belongs not only to the past, but to the past beyond my "death"—it should be remarked, however, that I have always had the ability to adapt myself to my environment. I share the talent of certain species of plants and animals for achieving, almost without design, a protective coloration, a cunning camouflage.)

Daily I walked about the many hills of the city, meditating upon my own survival and the tragedy of the others' deaths; tormenting myself with the thought that perhaps I could have saved them, had I had more faith in the validity of my own premonition; absolving myself, at last, of all guilt—for certainly my warnings would have had no effect. I read newspapers in four or five languages. I ate only twice a day, always at different cafés; I was perhaps unnecessarily careful about patronizing the same café more than once a week. If anyone spoke to me, I was courteous but said little, and of course I never approached anyone, even those occasional tourists—many of them American—who struck me as being particularly attractive. I fled from Germans, I fled from the French. Why? There was no need, surely. There was no need that I could determine. I sensed only a vague, primitive urgency that I keep my distance from everyone—even obvious strangers who would not know me. It seemed to me that someone or something (Death itself?) was hunting me; unless I was very prudent I would not thwart my destiny after all.

And so the weeks passed. Something stirred in my soul: a premonition of the design my life might take. But I did not feel any impatience; the impatience of youth was gone forever. It might be that I would take up another disguise . . . it might be that I would be a poet, or a writer, or an artist . . . or a musician . . . or a man of God, should I come to believe in God. . . . It might be that I would remain quite anonymous, living a placid and eventless life from day to day, utterly alone; or I might marry; or I might suddenly leave Portugal for another part of the world—for Rome, perhaps, or Tangiers. But in the meantime it was imperative that I live quietly, exulting simply in the fact that I had escaped, at least temporarily, the fate that had been intended for me.

It was in early December, I believe, that I saw, in the Cathedral of Santa Maria, my former mistress—her large, stern, melancholy face nearly hidden by a dark veil. She was alone, unaccompanied by either her husband or her charming daughter. My senses leapt; I wanted, of course, to approach her or to signal her; for a delirious instant it was as if no time at all had passed—only a day or two since we had declared our passionate love for each other, and stepped into our first embrace. But of course a great deal of time had passed. And I had not thought of her—had forgotten her entirely. And I was "dead" so far as she knew: the Marquis de Venosta who had been her feverish lover was dead, killed at sea. (The "Marquis de Venosta" was the identity I had had while in Lisbon; so far as I was concerned the young marquis was dead and there was no need to resurrect him now.)

I did not, therefore, approach her; I forced myself to look away from her stern, grieving figure. In the past the interiors of cathedrals had offended me with their ornate altars and statues and rose windows, but today the Cathedral of Santa Maria struck me as beautiful indeed, very nearly mesmerizing. If my northern, Protestant soul had been irritated previously by the South's shameless delight in the senses, and its random mixture of styles—pagan and Christian, Moorish and Greek—today I found the display splendid; I slipped forward onto my knees to pay it homage. My lips moved in prayer—a wordless prayer. As usual I offered thanks to the Presence that had saved my life, and in addition inquired about the purpose of my having been saved—what was I to do with the rest of my life?

By the time the answer suggested itself to me, my former mistress had left the Cathedral without my having been noticed. So unobtrusive was I in my dark, inexpensive clothes, so commonplace was my posture of unquestioning adoration, that had she paused to look at me I very much doubt that she would have recognized me. She had loved me—true enough; and I had felt a fierce, loving passion for her. But such matters come to seem insignificant once one has looked upon Death.

III

It was not until some months later—in late March—that another apparition from the past appeared, this time my father. And it was quite evident that he had come searching for me, his only son; that he had stirred from his place of repose in the Rhine Valley in order to seek me out and lay claim about me. A curious, frightful figure—almost comic in his rumpled, tight-fitting clothes—and heavier than I remembered him—his eyes ringed with fatigue and desperation and a peculiar *spitefulness* that alarmed me almost as much as the mere fact of his appearance in Lisbon.

By this time I had engaged a housekeeper and had settled into an almost bourgeois routine of work. The conviction that I was destined to be an artist, which had come to me in the Cathedral as I knelt with my hands pressed reverently against my eyes, had never left me—had been strengthened, in fact, by subsequent reflection; and not least by the initial and surprising success of my efforts. In order to make a little money (for my savings were running low) I did quick sketches of the kinds of sights tourists find pleasing—the market at its busiest; the baroque and rather ponderous monuments in the Anglican cemetery; small churches, monasteries, ruined cloisters; stone walls; fig trees; cypresses; sailing barges; ferries; Black Horse Square; priests and nuns and peasants and fishermen and fishwives and black-eyed charming urchins. These I managed without much difficulty to sell to tourists whom I was careful never to approach—instead, I allowed them to approach me as I stood in the open air, my easel before me. By now my disguise as an artist was complete: I did not need to take pains to disarray my hair or clothing. I *was* an artist. My little sketches were signed *Felix Krouveia*—a nonsensical polyglot name that served its purpose well enough. To the English and American and French and German tourists I was a Portuguese; to the Portuguese I was a foreigner, possibly French, more likely Italian. Though I often frequented cafés, I was careful to avoid the society of fellow artists—of whom there were a few in Lisbon—but I foresaw the time when my need for sympathetic and stimulating colleagues would outweigh my need for privacy. (In *Le Figaro* I had read a most astonishing manifesto by one Filippo Tommaso Marinetti, a name entirely new to me; with what bold, uncompromising energy did this poet set down the foundation of a revolutionary art!—remarkable, enviable—making my own customary amiability appear, by contrast, to be merely diffidence.)

It was in a small square near Coimbra that my father appeared—the apparition of my father, that is; for the poor man had been dead for years. I wore my dark overcoat and a cloth cap that had lost its shape and I was doing a very rough charcoal sketch of a bewhiskered Portuguese hero—a general on horseback—as a kind of exercise, simply to develop my skill; with one part of my mind I knew, and had known even before reading of the Futurists, that the sort of pleasant, innocuous work I was doing was no more than provisional and pragmatic: my true genius lay elsewhere. It was an unusually mild, sunny day, in mid-week, the square was by no means deserted, yet I picked out at once the awkward, ungainly figure of my father. For some seconds I stared at him, frozen. I could not believe what I saw. (And afterward, in reflecting upon the extraordinary visitation, I came to wonder if perhaps my poor eating habits—I often went without breakfast in my haste to get to work—had not caused me to hallucinate.) That obese, slow-moving man in the expensive, custom-made, but rather rumpled cashmere coat—that pale, solemn, peevish German who stopped passers-by frequently to ask them questions that (so I gathered) they could not comprehend: my poor father, dead by his own hand in my eighteenth year.

My surprise was such that, for several long minutes, I was not even terrified; I experienced a peculiar lightheadedness, an almost euphoric sensation, as if the apparition—or the man himself, for he certainly appeared solid—were proof of what I had suspected since early boyhood, *The world is a fathomless mystery.* My weeks of intensive artistic activity had also taught me to honor the unique, the odd, the surprising, even the perverse—for it is the unexpected that excites the artistic temperament. And here, not one hundred yards from the stately buildings and walls of Coimbra University, making his way along a wide graveled path in my general direction, was my poor father himself.

He had shot himself through the heart, one of the very few successful ventures he had ever undertaken. (Having inherited the firm of Engelbert Krull, makers of *Loreley extra cuvée* champagne, he had seen the business slide into bankruptcy and had been totally unable to alter the course of events.) The end of his life had, therefore, been especially unhappy, and perhaps it was for this reason that he did not resemble the father I knew so much as a vexed, fussing stranger. Of course it was the same man—there was no mistaking his fair, silken, thinning hair and his large morose features and his unconscious habit of stroking his round belly (which he did now though he was wearing an overcoat); I recognized him at once.

But, though he was obviously searching for me, he did not recognize *me.*

After I recovered from my astonishment I continued to

work at the sketch, despite my shaking fingers. The equestrian statue took shape; I then spent time trying to suggest, with soft feathery strokes, the lovely delicacy of the cypress trees in the background. At the same time I was well aware of my father, who stopped a middle-aged gentleman on the path and asked him a faltering question—in Spanish, I believe—and, receiving for reply a half-humorous gesture of total incomprehension, took out an already-soiled white handkerchief and passed it rapidly over his face and beneath his drooping chin. What must it mean, that my father had left his place of repose in order to seek me out . . . ? My inclination was to step forward and identify myself; for after all the man *was* my father, or had been. Yet for some reason I hesitated. I stood close to my easel, frowning, fussing over the sketch, even muttering to myself, for all the world like a self-absorbed, eccentric artist who would not welcome any interruption.

My father wandered near, still dabbling at his face. I saw that he was weary, perplexed, a little resentful. For a dead man he certainly perspired (as he had in life); his complexion was ruddy and flushed and quite damp. "Excuse me, sir," he would call out as someone passed near, and then, in his courteous but strained voice he would make inquiries about his son Felix who had been scheduled to meet with him some months ago but who had disappeared . . . had disappeared, evidently, somewhere in this city. He switched from Spanish to French and then to German, and then to a kind of French-English, always without success. Indeed it was kind of people not to laugh at him. I continued working at the sketch, able to control my trembling by supporting the wrist of my right hand with the fingers of my left; it seemed to me very important that I continue work, that I refuse to be frightened or even distracted by my poor father's presence. Was he a temptation that I betray my new calling by answering to my old name . . . ? That I thoughtlessly align myself with the dead . . . ?

Afterward I came to believe that the situation was more sinister. My father was searching for me in order to draw me into the other world with him; he didn't want to express his love for me but only his authority, his paternal right. A soft, slovenly, lazy, good-hearted man in life, he had become, in death, a malevolent figure—there was something mythically Teutonic about his manner, that perverse blend of cruelty and formality, as he made inquiries about his beloved son who had failed to meet with him on schedule.

By what power he was able to disengage himself from the Land of the Dead I cannot imagine. I do not wish to think of it, or of him—transformed as he is. Our fathers inspire our love only when they are truly fatherly; when they become *other,* greedy creatures from the night-side of the earth, we must stand fast against them, Teutonic, Germanic, an ostensibly life-affirming and life-honoring son of the fertile Rhine Valley, my father was nevertheless a ghoul—and I did right to resist him.

Sighing he passed near me. He paused to watch my fingers; he even bent close to the paper. "Very good, very good," he mumbled. "If only I had time . . . the luxury of time . . . to begin again, to see as you see . . . to *see* at all . . . If only . . . But . . ."

Though I made no encouraging response, he continued,

now in German, speaking irritably of his renegade son who had betrayed him It seems the son had simply disappeared —on the morning of October eighth—had not shown up where he was expected. "He was always a capricious boy," my father complained, "but I would not have thought he would go against *me*."

I nodded brusquely.

And he wandered away, he disappeared into the city; I never saw him again.

IV

Nor did I think of him again.

And, freed of him, of that mysterious "father" whose biological presence weighed heavily upon me, without my quite acknowledging it, I found myself thinking more and more seriously of leaving Lisbon. The kind of art I did was satisfactory on its own level, that of the picturesque representational; but more and more there crept into my paintings, and even into the most innocent of sketches, a certain impatience with the decorative, with familiar surfaces and textures. Was I, as an artist, to remain forever a *servant* of both the gullible public and the visual, three-dimensional world . . . ? I dreamed of locomotives rushing through exquisite gardens, of aeroplanes soaring above the golden crosses of cathedrals. I dreamed of Borghese Park crossed with ugly trenches and, in the background, immense buildings of granite and glass, of a kind never seen before on earth, rising into the smutty sky. Often, while awake, I had only to blink my eyes to see familiar streets and shops and people transformed into writhing patterns of energy, fairly pulsing with the angry joy of existence.

I yearned to visit Paris; and Rome; and perhaps Milan, where I might meet with the Futurist painters Boccioni and Carrà and Balla, whose work excited me more—perversely, perhaps—than that of the Parisians, whose fractured and cubed studies struck me as being oppressively intellectual, and in any case static. Even Picasso, whom I was to admire so fiercely in later life, did not much intrigue me at this time. My soul was stirred by what little I had seen of the Futurists: I was hungry to experience again and again the vertigo of Boccioni's *The City Rises*, to see it in person, to stand before it in homage.

Never had I been so wedded to life, never had my expectations been so various. My former existence faded and fell away; the old Felix seemed to me no more than a foolish child, intoxicated with the lush surfaces of the world and drawn away by them from his deepest self. Or was it the world that had enchanted me, really? I often thought it might have been my father's poor example; or the example of other adults; or a mysterious Presence that sought to guide me along pathways I would not have chosen for myself. (There were, I recalled in astonishment, several incidents in my life that were not characteristic of my life—I mean by that the half-dozen thefts I committed as if in obedience to a force outside my will. Thieving is base, dishonest, stupid, and degrading; I swear that it is not, and has never been, natural to my temperament. On the other hand, my artistic yearnings were never given adequate expression: were never taken seriously enough by myself and others. I was destroying my creative genius by performing in various masquerades, none of which expressed my own nature.)

In later years the conflicts within my soul were to be better understood by me, but at this time—during those bizarre months in Lisbon following my failure to "meet with my father on schedule"—I was often confused and discouraged. Only when I worked did I feel *myself*; only when I plunged into hours of activity, oblivious of my personal being, and of any dangers it might encounter, did I feel I moved with the pulse of life. This was the case despite the fact that my efforts at that time were crudely experimental —studies of raw undifferentiated motion, of blurred and frenzied moments not convincingly transcribed from the mind to the canvas.

And so I prepared to leave Lisbon in the spring. My fears about leaving were greater than I had supposed—like a child who has been terrified by an experience outside the home, I really wished to hide in my apartment on the Praça de São Pedro de Alcántara forever. (And it was out of the question for me to travel by water. Though in later years, airplane travel did not worry me in the slightest, but seemed, in fact, quite pleasant, crossing any body of water wider than a river was impossible.)

It was on a warm afternoon in April on the day before I was scheduled to leave, by train, for Madrid, that the most sinister of all imaginable apparitions appeared to me. For days I had been anticipating something of the sort—my dreams had been turbulent, filled with images of a formal, ritualistic death—my soul oppressed by the invisible weight of a Presence I could not fathom. Yet I never hesitated in my plans to leave. (It was as if I sensed, beyond the chill authority of that Presence, the warm, congenial, combative circle of fellow artists I was to meet in subsequent years.)

I was saying farewell to certain sights I supposed I would never visit again: squares, churches, marketplaces, the view of the Tagus from one of the hills, the Anglican cemetery. I wandered for some time in the cemetery, lost in thought, gazing at the tombstones, the broken columns, urns, crosses and spires and crude winged creatures squatting atop mausoleums. How lovely the April sunshine, after the damp, cold persistent winter! . . . I rejoiced simply in the familiar fact that nature had again revived and that all was well. (I have never been ashamed of sentiment and of expressing it.) Even the inscription on a time-darkened vault did not depress me: *We, the bones who are already here, wait patiently for yours.*

Is it possible to elude death?—if one is conscious of the imminent struggle? Or is it only possible when one has firmly envisioned in his soul a fate, a necessary destiny, that forbids premature extinction?

In the leafy sunshine of that mild spring day Death approached me. I glanced up, saw, stared. I realized that it was no accident, my wandering into the cemetery; it had been *his* design. . . . Death approached me in the figure of a distinguished elderly gentleman of about eighty. He wore a black topcoat and very white, blindingly white, linen; he was leaning heavily upon a gleaming black cane. Something about the austerity of his bearing, despite the difficulty with which he walked, made me think for a moment that he was English. As he drew nearer, however, I saw that he was of my own nationality—though, like me, he exhibited none of the more obvious characteristics of that nationality. His expression was dignified and stern, even severe. He wore glasses; he was clean-shaven and fastidiously groomed; his gunmetal-gray hair lay combed across his impressive skull in several damp strands. He had fixed his gaze upon me from the first and though I had the idea that his vision was badly deteriorated, I could not turn away. My impulse, of course, was to run like a terrified child—to rush past him and make my way frantically back to the street.

"Felix . . . ?"

The word was terrible: I had not heard it pronounced for so long.

"Felix?"

Death's voice was both curt and gentle; unlike my poor father, this gentleman knew exactly who I was, and what he wished of me. He could not be deceived.

"You *are* my Felix, my own child, are you not . . . ?"

"I . . . I don't . . ."

"Why do you shrink away like that?"

"I don't know you. . . ."

"Don't know me? My own Felix, my child, my most cherished son?"

He drew nearer; he leaned heavily on the cane. Through the thick lenses of his glasses he blinked at me, making an effort to smile. I was trembling violently. I wondered if he saw—if he could sense. My terror was his strength; in my malleability had been his authority.

"You must believe me when I say that you are my most cherished son," the gentleman said in his formal, ponderous voice. His narrow lips performed a smile; I could see now that he was very old—his face, though still handsome, was a mass of fine wrinkles. ". . . my most cherished creation. Though you have changed somewhat in the past few months, Felix, though you are no longer quite the . . . the work of art I had imagined . . . nevertheless you are . . . you are the child closest to my heart. You have been careless of your beauty, haven't you? The beauty with which I entrusted you? And your clothes . . ."

"But I don't know you," I said quickly. "My dear sir, you must be mistaken. I don't know you at all."

"Felix, that voice is my own! . . . it is yours, and mine. That marvelous soft voice I heard first in my imaginings, long before *you* drew breath. And your eyes, and your lean, graceful bearing, your beautiful lips, fingers . . . your soul itself."

"I don't know you. I have nothing to do with you," I said.

"Why are you trembling? Why are you frightened of me? You have everything to do with me," the gentleman laughed. "By which I mean—*everything*. You came into existence through my efforts, which should be perfectly obvious. And it should be perfectly obvious, as well, that your existence is bound up irrevocably with my own: that you must obey me in all matters. Therefore . . ."

I was shaking my head like an obstinate child.

"Therefore you had better surrender yourself to me, Felix. This latest disguise of yours is, I admit, a splendid one: the pretense of being an artist . . . an artist, moreover, with a curious bond of sympathy with a handful of barbaric Italians who have been (as you possibly don't know) a mere exercise in public relations. It is quite amazing, and quite unprecedented . . . rather ingenious, in fact. But contrary to nature. Contrary to the nature I have bestowed upon you."

"I reject that nature," I whispered.

"What are you saying?—I can't hear."

"I reject that nature," I said. Again I experienced the sickening desire to push my way past this old man, to rush headlong from the cemetery. We were alone; no one was watching. "I . . . I reject it and you . . . and everything you have planned for me. . . . I reject everything of yours," I said.

"That is not possible," he said curtly.

The effort of speaking with me was obviously tiring; he paused for a moment to regain his breath. Then he repeated in a softer tone, "*That is not possible*."

"My dear sir," I said, trembling now with a mixture of emotions—anger and frustration as well as fear—"I insist upon the fact that you and I are strangers. We share a common language, perhaps, and a common ancestry; but that hardly makes us kin, and it hardly gives you any authority over me. Moreover . . . In addition . . ."

"My dear child, you are beginning to sound exactly like my Felix! Sweet and histrionic and bold, with all the hyperbole of a favored son, not restrained by timidity from making the most stilted of speeches. . . . You have the self-consciousness of beauty, Felix; why do you want to betray your destiny, which is bound up with my own, and which will protect you from the vicissitudes of the world? Even if it were possible for you to have your own life, apart from my gentle nurturing, *why* should you wish it? You will grow old and decrepit, as I am now. You will never succeed in being more than a third-rate painter—of that I am certain. In fact I very much doubt whether anyone living in this era of ruins will be more than third-rate—"

"You don't understand them," I said. "You don't understand us."

"Felix, did not your Creator smile upon you, at your birth? Were you not destined for—for pleasures of the flesh, for boyish raptures—for adventures of the kind that I, burdened by the weight of my own genius, had to forgo? . . . What do you mean by *us*, who is this *us*? You belong to no one else; you know very well that you're mine."

"I know very well that I am not yours: I am my own person."

He adjusted his glasses and peered at me, smiling faintly. I was beginning to feel the injustice of it—the colossal injustice. That this elderly man should wish to claim the life he had created, that he should wish to draw *me* back into his head: what right had he? Simply because I had grown into an extraordinarly attractive young man and, for a while, mesmerized by *his* fantasies, had led a stupid, vain, frivolous life, trying on one costume after another like a monkey, performing in order to dazzle ignorant audiences—simply because I loved women solely in order to satisfy *his* base lusts, and his even baser desire to imagine himself as a successful lover: what right had he to appear now, on the eve of my departure, and make his claim? Granted he was an elderly man; granted, also, that he had labored to bring me to life, and might not be blamed, perhaps, for wishing to bring me to death—wishing me to accompany him to the Land of the Dead: I had achieved my own soul, nevertheless, during those months when I was freed of his authority. I was no longer his Felix—I was no longer that person at all. I belonged solely to myself.

As if sensing my thoughts, he began to speak. His manner was artificially genial; his fatherly smile did not call forth a smile from me. He spoke of the travails of artistic creation . . . of the artist's suffering, which is not unrelated to the suffering of a woman in childbirth. He spoke of the paradox that lies in the fact that the artist must create living beings, beings fully capable of drawing breath, and yet he must control them always; he *must* not allow them to escape the structure his imagination has created to sustain them. He spoke of the artist's altogether human desire to unleash, in his creations, those characteristics he does not possess, or does not dare acknowledge. . . .

"I have nothing to do with that," I cried. "I don't exist merely to fulfill *you*—to act out fantasies of yours you all but admit are infantile and unworthy of serious consideration—"

He stared at me, perplexed. It was obvious that my stubborn opposition was tiring him, yet he seemed unaware of his own quickened breath. Instead he stepped closer, now bent forward. I had to resist the desire to strike him. (What an imp Death is, taking on those forms that most intimidate us—stifling the natural impulse to lash out against what threatens to overwhelm and destroy!) Again he spoke: sadly, gravely. He spoke of the artist's necessary cruelty in bringing his creations to a finish, no matter how they might beg for life, no matter how boldly and prettily they might demand their freedom. It is an imitation of nature, no more and no less, and cannot be denied. The artist, far from transcending the sprawling drama of nature, is in fact a cunning servant of nature, and wishes merely to impose *his* design upon the larger, untidy design—and so the artist's authority must be obeyed, the life he brings into being must acquiesce to the death he ordains. It is unthinkable that a creature might rise up against his creator and demand his own autonomy. . . .

"I have nothing to do with this," I interrupted. I had taken a few steps forward; it was my intention to brush past him. "Even if I do acknowledge that there is a bond of some kind between us, a feeble sort of connection—frail as a cobweb; even if I do acknowledge that I am, of course, most grateful for your—for your perhaps involuntary generosity in giving me life: nevertheless I have forgotten most of my past; what I do remember I reject impatiently and irritably, having judged it to be a not-very-worthy prelude to my real life. And now if you will excuse me—"

"Felix, it simply isn't possible— What you are attempting is not possible—"

"You are going to die! You are an old man, and you are going to die! Can't you see that you want nothing more than to drag me with you?—there's nothing noble about it, nothing inevitable! It's selfishness! Vanity! I refuse—"

"Felix—"

He reached for me and, without thinking, I shoved him away. I shouted into his astonished face. "No! Never! I am not yours! *Not yours!*" Blinded with anger I shoved him again—I was only dimly aware of his having staggered backward. "I refuse to go with you—*I am not yours.*"

"But my boy, my dear— My dear one—"

"No."

He stared at me and a terrible, stricken look manifested

itself slowly in his eyes and in the slack flesh about his mouth. It was a look of recognition, of realization: I understood afterward that it was the old man's acknowledgment of my being, my ferocious and indomitable life. And that acknowledgment carried with it the necessity of his own death.

He collapsed in the cemetery but I ran away. Death blossomed in him, a void opening in his brain; but I ran, I escaped, I left Portugal that very evening.

V

Years passed and no one pursued me. No apparitions approached me, no "fate" claimed me; yet I was cautious still. (Of my life at the present time I will not speak—it is too complicated, too improbable; in many ways it is more astonishing than the story of my Portuguese adventure.) Someday, no doubt, I *shall* die: but I and I alone will determine when. My work draws me forward, teasing me with its enigmatic complexity. I cannot quite understand it. And so I am drawn forward, year after year, decade after decade. . . . I seem to know that so long as I am caught up in my work, I will not die; I am immortal.

The world is emptied now of all apparitions. No Presence directs me away from my truest self. Moment by moment, heartbeat by heartbeat, I live out the drama of my own life. Is this another masquerade? I grasp my brush, I plunge forward. Where I once questioned everything I now question nothing. I am supremely myself: the only immortality allotted to mankind.

STANISLAW LEM

THE MASK

In the beginning there was darkness and cold flame and lingering thunder, and, in long strings of sparks, char-black hooks, segmented hooks, which passed me on, and creeping metal snakes that touched the thing that was me with their snoutlike flattened heads, and each such touch brought on a lightning tremor, sharp, almost pleasurable.

From behind round windows eyes watched me, immeasurably deep eyes, unmoving, and they receded, but perhaps it was I who was moving on, entering the next circle of observation, which inspired lethargy, respect and dread. This journey of mine on my back lasted an indeterminate time, and as it progressed the it that was I increased and came to know itself, discovering its own limits, and I cannot say just when I was able to grasp its own form fully, to take cognizance of every place where I left off. There the world began, thundering, flaming, dark, and then the motion ceased and the delicate flitting of articulated limbs, which handed the me to me, lifted lightly up, relinquished that me to pincer hands, offered it to flat mouths in a rim of sparks, disappeared, and the it that was myself lay still inert, though capable now of its own motion yet in full awareness that my time had not come, and in this numb incline—for I, it, rested then on a slanting plane—the final flow of current, breathless last rites, a quivering kiss tautened the me and that was the signal to spring up and crawl into the round opening without light, and needing no urging now I touched the cold, smooth, concave plates, to rest on them with stone relief. But perhaps all that was a dream.

Of waking I know nothing. I remember incomprehensible rustlings and a cool dimness and myself inside, the world opened up before it in a panorama of glitter, broken into colors, and I remember also how much wonder there was in my movement when it crossed the threshold. Strong light beat from above on the colored confusion of vertical trunks, I saw their globes, which turned in its direction tiny buttons bright with water, the general murmur died down and in the ensuing silence the thing that was myself took yet another step.

And then, with a sound not heard but sensed, a tenuous string snapped within me and I, a she now, felt the rush of gender so violent that her head spun and I shut my eyes. And as I stood thus, with eyes closed, words came to me from every side, for along with gender she had received language. I opened my eyes and smiled, and moved forward, and her dresses moved with me, I walked with dignity, crinoline all around, not knowing where I was going, but continuing on, for this was the court ball, and the recollection of her own mistake a moment before, when I had taken the heads for globes and the eyes for wet buttons, amused me like a silly girlish blunder, therefore I grinned, but this grin was directed only at myself. My hearing reached far, sharpened, so in it I distinguished the murmur of courtly recognition, the concealed sighs of the gentlemen, the envious breathing of the ladies, and pray who is that young woman, Count? And I walked through an enormous hall, beneath crystal spiders, from their ceiling webs dropped petals of roses, I looked at myself in the disfavor creeping out over the painted faces of dowagers, and in the leering eyes of swarthy lords.

Behind the windows from the vaulted ceiling to the parquet gaped the night, pots were burning in the park, and in an alcove between two windows, at the foot of a marble statue, stood a man shorter than the rest, surrounded by a wreath of courtiers clad in stripes of black and bile, who seemed to press towards him, yet they never overstepped the empty circle, and this single one did not even look in my direction when I approached. Passing him, I stopped, and though he was not looking at all in my direction, with the very tips of my fingers I gathered up my crinoline, dropping my eyes, as if I wished to curtsy low to him, but I only gazed at my own hands, slender and white, I did not know however why this whiteness, when it shone against the sky blue of the crinoline, there was something terrifying in it. But he, that short lord or peer, surrounded by courtiers, and behind whom stood a pale knight in half-armor, with a bare blond head and holding in his hand a dagger small as a toy, he did not deign to look upon me, saying something in a low, boredom-muffled voice to himself, for to no one else. And I, not making my curtsy, but only looking at him a brief moment very fiercely, to remember his face, darkly aslant at the mouth, for its corner was turned up in a weary grimace by a small white scar, and riveting my eyes on that mouth, I turned on my heel, the crinoline rustled and I moved past. Only then did he look at me and I felt perfectly that fleeting, cold glance, such a narrow glance, as though he had an unseen rifle at his cheek and aiming for my neck, right between the rolls of golden curls, and this was the second beginning. I didn't want to turn back, but I did turn back and lowered myself in a deep, a very deep curtsy, lifting the crinoline with both hands, as if to sink through its stiffness to the sheen of the floor, for he was the King. Then I withdrew slowly, wondering how it was I knew this so well and with such certainty, and also strongly tempted to do something inappropriate, for if I could not know and yet did know, in a way inexorable and categorical, then all of this was a dream, and what could it hurt in a dream—to pull someone's nose? I grew a little frightened, for I was not able to do this, as if I had inside me some invisible barrier. Thus I wavered, walking unaware, between the convictions of reality and dream, and meanwhile knowledge flowed into me, somewhat like waves flowing up onto a beach, and each wave left behind new information, ranks and titles as if trimmed with lace; halfway through the hall, underneath a blazing candelabrum that hovered like a ship on fire, I already knew the names of all the ladies, whose wear and tear was smoothed away by careful art.

I knew so very much now, like one fully roused out of a

nightmare, yet with the memory of it still lingering, and that which remained inaccessible to me appeared in my mind as two dark shadows—my past and my present, for I was as yet in complete ignorance about myself. Whereas I was experiencing, in its totality, my nakedness, the breasts, belly, thighs, neck, shoulders, the unseen feet, concealed by costly clothing, I touched the topaz in gold that pulsed like a glowworm between my breasts, I could feel also the expression on my face, betraying absolutely nothing, a look which must have perplexed, for anyone who noticed me received the impression of a smile, yet if he searched my mouth more closely, my eyes, my brows, he would see that there was not a trace of amusement there, not even merely polite amusement, so he would gaze once more into my eyes, but they were completely tranquil, he would go to the cheeks, look for the smile in my chin, but I had no frivolous dimples, my cheeks were smooth and white, and the chin intent, quiet, sober, of no less perfection than the neck, which revealed not a thing. Then the gazer would be troubled, wondering why on earth he had imagined I was smiling, and in the bewilderment caused by his doubts and my beauty he would step back into the crowd, or render me a deep bow, in order that he might hide himself from me beneath that gesture.

But there were two things I still did not know, though I realized, if obscurely still, that they were the most important. I did not understand why the King had ignored me as I passed, why he had refused to look me in the eye when he neither feared my loveliness nor desired it, indeed I felt that I was truly valuable to him, but in some inexplicable way, as if he had no use for me myself, as if I were to him someone outside this glittering hall, someone not made for dancing across the mirrorlike, waxed parquet arranged in many-colored inlays between the wrought-bronze coats of arms above the lintels; yet when I swept by, not a thought surfaced in him in which I could divine the royal will, and even when he had sent after me that glance, fleeting and casual, though sighted along an invisible barrel, I understood that it was not at me that he had leveled his pale eye, an eye which ought to have been kept behind dark glasses, for its look feigned nothing, unlike the well-bred face, and stuck in the milling elegance like dirty water left at the bottom of a washbowl. No, his eyes were something long ago discarded, something requiring concealment, not enduring the light of day.

But what could he want of me, what? I was not able to reflect on this however, for another thing claimed my attention. I knew everyone here, but no one knew me. Except possibly he, he alone: the King. At my fingertips I now had knowledge of myself as well, my feelings grew strange as I slowed my pace, three-quarters of the hall already crossed, and in the midst of the multicolored crowd, faces gone numb, their side whiskers silvery with hoarfrost, and also faces blood-swollen and perspiring under clotted powder, in the midst of ribbons and medals and braided tassels there opened up a corridor, that I might walk like some queen down that path parted through humanity, escorted by watching eyes—but to where was I walking thus?

To whom.

And who was I? Thought followed thought with fluent skill, I grasped in an instant the particular dissonance between my state and that of this so distinguished throng, for each of them had a history, a family, decorations of one kind or another, the same nobility won from intrigues, betrayals, and each paraded his inflated bladder of sordid pride, dragged after him his personal past like the long, raised dust that trails a desert wagon, turn for turn, whereas I had come from such a great distance it was as if I had not one past, but a multitude of pasts, for my destiny could be made understandable to those here only by piecemeal translation into their local customs, into this familiar yet foreign tongue; therefore I could only approximate myself to their comprehension, and with each chosen designation would become for them a different person. And for myself as well? No . . . and yet, nearly so, I possessed no knowledge beyond that which had rushed into me at the entrance of the hall, like water when it surges up and floods a barren waste, bursting through hitherto solid dikes, and beyond that knowledge I reasoned logically, was it possible to be many things at once? To derive from a plurality of abandoned pasts? My logic, extracted from the locoweed of memory, told me this was not possible, that I must have some single past, and if I was the daughter of Count Tlenix, the Duenna Zoroennay, the young Virginia, orphaned in the overseas kingdom of the Langodots by the Valandian clan, if I could not separate the fiction from the truth, then was I not dreaming after all? But now the orchestra began to play somewhere and the ball careened like an avalanche of stones—how could one make oneself believe in a reality more real, in an awakening from this awakening?

I walked now in unpleasant confusion, watching my every step, for the dizziness had returned, which I named vertigo. But I did not give up my regal stride, not one whit, though the effort was tremendous, tremendous yet unseen, and given strength precisely for being unseen, until I felt help come from afar, it was the eyes of a man, he was seated in the low embrasure of a half-open window, its brocade curtain flung whimsically over his shoulder like a scarf and woven in red-grizzled lions, lions with crowns, frightfully old, holding orbs and scepters in their paws, the orbs like poisoned apples, apples from the Garden of Eden. This man, decked in lions, dressed in black, richly, and yet with a natural sort of carelessness which had nothing in common with artificial, lordly disarray, this stranger, no dandy or fop, not a courtier or sycophant, but not old either, looked at me from his seclusion in the general uproar—just as utterly alone as I. And all around were those who lit cigarillos with rolled-up bank notes in front of the eyes of their tarot partners, and threw gold ducats on green cloth, as if they were tossing nutmeg apples to swans in a pond, those for whom no action could be stupid or dishonorable, for the illustriousness of their persons ennobled everything they did. The man was altogether out of place in this hall, and the seemingly unintentional deference he paid to the stiff brocade in royal lions, permitting it to drape across his shoulder and bathe his face with the reflection of its imperial purple, that deference had the aspect of the most subtle mockery. No longer young, his entire youth was alive in his dark eyes, unevenly squinting, and he listened or perhaps was not listening to his interlocutor, a small, stout baldhead with the air of an overeaten, docile dog. When the seated one stood up, the curtain slid from his arm like false, cast-off trumpery, and our eyes met forcefully, but mine darted from his face in flight. I swear it. Still that face remained deep in my vision, as if I had gone suddenly blind, and my hearing dimmed, so that instead of the orchestra I heard—for a moment—only my own pulse. But I could be wrong.

The face, I assure you, was quite ordinary. Indeed its features had that fixed asymmetry of handsome homeliness so characteristic of intelligence, but he must have grown weary of his own bright mind, as too penetrating and also somewhat self-destructive, no doubt he ate away at himself nights, it was evident this was a burden on him, and that there were moments in which he would have been glad to rid himself of that intelligence, like a crippling thing, not a privilege or gift, for continual thought must have tormented him, particularly when he was by himself, and that for him was a frequent occurrence—everywhere, therefore here also. And his body, underneath the fine clothing, fashionably cut yet not clinging, as though he had cautioned and restrained the tailor, compelled me to think of his nakedness.

Rather pathetic it must have been, that nakedness, not magnificently male, athletic, muscular, sliding into itself in a snake's nest of swellings, knots, thick cords of sinews, to whet the appetite of old women still unresigned, still mad with the hope of mating. But only his head had this masculine beauty, with the curve of genius in his mouth, with the angry impatience of the brows, between the brows in a crease dividing both like a slash, and the sense of his own ridiculousness in that powerful, oily-shiny nose. Oh, this was not a good-looking man, nor in fact was even his ugliness seductive, he was merely different, and if I hadn't gone numb inside when our eyes collided, I certainly could have walked away.

True, had I done this, had I succeeded in escaping that zone of attraction, the merciful King with a twitch of his signet ring, with the corners of his faded eyes, pupils like pins, would have attended to me soon enough, and I would have gone back. But at that time and place I could hardly have known this, I did not realize that what passed then for a chance meeting of glances, that is, the brief intercrossing of the black holes in the irises of two beings, for they are—after all—holes, tiny holes in round organs that slither nimbly in openings of the skull—I did not realize that this, precisely this, was foreordained, for how could I have known?

I was about to move on when he rose and, brushing from his sleeve the hanging fringe of the brocade, as if to indicate the comedy was over, came towards me. Two steps and he stopped, now overtaken by the awareness of how impertinent was that unequivocal action, how very scatterbrained it would appear, to go walking after an unknown beauty like some gaping idiot following a band, so he stood, and then I closed one hand and with the other let slip from my wrist the little loop of my fan. For it to fall. So he immediately . . .

We looked at each other, now up close, over the mother-of-pearl handle of the fan. A glorious and dreadful moment, a mortal stab of cold caught me in the throat, transfixing speech, therefore feeling that I would not bring forth my voice, only a croak, I nodded to him—and that gesture came out almost exactly as the one before, when I did not complete my bow to the King who wasn't looking.

He did not return the nod, being much too startled and amazed by what was taking place within him, for he had not expected this of himself. I know, because he told me later, but had he not, even so I would have known.

He wanted to say something, wanted not to cut the figure of the idiot he most certainly was at that moment, and I knew this.

"Madam," he said, clearing his throat like a hog. "Your fan . . ."

By now I had him once more in hand. And myself.

"Sir," I said, and my voice in timbre was a trifle husky, altered, but he could think it was my normal voice, indeed he had never heard it until now, "must I drop it again?"

And I smiled, oh, but not enticingly, seductively, not brightly. I smiled only because I felt that I was blushing. The blush did not belong to me, it spread on my cheeks, claimed my face, pinkened my ear lobes, which I could feel perfectly, yet I was not embarrassed, nor excited, nor did I marvel at this unfamiliar man, only one of many after all, lost among the courtiers—I'll say more: I had nothing whatever to do with that blush, it came from the same source as the knowledge that had entered me at the threshold of the hall, at my first step upon the mirror floor—the blush seemed part of the court etiquette, of that which was required, like the fan, the crinoline, the topazes and coiffures. So, to render the blush insignificant, to counteract it, to stave off any false conclusions, I smiled—not to him, but at him, exploiting the boundary between mirth and scorn, and he then broke into a quiet laugh, a voiceless laugh, as if directed inward, it was similar to the laughter of a child that knows it is absolutely forbidden to laugh and for that very reason cannot control itself. Through this he grew instantly younger.

"If you would but give me a moment," he said, suddenly serious, as if sobered by a new thought, "I might be able to find a reply worthy of your words, that is, something highly clever. But as a rule good ideas come to me only on the stairs."

"Are you so poor then in invention?" I asked, exerting my will in the direction of my face and ears, for this persistent blush had begun to anger me, it constituted an invasion of my freedom, being part—I realized—of that same purpose with which the King had consigned me to my fate.

"Possibly I ought to add, 'Is there no help for this?' And you would answer no, not in the face of a beauty whose perfection seems to confirm the existence of the Absolute. Then two beats of the orchestra, and we both become dignified and with great finesse put the conversation back on a more ordinary courtly footing. However, as you appear to be somewhat ill-at-ease on that ground, perhaps it would be best if we do not engage in repartee . . ."

He truly feared me now, hearing these words—and was truly at a loss for what to say. Such solemnity filled his eyes, it was as if we were standing in a storm, between church and forest—or where there was, finally, nothing.

"Who are you?" he asked stiffly. No trace of triviality in him now, no pretense, he was only afraid of me. I was not afraid of him at all, not in the least, though in truth I should have been alarmed, for I could feel his face, with its porous skin, the unruly, bristling brows, the large curves of his ears, all linking up inside me with my hitherto hidden expectation, as though I had been carrying within myself his undeveloped negative and he had just now filled it in. Yet even if he were my sentence, I had no fear of him.

Neither of myself nor of him, but I shuddered from the internal, motionless force of that connection—shuddered not as a person, but as a clock, when with its assembled hands it moves to strike the hour—though still silent. No one could observe that shudder.

"I shall tell you by and by," I answered very calmly. I smiled, a light, faint smile, the kind one gives to cheer the sick and feeble, and opened up my fan.

"I would have a glass of wine. And you?"

He nodded, trying to pull onto himself the skin of this style, so foreign to him, poorly fitting, cumbersome, and from that place in the hall we walked along the parquet, which ran with pearly streams of wax that fell in drops from the chandelier, through the smoke of the candles, shoulder to shoulder, there where by a wall pearl-white servants were pouring drinks into goblets.

I did not tell him that night who I was, not wishing to lie to him and not knowing the truth myself. Truth cannot contradict itself, and I was a duenna, a countess and an orphan, all these genealogies revolved within me, each one could take on substance if I acknowledged it, I understood now that the truth would be determined by my choice and whim, that whichever I declared, the images unmentioned would be blown away, but I remained irresolute among these possibilities, for in them seemed to lurk some subterfuge of memory—could I have been just another unhinged amnesiac, who had escaped from the care of her duly worried relatives? While talking with him, I thought that if I were a madwoman, then everything would end well. From insanity, as from a dream, one could free oneself —in both cases there was hope.

When in the late hours—and he never left my side—we passed by His Majesty for a moment, before he was pleased to retire to his chambers, I felt that the ruler did not even bother to look in our direction, and this was a terrible discovery. For he did not make sure of my behavior at the side of Arrhodes—*that* was apparently unnecessary—as though he knew beyond all doubt that he could trust me completely, the way one trusts—in full—dispatched assassins, who strive as long as they have breath, for their fate lies in the hands of the dispatcher. The King's indifference ought to have, instead, wiped away my suspicions; if he did not look in my direction, then I meant nothing to him, nevertheless my insistent sense of persecution tipped the scales in favor of insanity. So it was as a madwoman of angelic beauty that I laughed, drinking to Arrhodes, whom the King despised as no other, though he had sworn to his dying mother that if harm befell that wise man it would be of his own choosing. I do not know if someone told me this while dancing or whether I learned it for myself, for the night was long and clamorous, the huge crowd constantly separated us, yet we kept finding each other by accident, almost as if everyone there were party to the same conspiracy—an obvious illusion, we could hardly have been surrounded by a host of mechanically dancing mannequins. I spoke with old men, with young women envious of my beauty, discerning innumerable shades of stupidity, both good-natured and malicious, I cut and pierced those useless dodderers and those pouting misses with such ease that I grew sorry for them. I was cleverness itself, keen and full of witticisms, my eyes took on fire from the dazzling quickness of my words—in my mounting anxiety I would have gladly played a featherbrain to save Arrhodes, but this alone I could not manage. My versatility did not extend that far, alas. Was then my intelligence (and intelligence signified integrity) subject to some lie? I devoted myself to such reflections in the dance, entering the turns of the minuet, while Arrhodes, who didn't dance, watched me from afar, black and slender against the purple brocade in crowned lions. The King left, and not long afterwards we parted, I did not allow him to say anything, to ask anything, he tried and paled, hearing me repeat, first with the lips, "No," then only with the folded fan. I went out, not having the least idea of where I lived, whence I had arrived, whither I would turn my eyes, I only knew that these things did not rest with me, I made efforts, but they were futile—how shall I explain it? Everyone knows it is impossible to turn the eyeball around, such that the pupil can peer inside the skull.

I allowed him to escort me to the palace gate, the castle park beyond the circle of continually burning pots of tar was as if hewn from coal, in the cold air distant, inhuman laughter, a pearly imitation from the fountains of the masters of the South—or else it was the talking statues like milky ghosts suspended above the flower beds, the royal nightingales sang also, though no one listened, near the hothouse one of them stood out against the disk of the moon, large and dark on its branch—a perfect pose! Gravel crunched beneath our steps, and the gilded spikes of the railing jutted up through wet foliage.

Ill-tempered and eager, he grabbed my hand, which I did not pull away immediately, the white straps on the jackets of His Majesty's grenadiers flashed, someone called my carriage, horses beat their hoofs, the door of a coach gleamed under violet lanterns, a step dropped open. This could not be a dream.

"When and where?" he asked.

"Better to say: never and nowhere," I said, speaking my simple truth, and added quickly, helplessly: "I do not toy with you, my fine philosopher, look within and you will see that I advise you well."

But what I wished to add I could not utter. I was able to think anything, strange as it may seem, yet in no way find my voice, I could not reach those words. A catch in my throat, a muteness, like a key turned in a lock, as if a bolt had clicked shut between us.

"Too late," he said softly, with his head lowered. "Truly too late."

"The royal gardens are open from the morning till the midday bugle call," I said, my foot on the step. "There is a pond there, with swans, and near it a rotten oak. At exactly noon tomorrow or in the hollow of the tree you will find your answer. And now I wish that by some inconceivable miracle you could forget we ever met. If I knew how, I would pray for that."

Most unsuitable words, banal in these surroundings, but there was now no way for me to break free of this deadly banality, I realized that as the carriage began to move, he could—after all—interpret what I had said to mean that I feared the emotions he aroused in me. That was true enough: I did fear the emotions he aroused in me, however it had nothing to do with love, I had only said what I *had been able* to say, as when in the darkness, in a swamp, one extends a careful foot, lest the next step plunge one into deep water. So did I feel my way in words, testing with my breath what I would be able—and what I would not be permitted—to say.

But he could not know this. We parted breathlessly, in dismay, in a panic similar to passion, for thus had begun our undoing. But I, willowy and sweet, girl-like, understood more clearly that I was his fate, fate in that terrible sense of unavoidable doom.

The body of the carriage was empty—I looked for the sash that would be sewn to the sleeve of the coachman, but it was not there. The windows also were missing—black glass, perhaps? The darkness of the interior was complete, as if partaking not of night, but of nonexistence itself. This was no absence of light, it was a void. I ran my hands along the curved walls upholstered in plush, but found neither window frame nor handle, found nothing but those soft, padded surfaces before me and above me, the ceiling remarkably low, as though I had been shut up not inside a carriage, but in a quivering, slanted container; no sound of hoofs reached me, nor the usual clatter of wheels in motion. Blackness, silence, nothing. Then I turned to myself, for that self was to me a darker and more ominous enigma than anything that had taken place so far. My memory was intact. I think it had to be that way, that it would have been impossible to arrange things otherwise, therefore I recollected my first awakening, as yet deprived of gender, so completely alien it was like remembering a dream of an evil metamorphosis. I recollected waking at the door of the palace hall, already in this present reality, I could even recall the faint creak with which those carved portals opened, and the mask of the servant's face, the servant who in his zeal to serve resembled a puppet filled with civilities—a living corpse of wax. All of this was a coherent whole now in my mind, and still I could reach back, there where I did not yet know what portals were, what a ball was and what —this thing that was I was. And in particular I remembered —and it made me shiver, it was so perversely mysterious— that my first thoughts, already half gathered into words, I had formulated in an impersonal, neuter mode. The it that was myself had stood, the I that was it had seen, I, it had entered—these were the forms used by me before the blaze of the hall, streaming through the open door, had struck my pupils and unlocked—it must have been the blaze, for what else?—and opened within me, I say, the bolts and latches from behind which there burst into my being, with the painful suddenness of a visitation, the humanity of words, courtly movements, the charm of the fair sex, and also the memory of faces, among which the face of that man was foremost—and not the royal grimace—and though no one would ever be able to explain this to me, I knew with unswerving certainty that I had stopped before the King by mistake—it had been an error, a confusion between what was destined for me and the instrument of that destiny. An error—but what sort of fate was it, that could make mistakes? No genuine fate. Then might I still save myself?

And now in this perfect isolation, which did not frighten me, on the contrary, I found it convenient, for in it I could think, could concentrate, when I made the wish to know myself, searching among my memories, now so accessible and neatly arranged that I had them all in easy reach like long-familiar furniture in an old room, and when I put forth questions, I saw everything that had transpired that night—but it was sharp and clear only as far as the threshold of the court hall. Before that—yes, exactly. Where was I—was it!?—before that? Where did I come from? The reassuring, simplest thought said that I was not quite well, that I was recovering from an illness, like someone returning from an exotic voyage filled with the most incredible adventures, that, as a highly refined maiden, much given to books and romances, reveries and strange whims, a young thing too delicate for this savage world, I had suffered visions, perhaps in a hysterical delirium I imagined that passage through metallic hells, no doubt while on a bed with a canopy, on sheets trimmed with lace, yes, brain fever would even be somewhat becoming in the light of the candle illuminating the chamber enough so that, upon waking, I would not take fright again, and in the figures leaning over me recognize at once my loving guardians. What a pleasant lie! I had had hallucinations, had I not? And they, sinking into the clear stream of my single memory, had split it in two. A split memory . . . ? Because with that question I heard within me a chorus of answers, ready, waiting: Duenna, Tlenix, Angelita. Now what was this? I had all these phrases prepared, they were given to me and with each came corresponding images; if only there had been a single chain of them! But they coexisted the way the spreading roots of a tree coexist, so then I, by necessity one, by nature unique, could I once have been a plurality of branchings, which then merged in me as rivulets merge into the current of a river? But such a thing was impossible, I told myself. Impossible. I was certain of that. And I beheld my life to the present divided thus: until the threshold of the palace hall it seemed to be made up of different threads, while from the threshold on it was already one. Scenes from the first part of my life ran parallel and belied each other. The Duenna: a tower, dark granite boulders, a drawbridge, shouts in the night, blood on a copper dish, knights with the aspect of butchers, the rusted ax heads of halberds and my pale little face in the oval, half-blind looking glass between the frame of the window, misty, filmy, and the carven headboard—was that where I came from?

But as Angelita I had been raised in the sweltering heat of the South and, looking back in that direction, I saw white walls with their chalky backs to the sun, withered palms, wild dogs with scraggly fur by those palms, releasing frothy urine on the scaled roots, and baskets full of dates, dried up and with a sticky sweetness, and physicians in green robes, and steps, stone steps descending to the bay of the town, all the walls turned away from the heat, bunches of grapes strewn in piles, yellowing into raisins, resembling heaps of dung, and again my face in the water, not in the looking glass, and the water pouring from a silver jug—silver but dark with age. I even remembered how I used to carry that jug and how the water, moving heavily inside it, would pull at my hand.

And what of my neuter self and its journey on its back, and the kisses planted on my hands and feet, and forehead, by the flitting serpents of metal? That horror had faded now completely and even with the greatest effort I could scarcely recall it, exactly like a bad dream one cannot put into words. No, it was impossible for me to have experienced, either all at once or in succession, lives so opposed to one another! What then was certain? I was beautiful.

As much despair as triumph had welled up within me when I saw myself reflected in his face as in a living mirror, for so absolute was the perfection of my features that no matter what madness I were to commit, whether I howled with the foam of frenzy at my mouth, or gnawed red meat, the beauty would not leave my face—but why did I think "my face," and not simply "me"? Was I a person at odds with, out of harmony with, her own face and body? A sorceress ready to cast spells, a Medea? To me that was utter nonsense, ridiculous. And even the fact that my mind worked like a well-worn blade in the hand of a rogue knight shorn of his nobility, that I cut asunder every subject without trying, this self-determined thinking of mine seemed in its correctness just a bit too cold, unduly calm, for fear remained beyond it—like a thing transcendent, omnipresent, yet separate—therefore my own thoughts too I held in suspicion. But if I could trust neither my face nor my mind, against what precisely could I harbor fear and suspicion, when outside of the soul and the body one had nothing? This was puzzling.

The scattered roots of my various pasts told me nothing of importance, inspection led to a sifting of bright-colored images, now as the Duenna of the North, now Angelita of the broiling sun, now Mignonne, I was each time another person with another name, station, descent, from under another sky, nothing had precedence here—the landscape of the South kept returning to my vision as if strained by a surfeit of sweetness and contrast, a color infused with azures too ostentatious, and if not for those mangy dogs, and the half-blind children with suppurating eyes and swollen bellies, silently expiring on the bony knees of their veiled mothers, I would have found that palmy coast overly facile, as slick as a lie. And the North of the Duenna, with her snow-capped towers, a sky churning leaden, the winters with tortuous shapes of snow invented by the wind, shapes which crept into the moat along the battlements and buttresses, emerged from the castle crenels with their white tongues across the stone, and the chains of the drawbridge as if in yellow tears, but it was only the rust coloring the icicles on the links, while in summer the water of the moat was covered by a sheepskin coat of mold: and all this, how well I remembered it!

But then my third existence; gardens, vast, cool, trimmed, gardeners with clippers, packs of greyhounds and the Great Dane of the harlequin that lay on the steps of the throne—a world-weary sculpture possessing the unerring grace of lethargy stirred only by breathing ribs—and in its yellowish, indifferent eyes gleamed, one might have thought, the reduced figures of the catabanks and grudgies. And these words, grudgies, catabanks, I did not know now what they meant, but surely I knew once, and when I delved thus into that past so well remembered, remembered to the taste of chewed blades of grass, I felt that I should not go back to the bootees I outgrew, nor to my first long dress embroidered all in silver, as if even the child that I had been concealed treason. Therefore I summoned a memory inhumanly cruel—that of the lifeless journey face-up, of the numbing kisses of metal which, touching my naked body, produced a clanking sound, as if my nakedness had been a voiceless bell, a bell unable to ring out because it had not yet its heart, its tongue. Yes, it was to this implausibility that I appealed, no longer surprised that that raving nightmare held on in me with such tenacity, for it must have been a nightmare. To assure myself of this certainty I took my fingers and with the very tips of them touched my soft forearms, my breasts; an intrusion, without a doubt, and I submitted to it trembling, as if with my head thrown back I had stepped beneath an icy torrent of reviving rain.

Nowhere an answer to my questions, so I retreated from the abyss that was myself and not myself. And now back to that which was one, only one. The King, the evening ball, the court and that man. I had been made for him, he for me, I knew this, but again with fear, no, it was not fear, rather the iron presence of destiny, inevitable, impenetrable, and it was precisely that inevitability, like tidings of death, the knowledge that one would now no longer be able to refuse, evade, withdraw, escape, and one might perish, but perish *in no other way*—I sank into that chilling presence breathlessly. Unable to endure it, I mouthed the words "father, mother, brother and sister, girl friends, kith and kin"—how well I understood those words, willing figures appeared, figures known to me, I had to admit to them before myself, yes but one couldn't possibly have four mothers and as many fathers, so then this insanity again? So stupid and so stubborn?

I resorted to arithmetic: one and one are two, from a father and a mother comes a child, you were that child, you have a child's memories . . .

Either I had been mad, I told myself, or I was mad still, and being a mind, was a mind in total eclipse. There was no ball, no castle, no King, no emergence into a state of being stringently subject to the laws of everlasting harmony. I felt a stab of regret, a resistance at the thought that I must part with my beauty as well. Out of discrepant elements I could construct nothing of my own, unless I were to find in the design already existing some lopsidedness, chinks I might penetrate, thereby to rend open the structure and get to the core of it. Had everything truly happened in the way it was supposed to? If I was the property of the King, then how was I able to know this? Even to reflect on it at night ought to have been forbidden me. If he was behind everything, then why had I wished to make obeisance to him but had not done so at first? If the preparations had been flawless, then why did I recall things I should not have recalled? For, surely, with only the past of a girl and child to turn to, I would not have fallen into that agony of indecision which brought on despair, a prelude to rebellion against one's fate. And certainly they should at least have wiped out that sequence on my back, the animation of my nakedness, inert and mute, by the sparking kisses, but that too had taken place and now was with me. Could it be that some flaw lay in the design and execution? Careless errors, an oversight, hidden leaks, taken for riddles or a bad dream? But in that case I had reason to hope again. To wait. To wait, as things progressed, for further inconsistencies to accumulate, and make of them a sword to turn against the King, against myself, it did not matter against whom, as long as it ran counter to the fate imposed. So then, submit to the spell, endure it, go to the assignation the very first thing in the morning, and I knew, knew without knowing how or why, that nothing would hinder me from doing *that*, on the contrary, everything would steer me precisely in that direction. And my immediately surrounding here and now was so primitive, yes, walls, pliant upholstery, yielding softly at first to the fingers, and underneath that a barrier of steel or masonry, I didn't know, but could have pulled apart the cozy softness with my fingernails, I stood up, my head touched the concave curve of the ceiling. This, around me and above me, but inside—I, I alone?

I continued to examine and expose this villainous inability of mine to understand myself, and since levels upon levels of ideas sprang up at once, one on top of the other, I began to wonder if I ought to trust my own judgment, when, drowning madwoman that I was, like an insect in clear amber, imprisoned in my *obnubilatio lucida,* it was only natural that I would—

One moment. Where did it come from, my so elegantly parsed vocabulary, these learned terms, in Latin, logical phrases, syllogisms, this fluency out of place in a sweet young thing, the sight of whom was a flaming pyre for masculine hearts? And whence this feeling of terrible tedium in matters of sex, the cold contempt, the distance, oh yes, he probably loved me already, was maybe even mad about me, he had to see me, to hear my voice, touch my fingers, while I regarded his passion as one might regard a specimen on a slide. Was not this surprising, contradictory, asyncategorematic? Could it be that I was imagining everything, that the ultimate reality here was an old, unemotional brain, entangled in the experiences of countless years? Perhaps a sharpened intellect was my only true past, perhaps I had arisen from logic, and that logic constituted my one authentic genealogy . . .

I did not believe it. I was guiltless, yes, and at the same

time full of guilt. Guiltless in all the tracks of time past-perfect merging towards my present, as the little girl, as the adolescent somber and silent through the gray-white winters and in the stifling must of the palaces, and guiltless too in that which had occurred today, with the King, for I could not be other than I was; my guilt—my hideous guilt—lay only in this, that I knew it all so well and considered it a sham, a lie, a bubble, and that wanting to get to the bottom of my mystery, I feared to make the descent and felt a shameful gratitude for the unseen walls that barred my way. So then I had a soul tainted and honest, what else did I have, what else was left, ah yes, there was something still, my body, and I began to touch it, I examined it in that black enclosure as a masterful detective might examine the scene of a crime. A curious investigation—for in searching by touch this naked body, I felt a faintly prickling numbness in my fingers, could this have been fear of my own self? Yet I was beautiful and my muscles were resilient, limber, and clasping the thighs in a way no one would hold them oneself, as though they had been foreign objects, I could feel in my tightening hands, beneath the smooth and fragrant skin, long bones, but the wrists and the inside of my forearms at the elbow for some reason I was afraid to touch.

I tried to overcome this reluctance, what could be there after all, my arms were swathed in lace, somewhat rough, being stiff, it was awkward going, so on to the neck. What they called a swan neck—the head set on it with a stateliness not assumed but natural, inspiring respect, the ears below the braided hair—small, the lobes firm, without jewelry, unpierced—why?—I felt my forehead, cheeks, lips.

Their expression, detected with the tips of my thin fingers, again disturbed me. A different expression from the one I had expected. Strange. But how could I have been strange to myself other than through sickness, madness?

With a furtive movement befitting the innocence of a small child prey to old wives' tales, I reached for my wrists after all, and for my elbows, there where the arm met the forearm, something incomprehensible was there. I lost all feeling in my fingertips, as if something had pressed against the nerves, the blood vessels, and once again my mind leaped from suspicion to suspicion: how did such information come to me, why did I study myself like some anatomist, this was hardly in the style of a maiden, neither Angelita nor the fair Duenna, nor the lyric Tlenix. But at the same time I felt a soothing compulsion: this is quite normal, don't be surprised at yourself, you eccentric, fanciful featherbrain, if you've been a bit unwell, don't return to that, think healthy thoughts, think of your rendezvous . . . But the elbows, the wrists? Beneath the skin—like a hard lump, was it swollen glands? Calcium deposits? Impossible, not in keeping with my beauty, with its absoluteness. And yet there was a hardening there, a tiny onc, I could feel it only with a strong squeeze, above the hand, where the pulse left off, and also in the bend of the elbow.

And so my body had secrets too, its otherness corresponded to the otherness of my soul, to its fear in my self-musings, there was in this a pattern, a congruency, a symmetry: if here, then there too. If the mind, then the limbs also. If I, then you as well. I, you, riddles, I was tired, an overpowering weariness entered my blood, I was supposed to submit to it. To fall asleep, to drop into the oblivion of another, liberating darkness. And then spitefully the sudden decision not to give in to that urge, to resist the confining box of this stylish carriage (but not so stylish on the inside!), and this soul of a maid too wise, too quick of understanding! Defiance to the physical self-beauty with its hidden stigmata! Who was I? My opposition was now a rage, which made my soul burn in the darkness, so that it seemed actually to shine. *Sed tamen potest esse totaliter aliter*, where was that from? My soul? *Gratia*? *Dominus meus*?

No, I was alone and alone I jumped up, to sink my teeth into those soft, shrouded walls, I tore at the padding, dry, coarse material crackled in my teeth. I spat out threads with saliva, my fingernails were snapping, good, that was it, that was the way, I didn't know whether against myself or someone else, but no, no, no, no, no, no.

I saw a light, something budded out in front of me, like the small head of a snake, except that it was metal. A needle? I was pricked, above the knee, in the thigh, from outside, a tiny, barely noticeable pain, a prick and then nothing.

Nothing.

The garden was overcast. The royal park with its singing fountains, hedges clipped down all to one same level, the geometry of the trees, shrubs and steps, marble statues, scrolls, cupids. And the two of us. Cheap, ordinary, romantic, filled with despair. I smiled at him, and on my thigh was a mark. I had been punctured. So my soul, there where I had rebelled, and my body too, there where I had learned to hate it, they had had an ally. An ally of insufficient cunning. Now I did not dread him as much, now I played my role. Of course he had been cunning enough to impose the role on me, and from within, having forced his way into my stronghold. Cunning enough, but not enough—I observed the trap. The purpose I did not know yet, but the trap was visible, palpable, and one who sees is no longer so frightened as one who must live by conjecture alone.

I had so much trouble, this struggling with myself, even the light of day was a nuisance with its solemnity, the gardens for the greater glory and admiration of His Majesty —not of the vegetation—I truly would have preferred my night now to this day, but the day was here and so was the man, who knew nothing, understood nothing, absorbed in the burning pleasure of his sweet insanity, in the enchantment cast by me, not by any third party. Traps, snares, a lure with a fatal sting, and was I all this? And did the lashing fountains also serve this end, the royal gardens, the haze in the distance? But really, how stupid. Whose ruin, whose death was at stake? Would not false witnesses have sufficed, old men in wigs, a noose, poison? Perhaps something bigger was involved. Some vicious intrigue, as on the royal parquets.

The gardeners in high leather boots, intent upon the verdure of His Gracious Majesty, did not approach us. I remained silent, silence being more convenient, we sat on the step of an enormous stairway, as though built in preparation for a giant who would descend some day from his cloudy heights in order to make use of it. The emblems embossed in stone, the naked cupids, fauns, sileni, slippery marble dripping water, as dull and dismal as the gray sky.

An idyllic scene, a Nicolette with her Aucassin, what utter bilge! I had come to my senses completely in these gardens, when the carriage drove off and I walked lightly, as if I had just stepped from a steaming, scented bath, and my dress was now different, vernal, with a misty pattern timidly reminiscent of flowers, it alluded to them, helping to inspire reverence, surrounding me with inviolability, Eos Rhododaktylos, but I walked between the dew-glistening hedges with a mark on my thigh, I did not need to touch it, I was unable to anyway, but the memory sufficed, they had not erased that from me. I was a mind imprisoned, chained at birth, born into bondage, but a mind still. And thus before he appeared, seeing that my time now was my own, that nearby was no needle nor sound detector, I began, like an actress readying herself for the performance, to say things in a whisper, the sort of things I did not know whether I would be able to utter in his presence, in other words I probed the limits of my freedom, in the light of day I searched for them blindly, by touch.

What things? Only the truth—first, the change of grammatical form, then the plurality of my past pluperfects, everything too that I had gone through and the prick that stilled rebellion. Was this out of sympathy for him, in order not to destroy him? No, since I did not love him, not at all. It was treachery: for no good purpose had we trespassed on one another. Then should I speak to him *thus*? That by sacrifice I wished to save him from myself as from a doom?

No—it was not that way at all. I had love, but elsewhere—I know how that sounds. Oh it was a passionate love, tender and altogether ordinary. I wanted to give myself to him body and soul, though not in reality, only in the manner of the fashion, according to custom, the etiquette of the court, for it would have to be not just any, but a marvelous, a courtly sinning.

My love was very great, it caused me to tremble, it quickened my pulse, I saw that his glance made me happy. And my love was very small, being limited in me, subject to the style, like a carefully composed sentence expressing the painful joy of a tête-à-tête. And so beyond the bounds of those feelings I had no particular interest in saving him from myself or another, for when I reached with my mind outside my love, he was nothing to me, yet I needed an ally in my struggle against whatever had pricked me that night with venomous metal. I had no one else, and he was devoted to me wholly: I could count on him. I knew, of course, that I could not count on him beyond the feeling he had for me. He would not rise to any *reservatio mentalis*. Therefore I could not reveal the entire truth to him: that my love and the venomous prick were from one and the same source. That for this reason I abhorred both, had hatred for both and wanted to trample both underfoot as one steps on a tarantula. This I could not tell him, since he would surely be conventional in his love, would not accept in me the kind of liberation I desired, the freedom that would cast him off. Therefore I could only act deceitfully, giving freedom the false name of love, and only in and through that lie show him to himself as the victim of an unknown someone. Of the King? Yes, but even were he to lay violent hands upon His Majesty, that would not set me free; the King, if the King was indeed behind this, was still so far removed that his death could not alter my fate in any way. So, in order to see if I would be able to proceed thus, I stopped by a statue of Venus, its naked buttocks a monument to the higher and lower passions of earthly love, so that in complete solitude I could prepare my monstrous explanation with its well-honed arguments, a diatribe, as if I were sharpening a knife.

It was extremely difficult. Repeatedly I found myself at an impassable boundary, not knowing where the spasm would seize my tongue, where the mind would stumble, for that mind was my enemy after all. Not to lie completely, but neither to get into the center of the truth, of the mystery. Only by gradual degrees then did I decrease its radius, working inwards as along a spiral. But when I caught sight of him in the distance, saw how he walked and began almost to run towards me, still a small silhouette in a dark cape, I realized that all this was for nothing, the style would not permit it. What sort of love scene is it, in which Nicolette confesses to Aucassin that she is his branding iron, his butcher? Not even a fairy-tale style, in removing me from the spell, if it could, could return me to the nothingness from which I had come. Its entire wisdom was useless here. The loveliest of maidens, if she considers herself to be the instrument of dark forces and speaks of pricks and branding irons, if she speaks *this* and *thus*, she is a madwoman. And does not bear witness to the truth, but instead to her own disordered mind, and therefore deserves not only love and devotion, but pity besides.

Out of a combination of such feelings he might pretend to believe my words, might look alarmed, assure me of steps taken to have me freed, in reality to have me examined, spread the news of my misfortune everywhere—it would be better to insult him. Besides, in this complex situation the more of an ally I had, the less of a lover filled with hopes of consummation—he would certainly not be willing to step far from the role of lover, his madness was normal, vigorous, solidly down-to-earth: to love, ah to love, scrupulously to chew the gravel on my path into soft sand, yes but not to toy with the chimeras of analysis concerning the origin of my soul!

And so it appeared that if I had been primed for his destruction, he must die. I did not know which part of me would strike him down, the forearms, the wrists in an embrace, surely that would have been too simple, but I knew now that it could not be otherwise.

I had to go with him, down alleys prettied by the skilled artisans of horticulture; we removed ourselves quickly from the Venus Kallipygos, for the ostentation with which she displayed her charms was not in keeping with our early-romance stage of sublime emotions and shy references to happiness. We passed the fauns, also blunt, but differently, in a way that was more suitable, for the maleness of those shaggy things of stone could not impinge upon my purity, which was sufficiently chaste as to remain unoffended even close to them: I was allowed not to understand their marble-rigid lust.

He kissed my hand, there where the lump was, though unable to feel it with his lips. And where was my cunning one waiting? In the dark of the carriage? Or could it be that I was merely supposed to worm out of Arrhodes some unknown secrets: a beautiful stethoscope put to the breast of the doomed wise man?

I told him nothing.

In two days the love affair had progressed in due form. I was staying, with a handful of good servants, at a residence four furlongs removed from the royal estate; Phloebe, my factotum, had rented this château the first day following the meeting in the garden, saying nothing of the means which that step had required, and I, as the maiden with no head for financial matters, did not ask. I think that I both intimidated and annoyed him, possibly he was not let in on the secret, most likely he was not, he acted on the King's orders, was respectful to me in words, but in his eyes I saw an impertinent irony, probably he took me for a new favorite of the King, and my rides and meetings with Arrhodes did not surprise him greatly, for a servant who demands that his King treat a concubine in accordance with a pattern he can understand is not a good servant. I think that had I bestowed my caresses on a crocodile, he would not have batted an eye. I was at liberty within the confines of the royal will, nor did the monarch once approach me. I knew by now that there were things which I would never tell my man, because my tongue stiffened at the very thought and the lips turned numb, like the fingers when I had touched myself that first night in the carriage. I forbade Arrhodes to call on me, he interpreted this conventionally, as the fear that he might compromise me, and the good fellow restrained himself. On the evening of the third day I finally set about discovering who I was. Dressed for bed, I stripped in front of the pier glass and stood naked in it like a statue, and the silver pins and steel lancets lay upon the dressing table, covered with a velvet shawl, for I feared their glitter, though not their cutting edge. The breasts, high-set, looked to the side and upwards with their pink nipples, all trace of the puncture on the thigh had disappeared; like an obstetrician or a surgeon preparing for an operation I closed both hands and pushed them into the white, smooth flesh, the ribs sank beneath the pressure, but my belly domed out like those of the women in Gothic paintings, and under the warm, soft outer layer I met with resistance, hard, unyielding, and moving my hands from top to bottom gradually made out an oval shape within. With six candles on either side, I picked up the smallest lancet, not out of fear but rather for esthetic reasons.

In the mirror it looked as if I intended to knife myself, a scene dramatically perfect, sustained in style to the last detail by the enormous fourposter and canopy, the two rows of tall candles, the glint in my hand and my paleness, because my body was deathly frightened, the knees buckled under me, only the hand with the blade had the necessary steadiness. There where the oval resistance was most distinct, not moving under pressure, right below the sternum, I thrust the lancet in deep, the pain was minimal and on the surface only, from the wound there flowed a single drop of blood. Incapable of showing the butcher's skill slowly and with anatomical deliberation, I cut the body in half practically to the groin, violently, clenching my teeth and shutting my eyes as tightly as I could. To look, no, I hadn't the strength. Yet I stood no longer trembling, only cold as ice, the room was filled with the sound, like something far from me and foreign, of my ragged, almost spastic breathing. The severed layers separated, like white leather, and in the mirror I saw a silver, nestled shape, as of an enormous fetus, a gleaming chrysalis hidden inside me, held in the parted folds of flesh, flesh not bleeding, only pink. What horror, terror, to look at oneself thus! I dared not touch the silvery surface, immaculate, virgin, the abdomen oblong like a small coffin and shining, reflecting the reduced images of the candle flames, I moved and then I saw its tucked-in limbs, fetal-fashion, thin as pincers, they went into my body and suddenly I understood that it was not *it*, a foreign thing, different and other, it was again myself. And so that was the reason I had made, when walking on the wet sand of the garden paths, such deep prints, that was the reason for my strength, it was I, still I, I was repeating to myself when he entered.

The door had remained unlocked—an oversight. He sneaked in, entered thus, intrigued with his own daring, holding out before him—as if in his justification and defense—a huge shield of red roses, so that, having encountered me, and I turned around with a cry of fright, he saw, but did not notice, did not yet understand, could not. It was not out of fear now, but only in a horrible, choking shame that I tried with both hands to cover back up inside of me the silver oval, it was however too large and I too opened by the knife for this to be done.

His face, his silent scream and flight. Let this part of the account be spared me. He'd been unable to wait for permission, for an invitation, so he came with his flowers, and the house was empty, I myself had sent out all the servants, that no one might disturb me in what I planned—by then there was no other way open to me, no other course. But perhaps the first suspicion had begun to grow in him back then. I recall how the preceding day we were crossing the bed of a dried-out stream, how he wanted to carry me in his arms and I refused, not out of modesty true or pretended, but because I had to. He noticed then in the soft, pliant silt my footprints, so small and so deep, and was going to say something, it was to have been a harmless joke, but he checked himself suddenly and with that now-familiar crease between his knitted brows went up the opposite slope, without even offering me, who was climbing behind him, a helping hand. So perhaps even then. And further, when at the very top of the rise I had stumbled and grasped—to regain my balance—a thick withe of hazel, I felt that I was pulling the entire bush out by its roots, so I dropped to my knees, ordered by reflex, releasing the broken branch, so as not to show the overpowering, incredible strength that was mine. He stood off to the side, was not looking, so I thought, but he could have seen everything out of the corner of his eye. Was it then suspicion that had sent him stealing in, or uncontrollable passion?

It didn't matter.

Using the thickest segments of my feelers I pressed against the edges of the wide-open body, in order to emerge from the chrysalis, and worked myself free nimbly, after which Tlenix, Duenna, Mignonne first sank to her knees, then tumbled face-down to the side and I crawled out of her, straightening all my legs, moving slowly backwards like a crab. The candles, their flames still fluttering in the draft raised by his escape through the open door, blazed in the mirror; the naked thing, her legs thrown apart immodestly, lay motionless; not wishing to touch her, my cocoon, my false skin, the she that was now I went around her and, rearing up like a mantis with the trunk bent in the middle, I looked at myself in the glass. This was I, I told myself wordlessly, I. Still I. The smooth sheaths, coleopterous, insectlike, the knobby joints, the abdomen in its cold sheen of silver, the oblong sides designed for speed, the darker, bulging head, this was I. I repeated it over and over as if to commit those words to memory, and at the same time the manifold past of Duenna, Tlenix, Angelita dulled and died within me, like books read long ago, books out of a children's room, their content unimportant and now powerless, I could recall them, slowly turning my head in either direction, looking for my own eyes in the reflection, and also beginning to understand, though not yet accustomed to this shape that was my own, that the act of self-evisceration had not been altogether my rebellion, that it represented a foreseen part of the plan, designed for just such an eventuality, in order that my rebellion turn out to be, in the end, my total submission. Since still able to think with my former skill and ease, I yielded at the same time to this new body, its shining metal had written into it movements which I began to execute.

Love died. It will die in you as well, but over years or months, this same waning I experienced in a matter of moments, it was the third in my series of beginnings, and emitting a faint, shuffling hiss, I ran three times around the room, touching with outstretched, quivering feelers the bed on which it was denied me now to rest. I took in the smell of my unsuitor, unlover, so I could follow in his track, I known to him and yet unknown, in this newly begun—and likely the last—game. The trail of his wild flight was marked first by a succession of open doors and the roses strewn, their smell could be of help to me, in that it had become, at least for a while, a part of his smell. Seen from below, from the ground, therefore from a new perspective, the rooms through which I scuttled seemed to me to be primarily too big, full of cumbersome, useless articles of furniture, looming unfamiliarly in the semidarkness, then there was the light scrape of stone steps, stairs, beneath my claws and I ran out into a garden dark and damp —a nightingale was singing, I felt an inner amusement, for that was now a wholly unnecessary prop, others were called for by this succeeding scene, I poked about in the shrubbery a good while, aware of the gride of the gravel underfoot, I circled once and twice, then sped straight ahead, having caught the scent. For I could not have helped but catch it, composed as it was of a unique harmony of fleeting odors, of the tremors of the air parted by his passage, I found each particle not yet dispersed in the night wind, and thus hit upon the right course, which would be mine now until the end.

I do not know whose will it was that I let him get a good head start, for until dawn instead of pursuing him I roamed the royal gardens. To a certain extent this served a purpose, because I lingered in those places where we had strolled, holding hands, between the hedges, therefore I was able to imbibe his smell precisely, to make sure I would not mistake it later for any other. True, I could have gone straight after him and run him down in his utter helplessness of confusion and despair, but I did not do this. I realize that my actions on that night may also be explained in an altogether different way, by my grief and the King's pleasure, since I had lost a lover, acquiring only a prey, and for the monarch the sudden and swift demise of the man he hated might had seemed insufficient. Perhaps Arrhodes did not rush home, but went instead to one of his friends, and there, in a feverish monologue, he answering his own questions (the presence of another person needed only to reassure and sober him), arrived at the whole truth by himself. At any rate my behavior in the gardens in no way suggested the pain of separation. I know how unwelcome that will sound to sentimental souls, but having no hands to wring, no tears to shed, no knees on which I might fall, nor lips to press to the flowers gathered the day before, I did not surrender myself to prostration. What occupied me now was the extraordinary subtlety of distinction which I possessed, for while running up and down the paths not once did I take a waft of even the most deceptively similar trace for that which was my present destiny and the goad of my tireless efforts. I could feel how in my cold left lung each molecule of air threaded its way through the windings of countless scanning cells and how each suspicious particle was passed to my right lung, hot, where my faceted internal eye examined it with care, to verify its exact meaning or discard it as the wrong scent, and this took place more rapidly than the vibration of wings on the smallest insect, more rapidly than you can comprehend. At daybreak I left the royal gardens. The house of Arrhodes stood empty, stood open, not bothering then even to ascertain if he had taken with him any weapon, I found the fresh trail and went with it, no longer delaying. I did not believe I would be searching long. However the days became weeks, the weeks months, and still I tracked him.

To me this seemed no more abominable than the conduct of any other being that has written into it its own fate. I ran through rains and scorching suns, fields, ravines and thickets, dry reeds slid along my trunk, and the water of the puddles or flood plains that I cut across sprayed me and trickled in large drops down my oval back and down my head, in that place imitating tears, which had however no significance. I noticed, in my unceasing rush, how everyone who saw me from a distance turned away and clung to a wall, a tree, a fence or, if he had no such refuge, kneeled and covered his face with his hands, or fell facedown and lay there for as long as it took me to leave him far behind. I did not require sleep, thus in the night too I ran through villages, settlements, small towns, through marketplaces full of earthen pots and fruits drying on strings, where whole crowds scattered before me, and children went fleeing into side streets with screams and shouts, to which I paid no attention, but sped on my trail. His odor filled me completely, like a promise. By now I had forgotten the appearance of this man, and my mind, as if lacking the endurance of the body, particularly during the night runs, drew into itself till I did not know whom I was tracking, nor even if I was tracking anyone, I knew only that my will was to rush on, in order that the spoor of airborne motes singled out for me from the welling diversity of the world persist and intensify; for should it weaken, that would mean I was not heading in the right direction. I questioned no one, and too no one dared accost me, somehow I felt that the distance separating me from those who huddled by walls at my approach or fell to the earth, covering the backs of their heads with their arms, was filled with tension and I understood it as a dreadful homage rendered me, because I was on the King's hunt, which gave me inexhaustible strength. Only now and then a child, still quite small, whom the adults had not had time to snatch up and clasp to their breasts at my silent, sudden appearance in full career, would start to cry, but I took no heed of that, because as I ran I had to maintain an intense, unbroken concentration, directed both outwards, at the world of sand and bricks, the green world, covered above with azure blues, and inwards into my internal world, where from the efficient play of both my lungs there came molecular music, very lovely, since so magnificently unerring. I crossed rivers and the coves of coastal bays, rapids, the slimy basins of draining lakes, and every manner of beast avoided me, withdrew in flight or frantically began to burrow into the parched soil, surely a futile effort were I to stalk it, for no one was so lightning-agile as I, but I ignored those shaggy creatures scrambling on all fours, slant-eared, with their husky whinnying, squeals and wailing, they did not concern me, I had another purpose.

Several times I plowed through, like a missile, great ant hills, and their tiny inhabitants, russet, black, speckled, helplessly slid across my shining carapace, and once or twice some animal of unusual size blocked my path, so though I had no quarrel with it, in order not to waste precious time on circling and evasions, I tensed and sprang, broke through in an instant, thus with a snap of calcium and the gurgle of red spouts splashing my back and head I hurried away so quickly, it was only later that I thought of the death that had been dealt in this swift and violent manner. I remember too that I stole across lines of battle, covered with a scattered swarm of gray and green surcoats, of which some moved, and in others there rested bones, putrid or completely dried out and thereby white as slightly grimy snow, but this also I ignored, because I had a higher task, a task made for me and me alone. For the trail would double back, loop around and cut across itself, and all but vanish on the shores of salt lakes, there parched by the sun into dust that bothered my lungs, or else washed away by rains; and gradually I began to realize that the thing eluding me was full of cunning, doing everything it could to baffle me and break the thread of molecules carrying the trace of its uniqueness. If the one whom I pursued had been an ordinary mortal, I would have overtaken him after a suitable time, that is, the time needed for his terror and despair to enhance duly the punishment in store, I would have surely overtaken him, what with my tireless speed and the unfailing operation of my tracking lungs—and would have killed him sooner than the thought that I was doing so. I had not followed at his heels at first, but waited for the scent to grow quite cold, so as to demonstrate my skill and in addition give the hunted one sufficient time, in keeping with the custom, a good custom as it allowed his fear to grow, and then sometimes I would let him put a considerable distance between us, for, feeling me constantly too near, he might in an access of despair have done some harm to himself and thus have escaped my decree. And therefore I did not intend to fall on him too quickly, nor so unexpectedly that he would have no time to realize what was awaiting him. So at nights I halted, concealed in the underbrush, not for rest, rest was unnecessary, but for intentional delay, and also to consider my next moves. No more did I think of the quarry as being Arrhodes, once my suitor, because that memory had closed itself off and I knew that it ought to be left in peace. My only regret was that I no longer possessed the ability to smile when I recalled to mind those ancient stratagems, like Angelita, Duenna, the sweet Mignonne, and a couple of times I looked at myself in a mirror of water, the full moon overhead, to convince myself that in no respect was I now similar to them, though I had remained beautiful, however my present beauty was a deadly thing, inspiring as great a horror as admiration. I also made use of these night bivouacs to scrape lumps of dried mud off my abdomen, down to the silver, and before setting out again I would move lightly the quill of my sting, holding it between my tarsi, testing its readiness, for I knew not the day nor the hour.

Sometimes I would noiselessly creep up to human habitations and listen to the voices, bending myself backwards, propping my gleaming feelers on a window sill, or I might crawl up on the roof in order to hang down freely from the eaves, for I was not (after all) a lifeless mechanism equipped with a pair of hunting lungs, I was a being that had a mind and used it. And the chase had already lasted long enough to become common knowledge. I heard old women frighten children with me, I also heard countless tales about Arrhodes, who was favored as much as I, the King's emissary, was feared. What sort of things did the simple folk say on their porches? That I was a machine set upon a wise man who had dared to raise his hand against the throne.

Yet I was supposed to have been no ordinary death machine, but a special device, one capable of assuming any form: a beggar, a child in a cradle, a lovely young lass, but also a metal reptile. These shapes were the larva in which the assassin emissary showed itself to its victim, in order to deceive him, but to everyone else it appeared as a scorpion made of silver, scurrying with such rapidity that no one yet had been able to count its legs. Here the story split into different versions. Some said that the wise man had sought to bestow freedom upon the people in opposion to the King's will, and therewith kindled the royal wrath: others—that he possessed the water of life and with it could raise up the martyrs, which was forbidden him by the highest authority, but he, while pretending to bow to the sovereign's will, in secret did marshal a battalion of hanged men, who had been cut down at the citadel after the great execution of the rebels. Still others knew nothing at all of Arrhodes and did not attribute to him any marvelous abilities, but only took him to be a condemned man, for that reason alone deserving their favor and support. Although it was unknown what had originally roused the King's fury, that he summoned his master craftsmen and commanded them to fashion him a hunting machine in their forge, everyone called it a wicked design and that command most sinful; for whatever the victim had done, it could not have been as awful as the fate the King had prepared for him. There was no end to these tall tales, in which the rustic imagination waxed audacious and unchecked, not changing in this one respect, that it conferred on me the most hideous qualities conceivable.

I heard, too, innumerable lies about the valiant ones hastening to relieve Arrhodes, men who supposedly barred my way, only to fall in uneven combat—lies, for not a living soul ever dared to do this. Nor was there any lack, in those fables, of traitors too, who pointed out to me Arrhodes's tracks when I was no longer able to find them —also an unmitigated lie. But as for who I was, who I might be, what occupied my mind, and whether or not I knew despair or doubt, no one said a thing, and this did not surprise me either.

And I heard not a little about the simple trailing machines known to the people, machines that carried out the King's will, which was the law. At times I did not hide myself at all from the occupants of the humble huts, but waited for the sun to rise, in order in its rays to leap like silver lightning on the grass and in a sparkling spray of dew connect the end of the previous day's journey with its new beginning. Running briskly, I was gratified when those I came upon prostrated themselves, when eyes turned glassy, and I delighted in the numb dread that surrounded me like an impervious aura. But the day came when my lower sense of smell went idle, in vain too did I circle the hilly vicinity seeking the scent with my upper smell, and I experienced a feeling of misfortune, of the uselessness of all my perfection, until, standing at the top of a knoll, my arms crossed as though in prayer to the windy sky, I realized, with the softest sound filling the bell of my abdomen, that not all was lost, and so in order that the idea be carried out I reached for that which long ago had been abandoned—the gift of speech. I did not need to learn it, I already possessed it, however I had to waken it within me, at first pronouncing words sharply and in a jangling way, but my voice soon grew humanlike, therefore I ran down the slope, to employ speech, since smell had failed me.

I felt no hate whatever for my prey, though he had shown himself to be so clever and adept, I understood however that he was performing the part of the task that lay to him, just as I was performing mine. I found the crossroads where the scent had gradually disappeared, and stood quivering, but not moving from my place, for one pair of legs pulled blindly down the road covered with lime dust, while the other pair, convulsively clawing the rocks, drew me in the opposite direction, where the walls of a small monastery gleamed whitely, surrounded by ancient trees. Steadying myself, I crawled heavily, almost as if unwillingly, towards the monastery gate, under which stood a monk, his face upraised, possibly he gazed at the dawn on the horizon. I approached slowly, so as not to shock him with my sudden appearance, and greeted him, and when he fixed his eyes on me without a word I asked if he would permit me to confess to him a certain matter, which I had difficulty dealing with on my own. I thought at first that he was petrified with fright, for he neither moved nor made an answer, but he was only reflecting and at last indicated his consent. We went then to the monastery garden, he in the lead, I following, and it must have been a strange pair that we made, but at that early hour not a living soul was about, no one to marvel at the silver praying mantis and the white priest. I told him underneath the larch tree, when he sat, taking on unconsciously—out of habit—the posture of father confessor, that is, not looking at me but only inclining his head in my direction, I told him that first, before I ever set out on the trail, I had been a young woman destined by the King's will for Arrhodes, whom I met at the court ball, and that I had loved him, not knowing anything about him, and without thought embarked upon the love that I had wakened in him, till from the puncture in the night I realized what I might be for him, and seeing no other salvation for either of us I had stabbed myself with a knife, but instead of death a metamorphosis befell me. From then on the compulsion which previously I had only suspected set me on the heels of my beloved, and I became to him a persecuting Fury. However the chase had lasted, and lasted so long, that everything the people said of Arrhodes began to reach my ears, and while I did not know how much truth lay in it, I began once more to brood on our common fate and a liking for this man rose up in me, for I saw that I wanted desperately to kill him, for the reason that I could not any longer love him. Thus I beheld my own baseness, that is, my love turned inside out, degraded, and craving vengeance on one whose only crime against me was his own misfortune. Therefore I wished now to discontinue the chase, and to cease arousing mortal fear around me, yes, I wished to remedy the evil, yet knew not how.

As far as I could tell, the monk by the end of this discourse had still not cast off his distrust, for he had straightway warned me, before I even began to speak, that whatever I might say would not bear the stamp of a confession, since in his judgment I represented a creature devoid of free will. And too, he might well have asked himself whether I had not been sent to him intentionally, indeed such spies existed, and in the most perfidious disguises, but his answer appeared to proceed from honest thought. He said: And what if you should find the one you seek? Do you know what you will do then?

I replied: Father, I only know what I do not wish to do, but I do not know what power slumbering in me might force its way out then, and therefore I cannot say that I would not be made to murder.

He said to me: What advice then can I give you? Do you wish that this task be taken from you?

Like a dog lying at his feet I lifted up my head and, seeing him squint in the glare of sunlight reflected off the silver of my skull, said: There is nothing I desire more, although I realize that my fate would then be cruel, as I would have no longer any goal before me. I did not plan the thing for which I was created, and will surely have to pay, and pay dearly, for transgressing against the royal will, because such transgression cannot be permitted to go unpunished, and so I shall in turn become the target of the armorers in the palace vaults and they will send a pack of metal hounds out into the world, to destroy me. And even should I escape, making use of the skills that have been placed in me, and go to the very ends of the world, in whatever spot I hide myself all things will shun me and I shall find nothing for which it would be worth continuing my existence. And too, a fate such as yours is closed to me, since each one in authority like yourself will tell me—as you have told me—that I am not spiritually free, therefore I cannot avail myself of the refuge of a cloister!

He grew thoughtful, then showed surprise and said: I am not versed in the construction of your kind, nevertheless I see and hear you and you seem to me, from what you say, to be an intelligent being, though possibly thrall to a limiting compulsion; yet if, as you indeed tell me, you struggle with this compulsion, O machine, and furthermore state that you would feel yourself delivered if the will to murder were to be taken from you, tell me then, just how does this will feel? How is it with you?

I replied: Father, maybe it is not well with me, but concerning how to hunt, track, detect, ferret out, lie in wait, stalk, sneak and lurk, and also smash obstacles standing in the way, cover traces, backtrack, double back and circle, concerning all of this I am extremely knowledgeable and to perform such operations with unfailing skill, turning myself into a sentence of relentless doom, gives me satisfaction, which no doubt was designedly inscribed by fire into my bowels.

"I ask you once again," he said, "tell me, what will you do when you see Arrhodes?"

"Father, I tell you once again that I do not know, for though I wish him no evil, that which is written within me may prove more powerful than what I wish."

Upon hearing this, he covered his eyes with his hand and said: "You are my sister."

"How am I to understand that?" I asked, astonished.

"Exactly as I say it," he said, "and it means I neither raise myself above you nor humble myself before you, for however much we may differ, your ignorance, which you have confessed to me and which I believe, makes us equals in the face of Providence. That being so, come with me and I shall show you something."

We went, one after the other, through the monastery garden, and came to an old woodshed, the monk pushed and the creaking door opened, in the dimness inside I made out a dark form lying on the bundle of straw, and a smell entered my lungs through my nostrils, a smell I had pursued incessantly, and so strong here that I felt my sting stir of its own accord and emerge from its ventral sheath, but in the next instant my vision grew accustomed to the darkness and I perceived my error. On the straw lay only discarded clothes. The monk saw by my trembling that I was greatly agitated, and he said: Yes, Arrhodes was here. He hid in our monastery a month ago, when he had succeeded in throwing you off the scent. He regretted that he was unable to work as before, and so secretly notified his followers, who sometimes visited him at night, but two traitors sneaked in among them and carried him off five days ago.

"Do you mean to say 'agents of the King'?" I asked, still quivering and prayerfully pressing to my breast my crossed arms.

"No, I say 'traitors,' for they abducted him by a ruse and using force; the little deaf-mute boy whom we took in, he alone saw them leave at dawn, Arrhodes bound and with a knife held to his throat."

"Abducted him?" I asked, not understanding. "Who? To what place? For what reason?"

"In order, I think, to have use of his mind. We cannot appeal to the law for help, for the law is the King's. Therefore they will force him to serve them, and if he refuses they will kill him and go unpunished."

"Father," I said, "praised be the hour in which I made so bold as to approach you and speak. I will go now on the trail of the abductors and free Arrhodes. I know how to hunt, how to track down, there is nothing I do better, only show me the right direction, known to you from the words of the mute!"

He replied: And yet you do not know whether you will be able to restrain yourself, you admitted as much to me!

To which I said: That is so, however I think that I will find a way. I have no clear idea as yet—perhaps I will seek out a skillful master craftsman, who will find in me the right circuit and change it, such that my desire becomes my destiny.

The monk said: Before you set out you may, if you like, consult with one of our brothers, because before he joined us he was, in the world, conversant with precisely such arts. He serves us now as a physician.

We were standing once more in the sunny garden, and though he gave no indication of it, I understood that still he did not trust me. The scent had dissipated in the course of five days, thus he could have given me the wrong as well as the right direction. I consented.

The physician examined me, maintaining the necessary caution, shining a dark lantern inside my body through the chinks of my interabdominal rims, and this with the utmost care and concentration. Then he stood, brushed the dust from his habit and said:

"It often happens that a machine sent out with these sorts of instructions is waylaid by the condemned man's family or his friends, or by other persons who for reasons unknown to the authorities attempt to foil their plans. In order to prevent this, the prudent armorers of the King lock such contents hermetically and connect them with the core in such a way that any tampering whatever must prove fatal. After the placing of the final seal even they cannot remove the sting. Thus it is with you. It also often happens that the victim disguises himself in different clothing, alters his appearance, his behavior and odor, but his mind he cannot alter and hence the machine does not content itself with using the lower and upper senses of smell to hunt, but puts questions to the quarry, questions devised by the foremost experts on the individual characteristics of the human psyche. Thus it is with you also. In addition, I see in your interior a mechanism which none of your predecessors possessed, a multiple memory of things superfluous to a hunting machine, for these are recorded feminine histories, filled with names and turns of phrase that lure the mind, and a conductor runs from them down into the fatal core. Therefore you are a machine perfected in a way unknown to me, and perhaps even an ultimate machine. To remove your sting without at the same time producing the usual result is impossible."

"I will need my sting," I said, still lying on my back, "as I must rush to the aid of the abducted one."

"As for whether you will succeed, if making every effort, in restraining the releases that are poised above the core of which we speak, I cannot tell you yes or no," continued the physician, as though he hadn't heard my words. "I can do—if you wish—one thing only, namely, I can sprinkle the poles of the place in question with finely ground particles of iron using a tube. This would increase somewhat the bounds of your freedom. Yet even if I do this, you will not know up until the last moment whether, in rushing to the aid of someone, you are not still an obedient tool against him."

Seeing them both look at me, I agreed to submit to this operation, which did not take long, it caused me no pain but then neither did it produce in my mental state any perceptible change. To gain their trust even more, I asked if they would allow me to spend the night in the monastery, the entire day having passed in talk, deliberations and auscultations. They willingly agreed, but I devoted that time to a thorough examination of the woodshed, familiarizing myself with the smell of the abductors. I was capable of this, because it sometimes happens that a King's agent finds its way blocked not by the victim himself, but by some other daredevil. Before daybreak I lay down on the straw where for many nights had slept the one allegedly abducted, and motionless I breathed in his odor, waiting for the monks. For I reasoned that if they had deceived me with some fabricated story, then they would fear my vengeful return from the false trail, therefore this darkest hour at early dawn would suit their purpose best, if they meant to destroy me. I lay, pretending to be deep in sleep, alert to the slightest sound coming from the garden, for they could barricade the door from the outside and set fire to the woodshed, in order that the fruit of my womb tear me asunder in flames. They would not even have to overcome their characteristic repugnance for murder, inasmuch as they considered me to be not a person but merely a machine of death; my remains they could bury in the garden and nothing would happen to them. I did not really know what I would do if I heard them approach, and never learned, since that did not come about. And so I remained alone with my thoughts, in which recurred over and over the amazing words spoken by the elder monk as he looked into my eyes, *You are my sister.* I still could not understand them, but when I bent over them something warm spread through my being and transformed me, it was as if I had lost a heavy fetus, with which I had been pregnant. In the morning however I ran out through the half-open gate and, steering clear of the monastery buildings according to the monk's directions, headed full speed for the mountains visible on the horizon—for there he had aimed my pursuit.

I hastened greatly and by noon more than one hundred miles separated me from the monastery. I tore like a shell between the white birches, and when I ran straight through the high grass of the foothill meadows, it fell on either side as if beneath the measured strokes of a scythe.

The track of both abductors I found in a deep valley, on a small bridge thrown across rapid water, but not a hint of Arrhodes's scent, so regardless of the effort they must have taken turns carrying him, which gave evidence of their cunning as well as knowledge, since they realized no one has the right to replace the King's machine in its mission, and that they were incurring the monarch's great displeasure by their deed. No doubt you would like to know what my true intentions were in that final run, and so I will tell you that I tricked the monks, and yet I did not trick them, for I truly desired to regain or rather gain my freedom, indeed I had never possessed it. However concerning what I intended to do with that freedom, I do not know what confession to make. This uncertainty was nothing new, while sinking the knife into my naked body I also did not know whether I wished to kill or only discover myself, even if one was to have meant the other. That step too had been foreseen, as all subsequent events revealed, and thus the hope of freedom could have been just an illusion, nor even my own illusion. but introduced in me in order that I move with more alacrity, urged on precisely by the application of that perfidious spur. But as for saying whether freedom would have amounted simply to renouncing Arrhodes, I do not know. Even being completely free, I could have killed him, for I was not so mad as to believe in the impossible miracle of reciprocated love now that I had ceased to be a woman, and if perchance I was yet a woman in some way, how was Arrhodes, who had seen the opened belly of his naked mistress, to believe this? And so the wisdom of my creators transcended the farthest limits of mechanical craftsmanship, for without a doubt in their calculations they had provided for this state also, in which I hurried to the aid of him who was lost to me forever. And had I been able to turn aside and go on wherever my steps led me, then too I would not be rendering him any great service, I big with death, having no one to whom to bear it. I think therefore that I was nobly base and by freedom compelled to do not that which was commanded me directly, but that which in my incarnation I myself desired. Thorny ruminations, and vexing in their uselessness, yet they would be settled at the goal. By killing the abductors and saving my beloved, in that way forcing him to exchange the disgust and fear he felt towards me for helpless admiration, I might regain—if not him, then at least myself.

Having forged through a dense thicket of hazels, beneath the first terraces I suddenly lost the scent. I searched for it in vain, here it was and there it vanished, as if the ones pursued had flown up into the sky. Returning to the copse, as prudence dictated, I found—not without difficulty—a shrub from which several of the thicker branches had been cut. So I sniffed the stumps oozing hazel sap and, going back to where the trail disappeared, discovered its continuation in the smell of hazel, because the ones fleeing had made use of stilts, aware that the trail of the upper scent would not last long in the air, swept away by the mountain wind. This sharpened my will; soon the hazel smell grew weak, but here again I saw through the ruse employed—the ends of the stilts they had wrapped in the shreds of a burlap sack.

By an overhanging rock lay the discarded stilts. The clearing here was strewn with giant boulders overgrown with moss on the north side and so piled up together that the only way to cross that field of rubble was by leaping from one rock to the other. This too the escapers had done, but not in a straight line, they had weaved and zigzagged, therefore I was obliged constantly to crawl down from the rocks, run around them in a circle and catch the particles of scent trembling in the air. Thus I reached the cliff up which they had climbed—so they must have freed the hands of their captive, but I was not surprised that he went with them of his own accord, for he could not have turned back. I climbed, following the clear spoor, the triple odor on the warm surface of the stone, though it became necessary to ascend vertically, by rocky ledges, troughs, clefts, and there was no clump of gray moss nestled in the crevice of a crag nor any tiny chink that could give a brief purchase to the feet which the fleeing ones had not used as a step, halting every now and then in the more difficult places to study the way ahead, which I could tell from the intensification of their odor there, but I myself raced up barely touching the rock and I felt my pulse strengthening within, felt it play and sing in magnificent pursuit, for these people were prey worthy of me and I felt admiration for them and also joy, because whatever they had accomplished in that perilous ascent, moving in threesome and securing themselves with a line whose jute smell remained on the sharp ledges, I accomplished alone and easily, and nothing was able to hurl me from that aerial path. At the summit I was met by a tremendous wind that whipped across the ridge like a knife, and I did not look back to see the green landscape spread out below, its horizons fading into the blue of the air, but instead, hurrying along the length of the ridge in either direction, I searched for further traces, and found them finally in a minute nick. Then suddenly a whitish scrape and a chipping marked the fall of one of the escapers, therefore leaning out over the brink of a rock I peered down and saw him, small, lying halfway down the mountainside, and the sharpness of my vision permitted me to make out even the dark spattering on the limestones, as if for a moment around the prone man there had fallen a rain of blood. The others however had gone on along the ridge, and at the thought that now I had only one opponent left guarding Arrhodes I felt disappointment, because never before had I had such a sense of the momentousness of my actions and experienced such an eagerness for battle, an eagerness that both sobered and intoxicated me. So I ran down a slope, for my prey had taken that direction, having left the dead man in the precipice, unquestionably they were in a hurry and his instantaneous death from the drop must have been obvious. I approached a craggy pass like the ruin of a giant cathedral, of which only the huge pillars of the broken gate remained, and the adjoining side buttresses, and one high window through which the sky shone, and silhouetted against it—a slender, sickly tree; in its unconscious heroism it had grown there from a seed, planted by the wind in a handful of dust. After the pass was another, higher mountain gorge, partly enveloped in mist, covered over by a trailing cloud out of which there fell a finely sparkling snow. In the shadow thrown by one turret of rock I heard a loose, pebbly sound, then thunder, and a landslide came rumbling down the slope. Stones pummeled me, till sparks and smoke issued from my sides, but then I drew all my legs under me and dropped into a shallow recess beneath a boulder, where in safety I waited for the last rocks to descend. The thought came to me that the hunted one guarding Arrhodes had chosen by design a place of avalanches he knew, on the chance that I, being unfamiliar with mountains, might set off an avalanche and be crushed—and though this was only a slight possibility, it raised my spirits, for if my opponent did not merely flee and evade but also could attack, then the contest grew more worthy.

At the bottom of the next gorge, which was white with snow, stood a building, not a house, not a castle, erected with such massive stones that not even a giant could have moved one single-handed—and I realized it had to be the enemy's retreat, for where else in this wilderness? And so, no longer bothering to find the scent, I began to lower myself, digging my back legs into the shifting rubble, with my front legs practically skimming over the powdered fragments, and the middle pair I used to brake this downward slide, in order that it not become a headlong plunge, until I reached the first snow and noiselessly now proceeded across it, testing every step so as not to drop into some bottomless crevice. I had to be cautious, for that one expected my appearance precisely from the pass, therefore I did not draw too near, lest I become visible from the walls of the fortress, and then, squeezing myself under a mushroom-shaped stone, I patiently waited for night to fall.

It grew dark quickly, but the snow still sifted down and whitened the gloom; because of this I didn't dare approach the building, but only rested my head on my crossed legs in such a way as to keep the building within view. After midnight the snow stopped, but I did not shake it from myself, for it made me resemble my surroundings, and from the sliver of moon between the clouds it shone like the bridal gown that I had never worn. Slowly I began to crawl towards the misty outline of the stronghold, not taking my eyes off the window on the second floor, in which a yellowish light was glimmering, but I lowered my heavy lids, for the moon dazzled and I was accustomed to the dark. It seemed to me that something moved in that dimly lit window, as if a large shadow had swept across a wall, so I crawled faster, till I came to the foundation. Meter by meter I began to scale the battlement, and this was not difficult, as the stones had no mortar joints and were held in place only by their enormous weight. Thus I reached the lower windows, which loomed black like parapet loopholes intended for the mouths of cannons. They all gaped dark and empty. And inside too such silence reigned, it was as though death had been the only occupant here for ages. To see better, I activated my night vision and, putting my head inside the stone chamber, opened the luminous eyes of my antennae, from which issued forth a phosphorescent glow. I found myself facing a grimy fireplace made of rough flagging, in which a few split logs and slightly charred twigs had grown cold long ago. I saw also a bench and rusted utensils by the wall, a crumpled bed and some sort of stone-hard rolls of bread in the corner.

It struck me odd that nothing here was preventing my entrance, I didn't trust this beckoning emptiness, and though at the other end of the room the door stood open, perhaps for that very reason sensing a trap, I withdrew as I had entered, without a sound, to resume my climb to the top floor. The window from which the faint light came—I did not even consider approaching it. Finally I scrambled up onto the roof and, finding myself on its snow-covered surface, lay down like a dog keeping watch, to wait for day. I heard two voices, but could not tell what they were saying. I lay motionless, both longing for and fearing the moment when I would leap upon my opponent to free Arrhodes, and tensed like a taut coil, wordlessly picturing the course of the struggle that would be ended by a sting; at the same time I looked within myself, now no longer seeking there a source of will, but trying to find some small indication, even the smallest, as to whether I would kill only one man. I cannot say at what point this fear left me. I lay, still uncertain, for not knowing myself, yet that very ignorance of whether I had come as a rescuer or as a murderess—it became for me something hitherto unknown, inexplicably new, investing my every tremor with a mysterious and girlish innocence, it filled me with an overwhelming joy. This joy surprised me not a little and I wondered if it might not be another manifestation of the wisdom of my inventors, who had seen to it that I find limitless power in the bringing of both succor and destruction, however I was not certain of this either. A sudden, short noise, followed by a babbling voice, reached me from below—one more sound, a hollow thud, as of a heavy object falling, then silence. I started to crawl down from the roof, nearly bending my abdomen in two, such that with the chest half of the body I clung to the wall, while my back pair of legs and the tube of the sting still rested on the edge of the roof, until with my head shaking from the strain I approached, hanging, the open window.

The candle, thrown to the floor, had gone out, but its wick still glowed red, and by exerting my nocturnal vision I saw beneath the table a body, recumbent, streaming blood—black in that light—and although everything within me yearned to spring, I first sniffed the air redolent of blood and stearin: this man was a stranger to me, therefore a struggle had taken place and Arrhodes slew him before me. The how, why and when of it never crossed my mind, for the fact that I was alone with him, and he alive, in this empty house, that there were now only the two of us, hit me like a thunderbolt. I trembled—bride and butcher—noting at the same time with an unblinking eye the rhythmic twitches of that large body as it breathed its last. If I could only leave now, steal softly away into the world of snow and mountains, anything rather than remain with him face to face—face to feeler, that is—I added, doomed to the monstrous and the comic no matter what I did, and the sense of being mocked and jeered at tipped the scale, pushed me so that I slid down, still suspended headfirst like a wary spider and, no longer caring about the screech of my ventral plates across the sill, in a nimble arc leaped over the corpse, and was at the door.

I don't know how or when I broke it down. Across the threshold were winding stairs and on them, on his back, Arrhodes, the head twisted back and propped against worn stone, they must have fought on these stairs, that was the reason almost nothing of it had reached me, so here at my feet he lay, his ribs were moving, I saw—yes—his nakedness, the nakedness I had not known, but imagined only, that first night at the ballroom.

He gave a rattle, I watched as he tried to lift his lids, they opened, first the whites, and I, rearing, with a bent abdomen, I gazed down into his upturned face, not daring to touch him nor retreat, for while he lived I could not be certain of myself, though the blood was leaving him with every breath, yet I clearly saw that my duty extended up until the very last, because the King's sentence must be executed even in the throes of death, therefore I could not take the risk, inasmuch as he was still alive, nor indeed did I know if I truly desired him to wake. Had he opened his eyes and been conscious, and—in an inverted view—taken me in entirely, exactly as I stood over him, stood now powerlessly carrying death, in a gesture of supplication, pregnant but not from him, would that have been a wedding—or its unmercifully arranged parody?

But he did not open his eyes in consciousness and when dawn entered between us in puffs of finely sparkling snow from the windows, through which the whole house howled with the mountain blizzard, he groaned once more and ceased to breathe, and only then, my mind at rest, did I lie down beside him, and wrapped him tightly in my arms, and I lay thus in the light and in the darkness through two days of snowstorm, which covered our bed with a sheet that did not melt. And on the third day the sun came up.

Translated from the Polish
by Michael Kandel

BIOGRAPHICAL NOTES ON THE AUTHORS

Ilse Aichinger (1921–) is an Austrian short-story writer, novelist, and radio playwright who now lives in Bavaria. A member of the influential Gruppe 47 of post–World War II writers and the recipient of many literary awards, she is particularly well known for her lyrical, symbolic short stories. "Story in a Mirror" is from the collection *The Bound Man* (1953), which describes the existential situation of modern man in a world without security.

J. G. Ballard (1930–), born in Shanghai, is an English writer. His fiction, which has been greatly influenced by surrealist writers and painters, characteristically uses landscape to reflect the inner state of characters. As a writer of science fiction, Ballard is admired by some and abused by others; his stories are usually dense symbolic constructs with images of sand dunes, wrecked spacecraft, and the rusting artifacts of human civilization. "The Drowned Giant" (1964) is an atypical story, impressive for its simplicity.

Donald Barthelme (1931–) is a distinguished American short-story writer and novelist who attempts to capture the chaotic events and pace of modern life. He depicts a world gone mad, in which lunacy appears to be the only sane response. Barthelme does not believe that the mysteries and miseries of human existence have any final resolution, and his stories can be quite cynical in outlook. He is fond of alluding to—and parodying—both popular and serious fiction, as can be seen from "The Emerald" (1979).

Jorge Luis Borges (1899–), Argentinian short-story writer, poet, and essayist, is perhaps the greatest living creator of metaphysical fantasy. Tellingly, he once declared theology and philosophy to be branches of fantastic literature. A professor of English literature and an ardent admirer of Poe, Chesterton, Wilde, and Wells, he is a man of universal erudition, masterfully expressing himself in ficition through parable and paradox. He delights in presenting the more heretical ideas of mankind in his fiction, mixing the real with products of his own fertile imagination. "The Lottery in Babylon" (1942) is one of his most celebrated stories.

Dino Buzzati (1906–72) was an Italian novelist, journalist, short-story writer, and painter whose fiction drew on a wide range of fantastic forms: horror, the occult, the absurd, science fiction, and the fairy tale. He preferred the extravagant, the outré, and the fantastic described in a commonplace manner. Buzzati's short stories are filled with bizarre events, catastrophes, and monsters; his characters are generalized types rather than psychologically analyzed individuals. "The Slaying of the Dragon" was first published in 1942.

Italo Calvino (1923–) is an Italian novelist, essayist, and short-story writer whose work has from the earliest contained many elements of the fantastic. In such novels as *The Cloven Viscount* (1952), *The Baron in the Trees* (1957), and *The Nonexistent Knight* (1959) the fantastic becomes dominant, as old myths are exploded in a pointed satire of the modern world and the human condition. In *Cosmicomics* (1965) and *t zero* (1967) he describes the creation and evolution of the universe through the eyes of a protean hero named Qfwfq. With time Calvino has written ever more complex narratives, blending the imaginary with the realistic, the metaphysical with the physical. "Adam, One Afternoon" (1949) is one of his earlier stories.

Julio Cortázar (1914–84), born in Brussels of Argentinian parents, lived in Argentina and, from 1952 until his death, in Paris. He achieved world renown with his volumes of fantastic short stories, which often describe the irruption of the uncanny into a decidedly commonplace, undramatic everyday world, frequently with an undertone of sardonic irony and cool satire. "Axolotl" is from *End of the Game and Other Stories*, a collection published in 1956.

Mircea Eliade (1907–), who was born in Bucharest, is a professor at the University of Chicago, a celebrated guest lecturer at many universities, and a leading authority on myth and the history of religion. Well known in the English-speaking world for his nonfiction, Eliade is also a prolific fiction writer; his first fantasy story, "How I Discovered the Philosophers' Stone," was written at the age of fourteen. His novels and short stories blend the real and the unreal, the autobiographical and the invented, the fabulous and the documentary, the mythological and the political. "With the Gypsy Girls" was written in 1959.

Carlos Fuentes (1928–), one of contemporary Mexico's most important writers, is a novelist, short-story writer, essayist, playwright, and author of film scripts. He is a master at combining reality and unreality in the modern Latin-American tradition. His deep concern with the political and social reality of Mexico, strikingly reflected in his short stories and novels, is also evident in the novella "Aura" (1962).

Stanislaw Lem (1921–), a Pole, is one of the world's most successful science-fiction writers, with translations in over thirty languages and worldwide sales of over eleven million. He is also one of the few science-fiction writers whose work is taken seriously as literature. Lem's novels, short stories, radio plays, and essays often focus on the cultural impact and moral consequences of modern science and technology, usually in an ironic and ambiguous manner that offers no easy answers. His best-known novel is *Solaris* (1961), with its insoluble puzzle of the living ocean that entirely covers another planet. Many of Lem's later works are hybrids that combine elements of fiction and nonfiction. "The Mask" was originally published in 1976.

Joyce Carol Oates (1938–) is a highly respected American novelist, playwright, short-story writer, poet, and essayist: A lecturer in creative writing at Princeton University, she is a recipient of the National Book Award and a member of the American Academy and Institute of Arts and Letters. Her subtle social and psychological analyses of everyday life in contemporary America are stylistically in the realistic tradition of Henry James and Edith Wharton, whose work also had a fantastic side. Perhaps her best fantasy stories are found in *The Poisoned Kiss and Other Portuguese Stories* (1975) and *Night-Side* (1977); "Further Confessions" is from the latter collection.